"It is not really so bad,

The duke said this ironically, after they had circled the room twice in silence. "I realize that, given a choice, you would not have danced with me, Miss Verey, despite your pretty little remark just now! You have a neat way of administering a set-down! It was a salutary experience for me!"

Jane raised her eyebrows, biting back a smile. The twinkle in his eyes was infectious. "You surprise me, Your Grace! I would imagine your self-esteem to be much more resilient than that!"

Alex Delahaye smiled, looking suddenly boyish. "But appearances can be so deceptive, Miss Verey! Do you not find that?"

Praise for Nicola Cornick's recent releases

LADY POLLY

"…a solid, cozy read with many delightful characters…"
—*Romantic Times*

THE VIRTUOUS CYPRIAN

"…this delightful tale of a masquerade gone awry
will delight ardent Regency readers."
—*Romantic Times*

THE LARKSWOOD LEGACY

"…a suspenseful yet tenderhearted tale of love…"
—*Romantic Times*

MISS VEREY'S PROPOSAL

Nicola Cornick

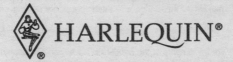

HARLEQUIN®

TORONTO • NEW YORK • LONDON
AMSTERDAM • PARIS • SYDNEY • HAMBURG
STOCKHOLM • ATHENS • TOKYO • MILAN • MADRID
PRAGUE • WARSAW • BUDAPEST • AUCKLAND

ISBN 0-373-29204-X

MISS VEREY'S PROPOSAL

First North American Publication 2002

Available from Harlequin Historicals and
NICOLA CORNICK

The Virtuous Cyprian #566
Lady Polly #574
The Love Match #599
"The Rake's Bride"
Miss Verey's Proposal #604

Please address questions and book requests to:
Harlequin Reader Service
U.S.: 3010 Walden Ave., P.O. Box 1325, Buffalo, NY 14269
Canadian: P.O. Box 609, Fort Erie, Ont. L2A 5X3

To my family

Prologue

'Say you'll do it, Jane! Oh, please say you will!'

Miss Sophia Marchment leant forward, blue eyes pleading, golden ringlets a-tremble.

Jane Verey bit her lip, looking troubled. 'Oh, Sophy, I would truly love to, but—'

But the truth was that Miss Verey liked her food all too well and her friend was suggesting the unthinkable. Sophia's face fell a little.

'But, Jane, it is such an adventure! If you go to bed without supper and do not look behind you, you will dream of your future husband!' Sophia clapped her hands. 'Why, to my mind it is worth any amount of food!'

Jane thought longingly of the fresh loaf she had watched Cook bake only that day, the newly churned butter and the thick slices of ham that had been steeped in ale. Her mouth watered. No, it was impossible…

Sophia was pushing the book of legends towards her. The binding was coming loose and there was a dusty smell and crackling paper that implied great antiquity. Reluctantly, Jane peered at the faded words.

'...for if you go supperless to bed on St Agnes Eve
and take care not to look behind, you will conjure
dreams of your future husband...'

The bare branches of the oak outside Jane's window tapped impatiently on the glass. She jumped. Sophia was leaning forward, her golden curls gleaming
in the candlelight.

'You see! Tonight is St Agnes Eve! Oh, Jane, do
not condemn me to do this alone!'

Jane could foresee all manner of practical difficulties. How was one to close the bedroom door without
looking behind? How was a dream to be interpreted
if it contained not one man, but two—or even three?
She was about to confront Sophia with these problems
when her friend spoke again.

'Molly, the second parlourmaid, *swears* that it is
true, Jane! Twice now she has tested the legend and
on both occasions she dreamed of Gregory Pullman,
the farrier, so she knows it must be true!'

Jane could not see the logic of this. The last time
she had seen the farrier he had been attempting to
tumble a maid behind the stables and the girl had
certainly not been Molly.

'Does Gregory realise yet that he is to marry
Molly?' she inquired practically. 'It might be twenty
years or more before he grasps the truth, by which
time she will have become a sour old maid! And is
this not the same girl who washed her face in dew on
a May morning, swearing it would make her beautiful, then caught the cowpox—?'

Sophia dismissed this with a wave of one white
hand. 'Oh, Jane, how you do run on! It will do you
no harm to miss your supper just this once.' Her blue
eyes considered her friend's more-than-ample form.

'And you may dream of some desperately handsome man! Oh, please…'

Jane's stomach made a monstrous rumbling noise. To starve herself voluntarily seemed an intolerable thought, but Sophia was looking quite wretched.

'Oh, very well,' she capitulated reluctantly, reflecting that Sophia would never know if she got up in the middle of the night and went in search of some food.

Three hours later, Sophia had returned to Penistone Manor and Jane had trailed off to bed, looking very sorry for herself, but remembering not to look behind her.

'It's not natural, madam,' Cook complained to Lady Verey. 'A growing girl of fifteen should not be refusing her food like that! Why, she'll waste away!'

'Jane's growing in more than one direction!' Simon, her elder brother, said heartlessly but with some truth. 'She can live off her fat for a while!'

In the middle of the night Jane awoke, suffering from huge hunger pangs. The wind had increased whilst it was dark and small flurries of rain hit the glass in the windows. Disappointingly, Jane could not remember having a single dream, despite the fact that she had followed her instructions exactly. But perhaps, on a full stomach, she might have more success…

She slid out of bed, shivering in her thin cotton nightdress. She almost changed her mind when she thought of the warm, downy nest of sheets and blankets she had just left. The door creaked a little on its hinges as she started to open it and the dark passageway stretched away towards the top of the stairs. Jane had never been a superstitious child, but suddenly the old house of Ambergate and its shadowy corners seemed unfamiliar and unfriendly. Jane braced herself. She was about to push the door wide and take her courage in both hands when she heard a step at the top of the stairs.

A man was just turning the corner and coming down the corridor towards her. Jane shrank back with a gasp. The door was only open a crack, but through the narrow aperture she could see him clearly, for he carried a candle in one hand. She knew that she had never seen him before in her life, for she would most certainly have remembered. He could not be a servant and, for a moment, she wondered if he was in fact an apparition conjured up by a fevered mind that had been weakened by lack of food.

The first impression that Jane had was that he seemed very tall in the flickering candlelight and was clothed with an informality suitable only to his own dressing-room. His cravat hung loose and his white shirt was unbuttoned at the neck, revealing the strong brown column of his throat. His pantaloons clung to muscular thighs and the candlelight reflected on the mirror-polish of his Hessians. Jane caught her breath, staring in strange fascination. He was very dark, with silky black hair that seemed to gleam in the faint light. One dark lock fell across his forehead and he flicked it back with an impatient hand. His black brows were drawn together in a frown that made the saturnine face seem even more forbidding. Then those dark eyes turned thoughtfully towards Jane's door and she shrank back even further into the shadows, convinced that he had seen her. For a long moment he seemed to hesitate, staring directly at her door, before disappearing. There was no sound but for the soft click of a door closing further down the corridor.

Some ten minutes later, Jane found that she was able to move again and dived into the refuge of her bed, all pangs of hunger banished by fright. It was even longer before she was able to sleep, convinced that she had definitely seen an intruder or a ghost and reluctant to leave her room for help against either. Eventually she fell into an uneasy sleep and dreamed of the dark stranger who stalked the corridors of Ambergate.

When she woke in the morning, both her common sense and her appetite were restored.

'Why did you not tell me that we had a house guest, Mama?' she inquired, at breakfast, helping herself to two portions of kedgeree. 'I saw a gentleman in the corridor last night and was almost caught in my shift!'

Lady Verey exchanged a look with her husband, who cleared his throat but said nothing.

'We have no guests, my love,' Lady Verey said, giving her daughter a sweet smile. 'You must have been dreaming. And if you will eat cheese before you go to bed...'

'I had no supper last night and I did not dream it!' Jane declared stoutly, but she knew she was fighting a losing battle. Her mother's face wore the gentle but stubborn smile that meant that a topic was closed. Her father rustled his newspaper loudly.

'Always has her nose in a book,' he said shortly. 'Mistake. Shouldn't let the girl read. Stands to reason.'

Lady Verey turned her sweet smile on her spouse. 'Just so, my dear. Do you go into Penistone today? Perhaps Jane could accompany you—I have an errand for her with Mrs. Marchment...'

A meaningful glance passed between husband and wife. 'Simon is out riding already,' Lady Verey continued contentedly. 'He will be gone hours, I dare guess...'

Thus it was that neither Jane nor her brother saw the lone horseman who made his way down the lime avenue some two hours later. And though the servants talked amongst themselves, they all heeded Lady Verey's stricture that no one was to tell Jane or Simon of the visitor on pain of dismissal.

'What did you dream about, Jane?' Sophia demanded, when Lord Verey had conveyed her friend to the Manor in the gig. She did not wait for a reply. '*I* had the most extraordinary dream about a young man—he was *so* handsome, fair haired and blue eyed, and most dashing. I declare...' she clasped her hands together '...he *must* be my future husband!'

'I did not dream,' Jane said firmly. 'I had no dreams all night long.' She resolutely pushed away the image of the man she had seen in the corridor. She was certain that she had been awake when she first saw him; though she had dreamed of him later, surely that could not count. Sophia's face fell.

'No dreams? But, Jane, how dreadful! That must mean you are destined to be an old maid!'

Jane shrugged her plump shoulders, a mannerism that her mother deplored. 'I am persuaded that it would be better for me not to marry,' she said, her mouth full of Mrs. Marchment's cake and jam. 'I should not make anyone a conformable wife.'

Sophia was on the verge of loyally disagreeing when something stopped her. There was no doubt that Jane was the best friend ever, but she was not like anyone else.

'Perhaps you might meet a gentleman willing to overlook your odd ideas—' She broke off, blushing a little. 'Oh, Jane, I am certain that there must be a gentleman suitable for you!'

Jane did not bother to argue. She already understood that it would only make Sophia uncomfortable if she insisted on being different. Besides, her friend's next words summed up Jane's dilemma and there was no arguing with them.

'Oh, Jane,' Sophia said sadly, 'you have to marry! You must! For what else would you do?'

Chapter One

Four years later

It was late at night when Miss Jane Verey's laggardly suitor finally arrived at Ambergate. Dinner had been held for hours until Cook had complained bitterly that the sauce béarnaise had curdled and the pheasant compote had dried out and stuck to the serving dish. With a sigh and a glance at the clock, Lady Verey had had the food brought in and had eaten alone with her daughter, both of them uncomfortable in the unaccustomed finery donned especially for their visitor.

After dinner, they had sat for another hour in virtual silence, broken only by Lady Verey's plaintive cry of, 'But why does he not come? I am certain that he said the fifteenth! Perhaps he has had an accident on the road...'

Jane had fidgeted with her needlework, but had said nothing at all. There seemed to be little to say. After two months of vague promises and broken arrangements, Lord Philip Delahaye had still not honoured their agreement and met his chosen bride. He seemed a reluctant lover indeed, which sat ill with the information Jane had been given that the Delahaye match, as well as having her late father's blessing, was Lord Philip's most earnest desire.

Eventually, when Jane's yawns had become too pronounced to be ignored and the clock had chimed twelve, Lady Verey patted her daughter's cheek.

'You had best retire for the night, Jane. I shall wait up in case Lord Philip comes. Such disappointment is hard to bear, I know, but perhaps the morning will bring better news.'

Jane kissed her mother and went off to bed. She did not feel it necessary to explain that her disappointment amounted to very little at all. She had been persuaded to receive Lord Philip's addresses since it had been made very plain to her that they were now quite poor and that her father's dying wish was that her future be secured. Her brother Simon, the new Lord Verey, had been fighting with Wellington's armies and had not been heard of for a twelvemonth. Ambergate was falling about their ears and the servants stayed only out of loyalty. It was a melancholy picture.

It is not that I do not wish to marry, Jane thought, as she climbed the stairs in the candlelight, for I know I have very little choice. It is just that I imagined— hoped—that it might be so very different... And she thought of her henwitted friend Sophia Marchment, and could not help smiling. Sophia had imagined herself in love with no less than four young gentlemen in the last six months, but then she had remembered that none of them resembled the young man she had dreamed of so long ago on St Agnes Eve...

Jane had no illusions that her marriage would be

other than a business arrangement, a matter for sound common sense, and yet part of her wished for, if not a romantic passion, at least a mutual regard.

If I can just like him, she thought, then matters need not be so bad. And I hope that I *do* like him, for Mama can be most determined and I know that she means for the match to be made...

She stood before her bedroom mirror for a moment and wondered whether Lord Philip would like *her*. So familiar was she with her own features that Jane could scarcely see their charm. She decided that she looked rather like a cat, though admittedly a sleeker creature than the mangy tom that patrolled their stables. Her face had lost all its childhood fat and was now almost triangular, tapering from wide-set hazel eyes to a pointed little chin. Her mother was always telling her that she had the Verey nose, a delicate little projection that always looked weak on the face of Jane's male ancestors but suited her own proportions far better. The whole was framed by thick black hair as dark as night.

Jane sighed and started to undress for bed. She could see little to commend herself and did not recognise her own intriguing mixture of innocence and allure. She donned her cotton nightdress hastily, for the spring evenings were still chilly and Ambergate had many draughts. Her best dress of slightly faded white silk was laid carefully aside, looking as forlorn as Jane felt.

It was five minutes after Jane had slipped into her bed that the front door bell pealed, harsh and loud in the night. It rang once, then several more times, with irritable repetition.

A loud male voice shouted, 'Deuce take it! Is the whole house asleep? Hello there! Wake up, I say!'

Jane slid out of bed and tiptoed along the corridor to the wide landing at the top of the stairs. She could see Bramson, the butler, hastily shrugging himself into his coat as he hurried to the door. The old man was almost visibly shaking at the shock of the sudden arrival and all the noise, and Jane could not but wish Lord Philip would leave the bell alone. The continuous jangling was giving her a headache.

Lady Verey herself now came running out of the parlour just as Bramson swung the door open. It was clear to Jane that her mother must have fallen asleep in front of the fire, for her coiffure had started to come down on one side and there was a vivid red mark on her cheek where it must have been pressed against the side of the chair. She had had no time to tidy herself and was straightening her dress with nervous fingers. Jane's heart went out to her as she saw the anxious look that creased Lady Verey's face. She was heartbreakingly eager for the visit to be a success.

'What the devil do you mean by keeping me standing out there in the cold!' The same loud, masculine voice demanded wrathfully, as Lord Philip stepped into the hall. 'You!' He pointed at Bramson. 'See to the stabling of my horses! They are worn to the bone by these devilish bad roads! And you...' he turned towards Lady Verey '...kindly take me to your mistress!'

With horror, Jane realised that he had mistaken her mother for the housekeeper. Fortunately, Lady Verey's good manners, if not Lord Philip's, were up to the occasion.

She dropped a slight curtsy.

'How do you do, sir. I am Clarissa Verey. I am sorry to hear you have had so poor a journey. Would you care for some refreshment before you retire?'

Jane waited to hear Lord Philip apologise for his late arrival, his poor manners or perhaps both. Instead, he looked down his nose as though he could not quite believe that the fright who was addressing him could really be the mistress of the house. He gave a slight bow. 'How do you do, ma'am. Some dinner would be excellent.'

'The servants are all abed,' Lady Verey said, colouring a little under Lord Philip's critical scrutiny. 'I hope a cold supper in your room will suit your lordship…'

Lord Philip gave a sigh. 'I suppose that will suffice! What extraordinary hours you do keep in the country, ma'am! Why, if this were London, we would only now be sitting down to our second course! Quite extraordinary!'

Jane shrank back into the shadows as her mother steered their guest towards the staircase, but she had ample chance to see Lord Philip's rather disparaging look as he took in the old-fashioned furnishings and the threadbare carpet. Something close to fury rose in her. She could see that Lady Verey was both offended and upset, but was bravely trying to maintain a flow of pleasantries as they mounted the stairs.

Lord Philip, however, was only concerned with the arrangements for his luggage and turned to shout over his shoulder at the footman, 'See to it that someone brings my bags up carefully, man! The last time I stayed in the country some dolt of a servant managed to ruin half my cravats with his man-handling!'

For a moment Jane indulged in the satisfying

thought of kicking Lord Philip's bags straight down
the stairs, then she dived for her bedroom door as her
mother ushered him down the corridor. She huddled
under her covers, knees drawn up to her chin, and
thought about what she had just seen and heard. How
could this be her intended husband, this arrogant,
boorish man who had made his contempt for country
manners and country living so obvious in the space
of only a few minutes? How could he humiliate his
hostess so? His rudeness and scorn were not to be
tolerated!

Her thoughts were distracted by the rattle of a tray
and the chink of china. Lady Verey had sent hotfoot
to the kitchens and even now she was labouring along
the corridor, weighed down with food. Jane slipped
out of bed again, opened her door a crack and pressed
her ear to the gap. She heard the door of the green
bedroom open and Lord Philip drawl in a tone very
different from the one last used,

'Well, my pretty, what good fortune can have sent
you to me?'

Jane pressed a hand to her mouth. Surely he could
not be addressing Lady Verey! Then she realised that
her mother must have left Lord Philip to the mercy
of the servants and it was Betsey, the prettiest of the
maids, who had run the errand. Betsey was giggling.

'I've brought your supper, sir!' There was a pert-
ness in her tone that Jane had heard before when Betsey was flirting with the youngest footman, or Jack
from the stables.

There was a crash and another giggle from the
maid. 'Oh, sir! And you come a-courting here, as
well! Whatever will Miss Verey say?'

'A pox on Miss Verey!' Jane heard Lord Philip say

lazily. 'What do I care for her? And a pox on this paltry dish! Here's one much more to my liking! You're a cosy armful—come and give me a kiss...'

The door swung closed. Jane, burning with a mixture of embarrassment and fury, slammed her own door, careless of the noise. How dared he! First to arrive so late that he missed dinner, then to scorn Lady Verey's hospitality and show his contempt for her home, and finally to seduce one of the maids before he was barely across the threshold! Jane knew that she would never accept Lord Philip now, even if he went down on bended knee.

Surely...*surely* Lady Verey would not insist on the match now... Jane shivered in the draught from the door. If only she could be that sure, but their situation was so perilous. With Simon missing, they had no one to protect them. The estate needed firm management and a great deal of hard work. Lord Verey's entire fortune was left to Simon, but for Lady Verey's widow's jointure and Jane's small dowry. It seemed inevitable that her mother would wish her to marry well and marry soon, perhaps so soon that she would be prepared to overlook Lord Philip's crass bad manners.

There was a crash in the corridor as Lord Philip ejected both the supper tray, contents scattered all over the floor, and a snivelling Betsey, who had evidently not received the reward she had expected for her services. Jane gritted her teeth as she heard the sobbing maid rush away downstairs. Enough was enough. She took a candle and crept through the adjoining door into the old nursery.

The nursery was cold and dark, the pale candle flame reflected in the window panes. Shivering, Jane tiptoed across to the huge Armada chest tucked into a corner, neglected for years since the Verey children had grown too old for dressing up. She dragged it out and threw back the lid. She was sure she remembered… Yes, there it was, the dress her governess, Miss Tring, had worn as the Wicked—and fat—Stepmother to Sophia's Cinderella. Sophia had made a lovely heroine, but Jane had preferred to play one of the Ugly Sisters, for she found the part more interesting. But Miss Tring's dress was perfect for her purpose. It had huge cushions sewn on the inside and had made her look outrageously obese. Then there were the little pads to fatten out the cheeks and the brown crayon for freckles. Jane gathered everything up into a hasty bundle and hurried back into her room. She had great deal to do before morning.

Lord Philip Delahaye was woken at some ungodly hour of the morning by a cock crowing outside his window. He groaned and turned over to bury his head in the pillow but the noise seemed to go on and on, skewering his brain. He vaguely remembered a pretty little maidservant and a large bottle of port… Groaning, he turned on to his back and flinched as the bed-curtains were flung wide and the light struck across his eyes.

'Good morning, my lord!' A voice trilled in his ear. 'Why, I declare you are quite a slug-a-bed! My mama said to let you sleep, but I declare you must be up and about and out riding with me before breakfast!'

Lord Philip opened his eyes very gingerly. Before him stood an apparition that seemed to have come straight from his feverish dreams. His incredulous gaze took in the mob-cap, perched on a frizz of black curls, the hugely fat figure and the mottled face. He goggled at her.

'Who the devil are you?'

'I am your affianced bride, my lord!' The apparition moved slightly so that the morning sun was directly behind her and gave a little simpering giggle. Lord Philip could see little more than a monstrous, dark shape menacing him from the side of the bed. He shrank back against the pillows.

'Beg you to retire, ma'am!' he stuttered. 'Whatever can your mama be thinking to allow you to visit a gentleman's chamber so early—'

'It is past six,' his future bride scolded, wagging a finger. 'What a shocking lazybones! Breakfast is served at seven and then we must be about to help with the milking and feed the pigs! This is a working farm, my lord, and there is much to be done!'

Lord Philip winced. The thought of breakfast brought on a rush of nausea and the sight of his bobbing, tittering bride made it much worse. He desperately tried to remember what his elder brother had told him about Miss Jane Verey. Alex had been very persuasive about the match, convincing him that it was the only way that he would have his debts paid and be given an increase in his allowance. Philip had reluctantly considered that a wife, provided that she was biddable and presentable, need not hamper his activities too much. Besides, the money had been the deciding factor.

He shuddered. He spent as little time as possible in the country and even its sporting pursuits did not interest him. He was a creature of the city, in thrall to the gaming tables and the clubs, shuddering at country taste and country manners. No wonder Alex had skated adroitly over the Vereys' situation! They were hardly in the first stare of fashion and he had known nothing of them before Miss Verey's name had been put forward as his potential bride. Now he could see why. Poor as church mice...working a farm to make ends meet...a shabby house, no food, a barely drinkable port... They evidently needed Alex's money as much as he did!

Miss Verey was hovering about his bed now, plumping his pillows, smoothing his sheets and all the while chattering on in a way that made his head ache abominably. Philip tried to concentrate on Alex's fortune and the improvements in his life when his brother deigned to grant him a small share in it. A wife could be *made* to look presentable, but he shuddered to think of the cruel amusement of the *ton* when he escorted Miss Verey to one of the exquisite Bond Street couturiers in the hope that they could work a miracle. Pride and appearance were everything in his circle. He would be a laughing-stock. He closed his eyes and concentrated hard on the money, but Miss Verey's chatter distracted him.

'Pray, ma'am, will you be quiet!' he snapped. 'All I require from you is that you summon my valet! Immediately!' Six in the morning—he knew that Gibson would be furious for, like his master, he was a late riser. Nevertheless, that could not be given consideration. Lord Philip knew that he simply had to get away from Ambergate.

Lady Verey did not wake until ten, for she had been exhausted by the events of the previous night and Jane had given the servants orders not to disturb her. The first thing she saw was her daughter, perched demurely on the end of her bed, face scrubbed and pale, black hair freshly washed and curling about her face.

'Lord Philip!' Lady Verey exclaimed, struggling upright. 'Have you seen to his lordship's requirements, Jane? He is most particular and I should not wish him to find fault with us—'

Jane came forward and patted her mother's hand. 'Do not distress yourself, Mama! I saw Lord Philip myself this morning—I went to his chamber to see that he had all that he needed—and alas, he told me that he must hurry back to London. He had some urgent and unexpected business, I understand.'

Lady Verey clapped her hand to her mouth in horror. 'Jane! You mean that he has left already?'

Jane nodded regretfully. 'I am sorry, Mama. He sent you his apologies and best wishes.'

'Did he say nothing of returning?' Lady Verey asked, clutching her head beneath its lacy bedcap. 'Surely he will be back with us soon?'

Jane shook her head. 'I fear he made no mention of it, Mama, and I did not wish to press him—'

'No, of course.' Lady Verey smiled distractedly at her daughter. 'Natural delicacy must prevent you from inquiring—' She broke off in exasperation. 'Oh, dear, this is so very unfortunate! What of the betrothal? He did not speak this morning? No, I can see that he would not have the time... Perhaps I should write... But if he did not seem anxious to return...'

Jane got up and made a business of brushing some imaginary dust from the skirts of her dress.

'I am persuaded that it would be best to let matters lie, Mama. I am sure that Lord Philip will come back to Ambergate if he wishes and that we should not importune him. As for the betrothal, well...' she tried to look suitably downcast '…we must bear the disappointment as well as we are able.'

'Yes, indeed!' Lady Verey took her wrap gratefully and slipped out of bed. 'What a sensible girl you are, Jane. Tell me, did you like Lord Philip?'

'I scarce had time to form an opinion, Mama,' Jane said carefully. 'His lordship is excessively handsome and seems most fashionable…'

Lady Verey's lips set in a thin line and for a moment her daughter thought that she was about to pass some criticism, but her innate courtesy triumphed over her feelings.

'Well, well, it is all most strange! He gave no indication of the business that had summoned him away so suddenly, I suppose? No, of course he would not. But perhaps he will return in his own good time…'

'Perhaps so, Mama,' Jane concurred. 'Perhaps so.'

Three weeks later, Simon Verey returned home.

'Is it not romantic, Jane?' Sophia Marchment exclaimed as the friends sat together in the parlour of the Manor. 'Your long-lost brother returned from the dead to save the estate from ruin! I declare you must be *aux anges*!'

Jane tried not to laugh. Sophia's flights of fancy were as extravagant as they were highly coloured, but she was the sweetest friend imaginable.

'I am very happy to have Simon back,' she agreed, 'for we were always close and to think him lost was a horrid thing! He has changed, Sophia, which I suppose is no surprise.' Jane wrinkled her brow. 'War has changed him. He seems older, not just in years but in attitude and experience.'

Sophia made a little noise of distress and took

Jane's hand in a comforting hold. 'Oh, Jane! Is he very sad?'

'Not precisely...' Jane smiled a little '...but he is serious and no madcap boy like he was before. He says he wishes to settle down! Imagine! He plans to go to London to find himself a suitable wife!'

Sophia coloured a little. She had been a little in love with Simon Verey for the last ten years.

Jane, realising she had been tactless, hurried on.

'Anyway, when Simon explained his plan to go up to Town, Mama decided that we should all go, for the Season. Apparently, Aunt Augusta Monckton has a house in Portman Square which she has offered to us and, although it is not the most fashionable of addresses, it is in a perfectly respectable area. Mama believes that we may afford it if we are careful and she is quite taken with the idea.'

'London!' Sophia breathed. 'Oh, Jane!' She looked round the manor parlour with its faded velvet and chintzes. 'The Season! Fashionable company! I declare you are the luckiest creature alive!'

Jane, reflecting how little she wished for her good fortune, gave her friend a smile. 'Well, it is not perfectly to my taste, for you know how I prefer the country, and I know you think me mad to do so! But what I really wished to ask was whether you would like to come with us? Mama thought it would be better fun for me if you were there and I should like it extremely—'

When Sophia had stopped screaming with excitement, had hugged her friend twice and had rushed off down the corridor to find the Squire and Mrs. Marchment, Jane sat back with a sigh.

She had spoken the truth when she said that she

was delighted to have her brother back, but his plans had taken her by surprise. She had expected him to want nothing but peace and rest after the privations and hardship of his life on campaign, but instead he had insisted on the entertainment and company of the capital. Lady Verey's enthusiastic acquiescence had made Jane's heart sink. She had not imagined that she would need to set foot in London.

She knew that her mother was thinking to bring her to Lord Philip's attention again in the hope that the Delahaye match might be saved, or, if that were not to be, that Jane might attract the interest of some other gentleman of means. Simon's return had staved off the most immediate threat of penury, of course, but she still had little alternative than to marry. She could not be a drain on her brother's limited resources indefinitely.

London. In view of the way she had disposed of Lord Philip, this was particularly awkward. Jane frowned. Her conscience had been troubling her, not about the way she had deceived Lord Philip by her appearance and behaviour, but over the necessity of omitting certain facts when she spoke of it to her mother.

For some reason, she had not anticipated ever having to see Lord Philip again and she was annoyed with herself for not considering the possibility. It would be very difficult to think up a convincing explanation for the sudden transformation in her appearance.

Of course, she might not even meet Lord Philip in London, but matters could become awkward if she did. Jane heaved another sigh. Thank goodness that no one else knew the embarrassing truth about Lord

Philip's foreshortened visit to Ambergate. It was not an episode of which she was proud but, given a little time, she was sure that she could come up with a plausible explanation for her behaviour.

The night watchman greeted the gentleman with the news that it wanted but ten minutes to two and the weather was fine. The butler at the house in Berkeley Square gave him the further intelligence that his brother was awaiting him in the library. Lord Philip Delahaye thanked both of them and tipped neither. The butler watched him go into the room and shook his head very slightly at the distinct unsteadiness of his lordship's gait.

The library was lit by the fire and one candle only. Lord Philip, coming to an abrupt halt just inside the door, said uncertainly, 'Alex?'

'Sit down, Philip.'

Alexander, Duke of Delahaye, spoke from the depths of the wing chair placed before the fire. He put his book to one side and got to his feet. 'A drink, little brother? Or have you already had enough for one evening?' There was the faintest, mocking undertone in his voice and, as always, it put Philip on the defensive.

'Devil take it, Alex, it's not even two o'clock yet! I'd only just got to Watiers as it was!'

'Not broached your third bottle yet? My apologies for finding you too soon,' his brother returned drily. 'Unfortunately, there was—is—a matter of some urgency I wished to discuss with you.'

There was silence. Philip watched a little sulkily as his brother crossed to the table and poured two glasses of brandy. He took one with a grudging word of thanks and sat down. Unlike the Duke, who was casually if elegantly attired, Lord Philip was in evening dress of a high dandyism. He felt rather than saw his brother's dark gaze skim him with thoughtful consideration and stiffened. Why was it, he wondered, that Alex could look so effortlessly elegant in his disarray whilst he had spent hours before a mirror and was still discontented with the result?

To make himself feel better he said spitefully, 'You look a little dishevelled, Alex. Been entertaining a lady?'

'No,' the Duke said indifferently. 'I have been waiting for you to come and explain to me why you are in Town rather than courting Miss Verey in Wiltshire.'

Lord Philip took a pull on his brandy. He felt he needed it. 'I did go to Wiltshire…'

'I know. And then you came back the following day. Why?'

There was nothing for it but the truth. 'The girl's a freak,' Lord Philip said viciously. 'A great, fat, whey-faced creature who can barely string two words together, and you and Lady Verey will not foist her on to me for the sake of any fortune! I'd rather starve!'

'And well you might.' There was still no inflection in Alex Delahaye's voice. The fire crackled. 'Have you forgotten that you'll not get another penny from me if you do not marry?'

'Marry, yes—but that?' Philip's eyes were wild. He slammed the glass down and the amber liquid jumped. 'Have you met Miss Verey, Alex? Do you really dislike me so much as to condemn me to that?'

Alex Delahaye raised his brows. 'I have not seen

her since she was fifteen and I'll allow she was a little on the plump side then—'

'Plump! Surely you mean monstrous fat! A great whale of a girl tricked out in pink satin!'

Alex winced. 'Must you always judge on appearance, Philip? I confess I have had no speech with her, but Verey assured me that she was of pleasant disposition and well to a pass—'

'Ha!'

'And that she was not unwilling to the match—'

'Maybe not, for what other chance will she get?' Philip drained the rest of his brandy in one gulp. 'No wonder she is not yet out! No wonder the Vereys had been hiding her away there in the country these years past! And now Lord Verey is dead and beyond retribution and I am promised to that fright!'

The Duke sighed with the first sign of irritation he had shown. 'As well he is dead, or you would be answering to him for your insults to his daughter! Philip, I will not carry on financing your escapades about town indefinitely. The alliance with Jane Verey is a sound one.'

'Oh, I know you want me to settle down.' Philip put his empty glass down with a sulky snap. All his remembered grievances were jostling in his mind, pushing forward, demanding to be heard.

'It is all very well for you to dictate to me, keeping me short of funds, making me beg to have my debts settled! You, with all the fortune and all the estates—'

'And all the responsibilities,' his brother finished, a little bitterly. 'Yes, it has been truly enjoyable for me, Philip, with five younger siblings to see settled creditably and three estates to return to profit! And then there have been fortune-hunting suitors to dis-

courage on behalf of my sisters and the extorting
landlords to deal with over breach of promise—'

'There was only one landlord,' Philip said crossly,
'and I never promised to marry his daughter!'

Alex did not trouble to reply. He stretched out his
long legs towards the fire and sighed. His brother
eyed him with disfavour.

'You have been married,' Philip said suddenly.
'How can you then condemn me to a loveless match?'

There was a sharp silence. 'I would have thought
that my own experiences were the perfect example of
the evils of a love match,' Alex said expressionlessly.
'I would spare you that, little brother.'

Philip said something very short and very rude. His
brother only smiled.

'I sometimes find it difficult to believe you are only
my senior by ten years,' Philip said, with a final vi-
cious spurt of malice. 'You seem so very much
older!'

Alex laughed. 'The weight of obligation!' he said
lightly, but his eyes were cold.

'But devil take it, Alex, you like living like this!
You choose it!' Philip reached for the brandy bottle,
staring at his brother aggressively. 'You never go out,
you never entertain… You cultivate your reputation
as a recluse! And yet the toadies still try to tempt you
with their daughters and their entertainments and their
wine cellars!'

Alex shrugged, indifferent again. 'A Dukedom is
perceived to be always in need of a Duchess,' he said.
'Unfortunately for the matchmakers, I am not in need
of a wife! Which is where you enter the play, Philip!'

'Damned if I see why I should marry just to oblige
you!' his brother said, aggrieved. 'I know Madeline

played fast and loose, and after she died you wanted no more to do with women! But you hold the Dukedom—you provide the heir! Damnation take it, there are hundreds of women panting after you!'

Alex Delahaye stretched, crossing one ankle over the other. 'You're wasting your time, Philip! I hold the purse strings and I want you to marry! It's as simple as that. Now, you will renew your courtship of Miss Verey—'

'I can't do that!'

'Because of your aversion to her appearance? You will find that there is more to marriage than a pretty face,' his brother said coldly.

'It's not just that.' Philip's face was turned away, suddenly suffused with colour. 'I have told everyone—told the others how it was with her. I shall be a laughing-stock if I renew my suit!'

'The others? Whom?' Alex's voice cut like a whip.

'Ponsonby and Malters and Cheriton,' Philip muttered. 'It seemed a good joke—Verey tricking you into agreeing an alliance between the Delahayes and that pudding-faced wench! They found it amusing, at any event...'

'No doubt,' Alex said, with biting sarcasm. He got to his feet, towering over his brother's chair. 'Your drinking cronies have seldom been graced with wit and taste! Well, you must make your choice, Philip! Either you are a rich laughing-stock or you are a penniless one!'

Philip was out of his chair in a second, confronting his brother. Alex had moved away and stood before the fireplace, one arm resting idly on the mantelpiece. He was the taller, which gave him an immediate advantage, but for once Philip was too angry to care.

'Damn you for dictating my life,' he said, real hatred lighting his blue eyes. 'I wish you had died along
with our parents!'

For a moment they stood as though frozen. Philip
was the first to look away.

'I'm going,' he muttered, 'and do not think to try
and pass off one of your candidates for matrimony on
to me again! Damned if I'll ever marry, to oblige you
or otherwise!'

'Damned if you don't,' Alex said expressionlessly,
moving over to the fireplace and pulling the bell for
the butler. 'Tredpole, my brother is just leaving. Be
so good as to lock up after him. You may go to bed.
I shall not need you again tonight.'

After the impassive Tredpole had shown Philip
out, Alex resumed his seat but did not pick up the book
that he had been reading. Instead, he sat staring into
the dying embers of the fire.

Miss Jane Verey... She had been little more than
a child when he had seen her at Ambergate, but she
had seemed a pleasant and unaffected girl. Alex
smiled a little as he remembered the first glimpse he
had had of her, riding across the fields close to her
home. She had had a good seat on the horse and was
clearly enjoying both the fresh country air and the
company of her brother, who rode alongside. She had
seemed exactly the type of sensible girl who would
best keep Philip's wilder excesses in check. Lord
Verey had been flatteringly eager for the alliance, but
they had agreed to wait a few years for Jane to reach
her eighteenth year. All had seemed set fair.

Verey's death had thrown the plan slightly, but
when the year of mourning had elapsed, Alex had
been glad to find that the widow was still as receptive

to the match. Philip had been giving increasing cause
for concern over the years, with his deep play and
unsuitable friends, and now that he had attained the
age of four and twenty, Alex had decided it was high
time that his brother settled down. Nor had Philip
seemed particularly reluctant at first. Alex gave a rueful grimace. Money was the only currency that Philip
understood and the inducements that he had offered
alongside Miss Verey had obviously been attractive.
More attractive than the girl herself, evidently!

Alex sighed. Perhaps he had been mistaken, in both
Miss Verey and in the strength of Philip's feelings. It
was not always easy to know what was best in the
matter of his brother and sisters. There had been an
ageing roué whom his sister Eliza had sworn was the
love of her life. Alex had disapproved of the man but
had not liked to oppose the match when he could see
that his actions made Eliza so unhappy. Yet the very
next season she had met a young baronet and was
now happily married and living in Herefordshire. The
other two girls were also married and the middle
brother, George, was serving with Wellington's army.
There was only Philip…

Alex strode over to the bureau beside the window.
One of the desk drawers was half-open, a pile of pa-
pers almost spilling over the top. His expression hardened. Philip had been granted endless credit on the
strength of the Delahaye fortune and now he was the
one they were dunning for payment. He slammed the
drawer closed, sending several of the bills tumbling
onto the carpet. He would not stand for any more
nonsense. The Verey match would be put forward
once again and Philip forced to comply. Alex's jaw
tightened. His brother's day of reckoning was approaching in more ways than one.

Chapter Two

'It's true, I'm afraid,' Lady Eleanor Fane said bluntly. 'It's the *on dit* all over Town, Alex, even eclipsing poor Maria Scrope's elopement with the footman! Everyone knows that Philip described Miss Jane Verey as an ugly, illiterate brood mare! Which,' Lady Eleanor added fairly, 'would be bad enough even without the rest!'

She removed her gloves, discarded her parasol and collapsed into an armchair with a heavy sigh.

Lady Eleanor, the Duke of Delahaye's aunt and godmother, was one of the few women allowed past the portals of Haye House. Impeccably connected and with a wide circle of friends, Lady Eleanor often acted as the Duke's eyes and ears in Society. And her intelligence system was faultless. Which was why Alex Delahaye did not interrupt, but simply waited for her to continue.

'Lady Verey has brought her daughter up to Town,' Lady Eleanor went on, reaching for the silver teapot and pouring herself a generous cup. 'Jane is not out yet—she makes her debut at Almack's next week. When I met Clarissa Verey in Bond Street she had not yet heard the rumours, but it can only be a matter of time before some spiteful scandalmonger stirs up trouble!' She watched Alex's face set in lines of deep displeasure. 'The girl is practically ruined before she starts! It was the utmost folly of Philip to speak as he did.'

'I know it.' Alex got up from the desk and strode across to the window, hands in his pockets. 'The foolish young cub! He could never resist bragging to his cronies. No doubt they all thought it a great jest, but if the Vereys hear of it—'

'If! When!' Lady Eleanor said energetically. 'The presence of Jane Verey in Town will stir the gossip to a positive maelstrom! Oh, Clarissa Verey glossed over Philip's desertion, claiming that the betrothal had been a mere suggestion rather than a definite match, but she will not be so kind when she hears what Philip has been saying about her daughter! And there is worse, Alex, far worse!'

Alex raised one black brow, a look of faint amusement on his face. 'What could possibly be worse?'

'Simon Verey has returned from the wars and is accompanying them to Town,' Lady Eleanor said, grimly. 'They are not without protection! If he should hear of the slur cast on his sister's name—'

'Scarcely her name,' Alex said mildly. 'Even Philip has not suggested Miss Verey is anything but virtuous!'

'Her intellect, her appearance!' Lady Eleanor amended crossly. 'Must you be so literal, Alexander? Simon—Lord Verey, I suppose we must now call him!—will hear some mention of it in the clubs and we will all be in the suds!'

'Very poetic, Aunt Eleanor!'

Lady Eleanor gave a snort of disgust. 'Upon my word, you are in an odd mood today, Alex! But I know that you have always rated Simon Verey most highly!'

'I have indeed—he is spoken of as a most intelligent and sound man!'

'But wait,' Lady Eleanor said impatiently, 'you have not heard the final piece of news!'

'I am all attention, ma'am,' her nephew murmured politely, betrayed only by the twinkle in his eye. Lady Eleanor let it pass in the interests of conveying her information.

'On the strength of our old friendship, Clarissa Verey invited me back to Portman Square,' she said. 'Well, of course, I could scarce decline, although I hoped she would not ask my advice on how to make her hideous daughter presentable. Don't smile at me, Alex, this is serious! Try to follow my chain of thought!'

'Yes, ma'am!' the Duke said meekly.

Lady Eleanor looked suspiciously at him but his expression remained quite bland.

'Well, naturally enough, Clarissa Verey suggested that both Jane and the friend she has brought with her from the country should make their curtsies to me! Clarissa had already ordered tea, and mentioned in passing that Jane had a sweet tooth so, coupled with Philip's comments, I made the obvious connection that the girl ate too many cakes!'

'Naturally enough!'

'Then the door opened, and a divine child tiptoed in and curtsied to me! She was tiny, all pink and white, with golden curls! A veritable angel!'

'The friend from the country?'

'Of course,' Lady Eleanor said, discontentedly. 'Miss Sophia Marchment! It's a tragedy!'

'That the friend is so pretty and Miss Verey not?'

'No!' Lady Eleanor glared. 'Really, Alex, how you do leap to conclusions! No, the tragedy is that Philip has made even more of a fool of himself than we had imagined. For then, Miss Verey herself came in. Oh, dear!'

'Pray compose yourself, ma'am,' the Duke said, lips twitching. 'I am desperate to hear the end of the tale!'

'Why, but she is quite beautiful! Quite distractingly lovely!' Lady Eleanor said crossly, reaching for a handkerchief and blowing her nose hard. 'And the sweetest of girls! How could Philip do such a thing? How *could* he?'

The Duke was accustomed to his aunt's slightly long-winded and sometimes circuitous route when approaching a subject. There was no doubt, however, that he had not been expecting this.

'The girl is beautiful?' he echoed, dumbfounded. 'Are you sure?'

'Of course I am sure! How can you be so nonsensical? She is beautiful and charming and intelligent! They are the perfect foil for each other, the one so fair and the other so dark! They'll break all the hearts in Town!'

There was a silence. Alex got to his feet and strolled over to the window, hands in the pockets of his beautifully cut bottle-green coat. Lady Eleanor viewed his tall figure hopefully. If anyone could think of a way to bring them out of this mess, it had to be Alex. He was as cool-headed and resourceful as Philip was rash and quixotic. In fact, Lady Eleanor regretted that he sometimes seemed too cold, too passionless.

It had not always been thus. She could remember the youthful Alexander, Marquis of Hawarden as he was then, flushed with happiness and good humour on his wedding day some fourteen years before. Before his parents had died so tragically in a carriage accident, before he had had to take on the upbringing of his five siblings and before his beautiful young Duchess had disgraced his name with her open affairs, her gambling and the drinking which had lead to her premature death some six years after their marriage…

'Are you still of a mind for Philip to wed, Alex?' she asked a little hesitantly, as her godson seemed sunk deep in thought.

'I am.' Alex shook himself, turning away from his contemplation of the view of Berkeley Square. 'He has to be made to conform, Aunt Eleanor, and what better way than by a respectable marriage and a brood of infants? And the Verey match is a good one! You may remember that it was my grandfather's dearest wish that there should be an alliance between the Delahayes and the Vereys! I even went to Ambergate myself a few years ago to speak to Verey about it! All was set fair, and now Philip—' He broke off, his lips tightening in exasperation.

'You went to Ambergate?' Lady Eleanor sat forward. 'I had no notion! Did you meet Miss Verey whilst you were there?'

'I did not. I saw her, but I did not speak to her. She was unaware of my visit since her father wished to keep the proposed marriage a secret from her at the time. I believe she was but fifteen and no doubt he did not judge her of an age to be considering her future husband!'

Lady Eleanor raised her brows. In her experience young ladies with far less than fifteen years in their dish were pre-occupied with their marriages.

'What was your opinion of her?'

Alex shrugged as though he did not have an opinion. 'Her looks were pleasant enough, I suppose, although she was a little plump. She seemed a bright, lively girl and hardly the frumpish dullard Philip is suggesting!'

Lady Eleanor frowned. 'How could he have been so mistaken in her? I can scarce believe it! Why, the girl he described and the one that I met cannot be the same person!'

Alex was also frowning now. 'Yes, I confess that that is the part that exercises me the most! I have every respect for your judgement, Aunt—' he flashed her a grin '—and were it a choice between your assessment and Philip's, I should settle for yours any time! But the fact remains that Philip describes Miss Verey in terms of pungent denunciation whilst you have seen her to be a veritable angel! One of you must be mistaken!'

'My dear Alex,' Lady Eleanor said trenchantly, 'the whole Town will shortly see that *my* description is the accurate one! And not only can I vouch for Miss Verey's personal charms, I know she has wit and style to match!'

'Then,' Alex Delahaye said slowly, 'Philip must be lying. I can only assume he made up this outrageous fabrication to strengthen his refusal of the match. Perhaps he thought that I would relent if I believed Miss

Verey to be utterly unpresentable! Evidently he is prepared to go to extreme lengths to avoid the marriage!'

'Foolish,' Lady Eleanor said shortly, 'and dangerous. It only needed for Miss Verey to come to Town for him to be seen to be a liar and a scoundrel! I am surprised at Philip! He may be a loose fish but he is no fool!'

'No,' Alex said, 'he is no fool. Which is why—' He broke off and Lady Eleanor looked at him curiously.

'What is in your mind, Alexander?'

'I am thinking that there are various strands to be resolved here,' the Duke said thoughtfully. 'I am still of a mind to try to save the Verey match if I can. More importantly, I must speak to Philip about the sudden transformation in Miss Verey's person and character. It is that, dear ma'am, which interests me the most.' His dark gaze, reflective but with a faint hint of humour, rested on Lady Eleanor's puzzled face.

'We have assumed that it is Philip who is at fault here,' he enlarged, 'but no one has yet thought to ask of Miss Verey's reaction to the proposed match. I imagine that you had too much delicacy to mention it to her, Aunt?' Then, as Lady Eleanor nodded in bewilderment, he continued.

'You say that she has wit and charm. Supposing, dear Aunt…just supposing…that Miss Verey herself has objections to Philip's suit, objections that have been set aside by those making the match. She might have told her mother that she did not wish to marry, only to be overruled. Would she perhaps take matters into her own hands? And take any steps within her power to make herself displeasing to him?'

Lady Eleanor gasped, recoiling, grasping her parasol as if for comfort. 'Alex! What a suggestion! How could she possibly—?'

'Anyone may play the fool if they choose,' Alex said drily. 'It is more difficult to appear ugly if one is not, but scarcely impossible with a little disguise! And Philip is not very discerning! I wonder...'

'Are you truly suggesting that Miss Verey has tricked Philip?' Lady Eleanor looked as though she would be reaching for the hartshorn next. 'No! Oh, no, I cannot credit it!'

Alex smiled. 'I may, of course, be doing Miss Verey the greatest injustice. But it should be possible to discover the circumstances under which she and Philip met, the witnesses, the words that passed between them. I believe that I could find out quite easily whether or not Philip has been cozened!'

Lady Eleanor was still looking confused and deeply reproachful. 'Alex, you have the cunning of the devil even to think of it!'

'Thank you, Aunt Eleanor!' Once again, Alex grinned at her. 'I confess to a certain curiosity about Miss Jane Verey! It is stimulating to suspect that I may have met an adversary as devious as I!'

'No, it is impossible! Not that sweet girl!'

'Well, we shall see!'

'How do you intend to go about it?' Lady Eleanor asked with misgiving.

'I will make inquiries,' Alex said slowly, 'and I intend to meet Miss Verey. I will judge for myself if she be innocent angel or cunning jade!'

'Oh, Jane, is this not fine?' Sophia sighed in ecstasy. 'Such beautiful shops! Why, not even Bath can rival it! I declare, I could spend an entire day just looking!'

Jane stifled a yawn. She already felt as though she had spent a whole day doing precisely that. This had to be the twentieth shop that they had visited that afternoon.

When the shopping trip had been mooted after breakfast, Jane's brother Simon had looked horrified and had taken refuge at his club. Jane wished that she had a similar choice. It was not that she disliked shopping, precisely—she paused to watch her mother and Sophia agonising between two exquisitely painted fans—it was simply that she grew bored with it so very quickly. The silks and taffetas, slippers and shoes, hats and gloves that so fascinated her friend could not hold her attention for long. Now, if only it had been books... Jane smothered a giggle as she remembered the look of pained disapproval on her mother's face when she had tentatively suggested that they visit James Lackington's 'Temple of the Muses' in Finsbury Square.

'Temple of the Muses!' Lady Verey had repeated. 'Why, it sounds like a house of ill repute rather than a bookseller's! I cannot believe it a suitable place for us to visit unescorted!'

So Jane had been obliged to enlist her brother's help to buy the books she wanted and was denied the pleasure of browsing amongst the galleries of bookshelves and of watching the other bibliophiles thronging Mr Lackington's 'lounging-rooms.'

Lady Verey and Sophia had moved on to consider a very pretty straw hat adorned with blue ribbons. Jane's eye was caught briefly by a silky scarf of emerald green, and she moved over to take a closer look,

letting it run through her fingers like water. Beyond
the wide bow windows, Charles Street was busy with
ladies and gentlemen strolling in the sunshine. Across
the road was a spirit booth, with crystal flasks of
every shape and form, cunningly lit from behind so
that the different coloured spirits sparkled alluringly.
Jane smiled. Now there was something worthy of her
time; glass and china were fascinating commodities
and she hoped to visit Mr Wedgwood's emporium in
Great Newport Street, where she had heard that the
displays of china were arranged especially to amuse
and intrigue the visitor...

There was a gentleman standing across the road
just to the left of the spirit booth. His very stillness
caught Jane's notice and, once she had looked up, she
found that his intent gaze appeared to be directed
through the bow windows of the shop and fixed upon
her person. It was oddly disconcerting, not least because she was certain that she had seen him before.
He was very tall and very dark, and his penetrating
gaze locked with her own. Suddenly it was as though
they were only a matter of feet apart, with no glass
window between them, nor bustling street, nor indeed
any barrier of any kind. Jane found herself unable to
look away and break the spell.

His gaze pinned her to the spot, so searching and
intent that Jane felt the colour coming up into her
cheeks.

Then a dray cart came between them, the carter
shouting to his horses and blocking the view, and Jane
drew a shaky breath and turned away from the window.

'Jane?' Lady Verey had noticed nothing amiss.
'Come here, my love, and tell us which is the finer

of these two shawls. Sophia has a fancy for the pink with the lace, but I am not sure—' Her eye fell on the scarf, which Jane was still clutching unknowingly in her left hand.

'Oh, how pretty! You must have it, my love, for it matches your eyes to perfection! What excellent taste you do have, Jane! Now, tell me what you think of this shawl...'

Both the shop assistant and Sophia were looking at her expectantly. Jane obediently looked where her mother pointed but she was scarcely thinking of fripperies and furbelows.

It was him! she thought, still a little breathless inside. I recognised him. I *know* it was him.

Gradually her fluttering pulse stilled and her breathing slowed. No doubt she had imagined it. One dark stranger might look very like another and London was full of people. It seemed foolish to think that she would recognise one man, glimpsed four years before at Ambergate and never seen again. All the same...

She was still puzzling over it as they came out of the shop and on to the sunlit pavement.

'Now then, girls,' Lady Verey said, shepherding them into the street, 'the milliner's is just across from here—'

'Oh, look, ma'am!' Sophia exclaimed, clutching Lady Verey's arm. 'I did not see those gloves! Oh, they would be perfect for tomorrow night! I positively must have them! Jane—' she turned anxiously to her friend '—you do not mind?'

Jane smiled a little. Sophia would be spending all her allowance in one morning at this rate!

'I shall wait for you out here in the sun,' she said. 'It is a pleasant day and there is no need to hurry.'

'Stay in sight of the window, Jane,' Lady Verey instructed, turning to follow Sophia into the shop. 'I wish to keep you in view. And should anyone accost you, I pray you to come straight back into the shop—'

'Yes, mama,' Jane said patiently, gesturing to her mother to follow Sophia. 'I can come to no harm in full view!'

The shop door closed behind Lady Verey and Jane turned to scan the street. Although her acquaintance in London was still small, she recognised the lady and gentleman who were strolling along the opposite side of the road, for they were neighbours of the Vereys in Portman Square and had been most welcoming. And just beyond them… Jane took an involuntary step forward as she saw the dark gentleman again, pausing before a gunsmith's, his back turned to her.

There was a sudden, irate shout and she spun around in alarm. A cart was passing close by and she felt her skirts snag on something, tugging hard and catching her off balance. She slipped on the cobbles, her skirt hopelessly entangled in the cart's left wheel, and felt herself dragged to the ground. It all seemed to happen in the blink of an eye before Jane could scramble back to safety.

'Oh!' It was Jane's dignity that had suffered most, but tears of shock swam in her eyes. Her hands felt bruised from the sudden contact with the ground and she had bumped one knee painfully as she fell. Tumbled in the gutter in a heap of petticoats and rubbish, she struggled to recover herself.

'Allow me to help you, ma'am.' A quiet voice spoke in her ear at the same time as the gentleman slid a supportive hand under her elbow and helped her to her feet. 'Are you injured at all?'

Jane looked up and experienced her second shock. This time there could be no mistake. It was certainly the man that she had seen at Ambergate, though this time more formally dressed in immaculate buckskins, top-boots and a mulberry-coloured jacket. At such close quarters he was disturbingly attractive, a man quite outside Jane's limited experience. He was certainly handsome, with wicked, dark good looks that quite took her breath away, but there was a rather austere expression in those very dark eyes that contradicted the impression of slightly rakish attraction. There was also an aura of strength about him and an impression of power held under tight control that was instantly reassuring.

He was holding her very gently with an arm supporting her about the waist and there was concern in his face and something else…an extraordinary tenderness, surely, that made Jane feel suddenly faint. She swayed a little and his arm tightened.

'You should sit down, I think, to recover from the shock. Where did your companions go?'

'I thank you, sir, I am quite well,' Jane said shakily, catching sight of her mother's face peering in horror through the shop window. The carter chose the same moment to start justifying himself to the gathering crowd. His diatribe on foolish young women who did not look where they were going was silenced by one glance from the gentleman.

Jane realised that she was bruised but not badly injured. She felt foolish and embarrassed. She noticed that one of her hands was resting confidingly against the lapel of the mulberry jacket, whilst the gentleman's arm still held her close. It was most comforting, but surely rather improper. Dark eyes smiled down into her hazel ones. Jane felt her knees tremble again.

'Thank you for your help, sir,' she said again, trying to extricate herself. 'You have been most kind, and I am quite well enough to—'

'Jane!' Lady Verey and Sophia came dashing out of the shop, accompanied by the modiste and half of the staff, adding to the confusion on the pavement. The carthorse started to stamp and rear, disturbed by the noise. Sophia helpfully removed a cabbage leaf from her friend's skirt.

'Jane!' Lady Verey said again. 'Are you hurt? Whatever has happened—' She broke off, staring in sudden confusion at the gentleman. 'Your Grace!'

The gentleman removed his arm from Jane's waist at last and executed a bow. 'Lady Verey. How do you do, ma'am.' Jane thought that she could detect the very slightest hint of rueful amusement in his voice. 'I do not believe that Miss Verey has come to any lasting harm, but perhaps she should be conveyed home for a rest. I shall call a hack for you.'

'Yes of course, but—' Lady Verey's gaze was darting from Jane to her rescuer. 'I had no notion that you were the gentleman who had come to Jane's rescue. We had no idea that you were even in Town! Is your brother with you? You must permit us to call and express our sense of obligation—'

'Of course, ma'am, I should be delighted.' The gentleman cut her short in the politest, most deferential manner possible. 'I shall not detain you any longer. Good day…'

He bowed again and the crowd parted to let him

pass as though obeying some unspoken authority. The cart pulled away and a hackney cab took its place. Jane, bewildered and shaken, allowed Sophia to help her solicitously inside.

'Who was that gentleman, ma'am?' she heard Sophia ask Lady Verey as the cab set off in the direction of Portman Square. 'He seemed quite...' Sophia hesitated, but Jane knew just what she meant. The gentleman in question had seemed quite awesome. She felt again the power of his glance, the tender strength with which he had held her. Jane shivered.

'That was the Duke of Delahaye,' Lady Verey was saying composedly, 'the elder brother of Lord Philip. Jane...' she saw her daughter's pale, stricken face '...are you sure that you are quite well? You must go to bed as soon as we reach home or you will not be well enough for Almack's this evening! I am sure that the accident must have overset you!'

'Yes, Mama,' Jane said submissively. 'I confess I feel a little shaken.'

'Well, perhaps we should not go tonight—' Lady Verey broke off, looking torn. 'But on the other hand it could be construed as a snub to the patronesses...oh, dear, how provoking! I do not know what to do!'

'I shall be better directly, Mama!' Jane said, leaning back and closing her eyes. 'I pray you, do not consider cancelling our attendance...'

'I had no notion that the Duke was in Town,' Lady Verey said, smoothing her gloves. 'He is seldom in London, you know, for he much prefers the country!' She frowned. 'How odd! And how curious that he should be passing just when you fell, Jane!'

Jane, remembering the way in which the Duke of

Delahaye had stood watching her from across the road, was tempted to say that he had hardly been passing. She held her peace. The whole episode had been most disconcerting. Why had the Duke been watching her beforehand and what could account for her strange reaction to him? The colour flooded her face as she remembered the sensation of his arm about her. She had met plenty of personable gentlemen in the past week, but never before had she been so aware of a man's touch. She closed her eyes. It was best to forget it, best to forget him. It seemed that, between them, the Delahaye brothers were causing her nothing but trouble.

It was Simon Verey who heard the rumours first. Whilst the ladies were out shopping he had had a meeting with Pettishaw, his man of business, and had then spent a convivial afternoon with Lord Henry Marchnight, one of his oldest friends. They had met by chance at Tattersall's and, as the evening advanced, made their way to Brooks.

'Covered yourself with glory on campaign, I hear,' Henry said with a lazy grin, after they had tried the claret and considered it more than tolerable. 'Whatever will you find to do with yourself here that could compare?'

Simon laughed. 'I intend to enjoy the pleasures of Town for a little, then turn into the complete country squire! Ambergate will be back in good order soon, but I don't want to be an absentee landlord for too long!'

'A country squire needs a wife and brood to look the part!' Henry observed. 'Plenty of pretty girls out this Season!'

Simon grimaced. 'So my mama keeps reminding me! She is forever pushing likely heiresses under my nose! It will be a little while yet before I set up my nursery, though I don't deny I'm looking out for a potential bride!' He shot his friend a look. 'If Mama becomes too pressing I suppose I could always offer my hand and heart to Lady Polly Seagrave—'

Lord Henry's gaze narrowed. 'She wouldn't have you! Lady Polly has just turned down her seventh suitor this Season!'

'And it would be a shame to ruin our good friendship,' Simon murmured, signalling for more wine.

Lord Henry relaxed infinitesimally. 'As you say...'

'Are you settled in Town for the Season or do you travel again?' Simon thought it wise to turn the conversation away from his friend's unrequited passion for Lady Polly. The Earl of Seagrave's daughter had rejected Henry's plea to elope some three seasons before, but Simon knew that, despite Henry's apparent indifference, his friend's feelings were still deeply engaged.

Lord Henry shook his head slightly. 'My plans are uncertain...I must go abroad again shortly and I think that there may be trouble brewing closer to home but...' he shrugged '...I seldom know where I will be sent from week to week!'

Simon let it pass. He knew that Lord Henry worked for the government in various shadowy capacities and equally knew that his friend wished that to remain a well-kept secret. They paused in their conversation as a couple of slightly inebriated young men staggered past on their way to the card tables.

'Are you staying for a hand of whist?' Henry asked.

Simon shook his head. 'Promised to look in at Almack's tonight. M'sister and Miss Marchment are making their debut. Bound to be a crush!' He put his glass down and got to his feet. 'Damned slow, squiring one's own sister about Town!'

'You're too kind-hearted,' Henry mocked. 'Can Miss Marchment be the reason for this generosity?'

Simon stared. 'Sophia? Hardly!' He realised that he sounded less than gallant and flushed at the sardonic light in Lord Henry's eyes. 'Miss Marchment is a charming girl, but I know her like my own sister and besides...I prefer women a bit more—'

'Voluptuous?'

'Intelligent!' Simon finished, on a note of rebuke. 'Unfashionable it may be—boring it ain't!'

'Miss Verey is highly intelligent,' Lord Henry murmured.

'Jane?' Simon paused. 'Well, I suppose that she reads a lot—'

'Not just intelligent—clever. Clever enough to evade marrying Philip Delahaye, by my reckoning, and making him look churlish into the bargain!'

Simon sat down again. 'You've lost me, Harry. What are you trying to tell me?'

'You were still away when Delahaye went to Ambergate to pay court to your sister, weren't you?'

'Came back a few weeks later,' Simon confirmed. 'Mama said Philip Delahaye had cried off. Jane didn't seem to mind and I was always a bit uncomfortable about the match, to tell the truth. I knew it was mooted—knew m'father had been keen and that the Duke was pushing for it to go ahead.' He shifted in his chair. 'Thought that was the end of the matter.'

Lord Henry shook his head slowly. 'Better that you

hear it from me, Simon, than through rumour and falsehood. There are a hundred-and-one stories circulating about Philip Delahaye's visit to Ambergate because he arrived and left again so swiftly. Everyone knows that he intended to make Jane an offer and the speculation is all about what made him change his mind. The worst matter is that Philip himself appears to have encouraged the rumours by saying that he cried off because—'

'Verey!' Lord Henry had broken off as someone stumbled against Simon's chair and hailed him at a volume more suited to a hundred yards than the three feet actually involved.

'Cheriton,' Simon said, with a cold inclination of the head for the painted dandy before him, 'how do you do?'

'Well, old fellow, very well! I'm for Almack's—I hear that your lovely sister is to be there! I can barely wait to make her acquaintance!' Lord Cheriton gave a crack of laughter. 'You will have heard what a fool Philip Delahaye has made of himself by disparaging Miss Verey! The *on dit* is that Delahaye was so foxed when he arrived at Ambergate that he mistook some pox-faced serving wench for your sister! We had a fine laugh at his description of her! Pudding-faced, freakish, barely literate—' Cheriton's shoulders shook. 'He said that he would rather starve than tie himself to her in marriage! Then Freddie Ponsonby met Miss Verey in Charles Street and said that she was divinely beautiful with a wit to match, don't you know! Philip could not believe it and swears he'll be at Almack's to see for himself! We gave him a roasting he'll never forget and all he could think of was that he must have confused her with some serving

doxy! He was paying his addresses to a damned serving maid!' Cheriton sauntered away, still chuckling.

The detail might have been confused but the gist
of Cheriton's words was all too clear. Simon was half
out of his chair and Henry Marchnight laid a restrain-
ing hand on his arm. As was often the way, a hush
had fallen over the room as everyone else, sensitive
to the slightest scandal, strained to hear what was going on.

'Simon, think a little!'

Simon sank back into his chair, his face flushed
with sudden fury. 'I suppose that this was what you
were about to tell me, Harry? That Philip Delahaye
has been bandying my sister's name about Town—'

'Well, not precisely…' Lord Henry bit his lip.
Cheriton's tactless interruption had made it well-nigh
impossible for him to explain to Simon that he suspected Jane of tricking Philip Delahaye. Henry had
known Jane since childhood and had the greatest respect for her quick mind. As soon as he had heard
Philip's lurid description of his encounter with Miss
Verey, Henry had immediately remembered the ugly
stepmother of the pantomime held at Ambergate so
long ago. After serious consideration, he had thought
it only fair to warn Simon. His friend needed to know
of Philip's inexcusable slander, but also to be alerted
to the fact that Jane might have deceived him. Matters
seemed somewhat delicate. It only needed for Jane
and Philip Delahaye to meet for the most almighty
row to develop.

As Henry hesitated over his potential disclosure,
another voice broke the silence.

'May I have a moment of your time, gentlemen…?'

Neither Simon nor Lord Henry had noticed the arrival of the newcomer, yet when they looked up they both wondered how they could have missed the atmosphere of tension in the room. The slightly malicious eavesdropping of a few minutes before had given way to something approaching incredulity. Astonishment was mingled with awe. Then Simon caught the whisper:

'It is the Duke of Delahaye—Alexander Delahaye…'

A faint smile touched Alex's mouth as he took the third chair at the table. 'I must apologise for interrupting your conversation, gentlemen, but my business is pressing.'

'Simon, this is Alex Delahaye,' Henry murmured, covertly assessing the interest they were arousing from their peers and smiling wryly. Any minute now, Cheriton would be offering to serve the wine in his attempts to overhear. 'Alex, Simon Verey. Forgive my informality but I guessed that you would wish to cut straight to your business!'

The two men shook hands. 'You were correct, Harry,' Alex said drily. ' A pleasure to meet you, Lord Verey. I have heard a great deal about your exploits on campaign. Just now, however, there are matters closer to home that demand our attention! Have you, perhaps, heard the rumours?'

'Heard about them just this instant,' Simon confirmed grimly. 'A small misunderstanding over your brother's courtship of m'sister!'

'You are all generosity to describe it thus,' Alex said ruefully. 'I am most concerned to avoid any further cause for general speculation. The rumours are highly coloured and as inaccurate as these things usually are! My major preoccupation, however, is that

Philip is to be at Almack's tonight, where, I understand, he will undoubtedly meet Miss Verey again. I
do not wish it to be turned into a public spectacle!'
He cast a quick look round the crowded room and
drew his chair in closer. 'Every ear in the place is
strained to overhear us, I see!'

'They're taking bets,' Henry said cheerfully.
'Evens on a public row in Almack's, two to one that
Miss Verey will cut Lord Philip dead and twenty to
one that Philip's description was accurate after all—
saving your presence, Simon!'

Both Simon and Alex Delahaye winced.

'How did this happen in the first place?' Simon
demanded. 'Pudding-faced, freakish, illiterate…
Those were Cheriton's words and, devil take it,
there's no smoke without fire! Your brother must
have been damned disparaging, Delahaye!'

Alex gave him an enigmatic glance. 'I confess that
that is one aspect of the case that does interest me.
Without a doubt, Philip has been more outspoken in
his opinions than he should have been, although I am
persuaded that the *ton* has far exaggerated his comments and turned the whole thing into a bear garden.
But having met your sister, Lord Verey, I can see that
the description could not be less appropriate!'

Simon grinned, not noticing that he had been de-
flected from his original question. 'Well, for all that
I'm her brother, I can see that Jane's grown into a
devilish attractive girl! The only effect of this is to
make your brother look foolish, Delahaye!'

'Absolutely,' Alex Delahaye murmured. He
drained his glass. 'I hope that Philip will accept that
he has only himself to blame. But in case he does not,
I believe we should have a plan.'

Henry raised a brow. 'You mean to stage a diversion, distract attention?'

'Precisely. If we three go to Almack's, make an entrance, draw attention to ourselves and spike Philip's guns, I think that we may successfully defuse the situation. What do you say? It is almost eleven and they will be closing the doors on us if we are not careful!'

There was general acquiescence to the plan.

'I did not think to see you turning your attention to domestic disputes, Alex!' Lord Henry said pensively, as they got up to leave. Alex flashed him a smile of genuine amusement.

'More difficult than diplomacy between nations, Harry, I assure you!'

'I had no notion that the two of you were in the same line of business,' Simon observed quietly to Henry as Alex paused for a word with an old friend on his way to the door.

'Oh, Alex is way above my humble station,' Henry said cheerfully, eyes twinkling, 'but keep it to yourself, old fellow! He wouldn't thank me for giving the game away!'

'He is somewhat forceful,' Simon said, with a grin. 'I imagine it would be uncomfortable to be in opposition to him!'

Lord Henry held his tongue. He could have said that Miss Jane Verey was the only person he knew who had successfully opposed the Duke of Delahaye's plans. Despite Alex's self-proclaimed desire to prevent further gossip, Henry reckoned that he had a secondary motive. He was almost certain that Alex intended to get to the bottom the mystery of Jane's apparent change of appearance and personality. Stifling a grin, he found himself possessed of a sudden, surprising enthusiasm to visit Almack's again. He had a healthy regard for Jane Verey's wit and charm, but if they were placing bets on who would prevail in this struggle, his money would have to be on Alex Delahaye every time.

Chapter Three

Jane was dreading her come out at Almack's. Her encounter with the Duke of Delahaye had made her realise that she had been naïve in the extreme to imagine that she could avoid Lord Philip. In such a small circle of society, where one brother went the other must inevitably follow. She had already heard that, although Lord Philip was generally held to be a rake and a gambler, all but the highest sticklers opened their doors to him. Perhaps he might even be at Almack's that very evening.

Jane could imagine all too well what might happen when they finally met. She knew that it would be dreadful. They might come upon each other in a crowded ballroom and Lord Philip would declare before hundreds of onlookers that she was an impostor and not the real Jane Verey at all. Or perhaps he would denounce her for playing a trick on him and the *ton* hostesses would turn their backs on her. He might demand an explanation that would be almost impossible to give and Lady Verey and Simon would be both horrified and disappointed in her when they knew the truth. She would be packed off back to Ambergate in disgrace and would have ruined matters for Sophia as well as herself.

Then there was the Duke of Delahaye himself, a man who had come to Ambergate to look her over as though she had been a prize horse. Whilst Jane was supposed to be resting that afternoon, she spent the whole time thinking about him. There was no doubt that the Duke was the man she had seen four years previously at Ambergate. The memory of that night was etched on her mind forever; the candlelight, the handsome stranger, the mysterious way in which he had appeared and then vanished. It had all seemed so romantic, and yet it was proved to be nothing but a sham. He had come to do business with her father, come and gone again in secret, and his sole intention had been that she should marry his brother. Everything that had followed was his fault. Jane felt this very strongly. The unwelcome proposal, the necessity of deceit, the problems that now arose…the blame for all of this could be laid directly at Alex Delahaye's door. Arrogant, overbearing man! Jane sat up, all prospect of rest vanishing. She could feel her anger swelling again, and with it a curious feeling of desolation that she should have come to know Alex Delahaye through this particular set of circumstances.

She started to prepare for the ball as slowly as possible, in the hope that something untoward would happen to prevent their departure. Perhaps the carriage would have a wheel loose, or the horses would have colic, or Lady Verey would decree that Jane was too ill to go, although this was unlikely in view of the fact that she had told her mother that she was very well…

Jane frowned a little as she allowed the maid to

help her into an exquisite white dress embroidered with tiny violet flowers. For some reason she had started to think of the Duke of Delahaye again, remembering how powerfully attractive she had found him. Honesty prompted her to admit that this was the other reason that she dreaded her come out. The thought of meeting Alex again was a disturbing one, filling her with a mixture of anticipation tinged with fear that was entirely uncomfortable. She could not account for the effect the Duke had had on her other than to hope rather half-heartedly that it had in fact been the shock of the accident that had made her pulse race in his presence.

'Oh, if only we had not come to Town!' Jane lamented, as she watched the maid finish dressing Sophia's hair. 'I feel quite *sick* with nerves!'

Sophia checked her reflection for one last time and thanked the maid prettily. She patted Jane's hand, giving her an anxious look.

'Oh, Jane, but it is all so thrilling! You must try to enjoy yourself! Why, I declare I do not know whether to faint with nerves or burst with excitement!'

Even Sophia's high spirits seemed a little dampened, however, as they crossed the famous threshold. Jane, for her part, was almost silent, a state of affairs so unusual that even Lady Verey noticed and fretted.

'Come along, girls! Try to look animated! No, not like that, you merely look half-witted! Oh, dear...'

The rooms were decidedly shabby but the company clearly had a good opinion of itself. Young ladies stood about in small groups, their eyes bright and malicious as they surveyed new arrivals. Their mamas looked harder and more acquisitive still and the young

men appraised the girls boldly but without warmth.
Snatches of conversation ebbed and swirled around
them.

'Thirty-two if she's a day…'

'Only two thousand a year, my dears, and who is
to make a respectable match on that?'

'They say her grandfather was a coal merchant…'

'Positively paints her face, but should try to make
a better attempt at it. One can see where the face ends
and the neck begins, for they are two different col-
ours!'

The spiteful words cut like shards of glass.

'Oh, dear,' Sophia said under her breath, and Jane
knew from her tone that her friend suddenly felt as
small and uncertain as she, 'I am not sure that I shall
like this place after all!'

They were greeted fulsomely by Lady Jersey, who
swam towards them in a diaphanous robe of eau-de-
nil, brown eyes alight with excitement and intrigue.
The sophistication of her dress made Jane feel like a
frump in her debutante white and the warmth of her
greeting seemed suspicious in itself.

'My dears!' Lady Jersey took Jane's hand in one
of hers and Sophia's in the other. 'I am so very glad
that you have decided to come! What courage in the
face of such unkind gossip! I do so admire you! And
how charming you look, Miss Verey! All the gentlemen will soon see that Lord Philip was fair and far
out in his remarks! Still, he is such a slow-top that I
dare swear 'tis true he mistook the serving maid for
a lady!'

She wafted away, leaving Jane, Sophia and Lady
Verey to look at each other in consternation.

'Whatever can she mean?' Lady Verey fretted,

fidgeting with the beaded fringe on her shawl. 'Oh, I do wish that Simon were here! He promised! Everyone is looking at us and this is so awkward!'

Jane knew that her mother was feeling countrified and dowdy amongst the exotic throng and it was true that everybody did appear to be paying them a great deal of attention. It was early, so the rooms were not yet crowded, and they could see few of their acquaintance amongst the assembled guests. It was many years since Lady Verey had been to Town and she had no fashionable relatives to sponsor them. Jane began to perceive that it might be awkward to be an object of curiosity and yet to see no friendly face ready to help them. Then Lady Verey sighed with relief.

'Oh, thank goodness! It is Lady Eleanor Fane!'

The redoubtable Lady Eleanor came up and kissed Lady Verey, bestowing a look of approval on Jane and Sophia. 'Charming,' she observed. 'Quite charming and a credit to you, Clarissa!'

'Eleanor, the most extraordinary thing!' Lady Verey began. 'Lady Jersey made some strange remark about Lord Philip Delahaye and some rumours about Jane! And everyone is staring! Do you know—?'

Jane saw a look akin to annoyance cross Lady Eleanor's face. 'That woman!' she said crossly. 'There has been a little talk about Lord Philip's hasty departure from Ambergate, Clarissa, that is all!' She smiled approvingly at Jane and Sophia. 'The best way to refute the gossip is simply by being here and looking so delightful. I know I can rely on you girls! Now, look—' she took Lady Verey's arm in a firm grip '—my cousins the Applefords are approaching. Do smile, Clarissa! You would not wish to put off the girls' partners with that mournful face!'

Mrs Appleford, her daughter Paulette and son Roger arrived at that moment. Roger soon asked Jane to dance and from that moment both girls seemed to be besieged by a flood of eager admirers. Lady Verey's strained social smile soon relaxed into one of genuine enjoyment as Lady Eleanor introduced her to what seemed like half the *ton*, all of whom seemed flatteringly eager to make her acquaintance.

Jane, dancing with young Lord Blakeney, had almost forgotten her apprehension about the evening when fate finally caught up with her. A group of four young men had come into the ballroom; even from her place amongst the dancers, Jane could see everyone craning to watch. A few glances were cast in her direction and with a sinking heart she realised that one of the men was Lord Philip Delahaye. She saw one of the others lean close to Lord Philip and he turned towards her, scanning the ballroom.

Jane tried to make herself as inconspicuous as possible, shrinking amongst the other dancers. Unfortunately the set was coming to an end and she was obliged to accept Lord Blakeney's escort back to her mother and Lady Eleanor. She watched Lord Philip draw closer, he and his cronies strolling with lazy disdain across the floor towards them. Her breath caught in her throat. What on earth was she going to say?

'Lady Verey.' Lord Philip's bow was much more punctilious than on the occasion of their previous meeting. 'Aunt Eleanor.'

Lady Eleanor frowned slightly. Lord Philip was no favourite of hers. 'How do you do, Philip? It is a surprise to see you here! I thought that you had little time for Almack's!'

Lord Philip looked vaguely discomfited. A hint of colour came into his face. Jane suddenly thought how young he looked, for all his dandified appearance. He could only be a couple of years older than she was. His fair hair flopped across his brow with carefully arranged disorder and his shirt points inhibited him from turning his head too much. He looked a little like a schoolboy trying to appear grown-up. Jane stifled a smile.

'Came to pay my respects to Miss Verey again,' he muttered, his colour rising higher. He turned to Jane. 'How do you do, ma'am? I hope that you will spare a dance for me later.'

Jane dropped a slight curtsy, avoiding his gaze. 'How do you do, sir,' she responded colourlessly. 'I should be delighted.'

There was an awkward silence. Lord Philip's friends began to fidget behind him. They had expected far greater sport than this. Murmuring their excuses, they drifted away, leaving Lord Philip marooned and looking very uncomfortable.

'Very pretty, Philip,' Lady Eleanor approved with deliberate tactlessness. 'Everyone will see now that those silly rumours are nothing more than empty gossip! Now, may I make you known to Miss Sophia Marchment, a friend of Miss Verey's from Wiltshire? Miss Marchment—Lord Philip Delahaye.'

Lord Philip turned to look at Sophia properly for the first time. Jane, watching with sudden sharpened interest, saw the first moment that he truly saw Sophia and the arrested expression that came into his eyes.

Sophia, for her part, blushed adorably and curtsied most gracefully.

'How do you do, sir? I am most happy to meet you!'

Lord Philip was still holding Sophia's hand as though he had forgotten that it rested in his. His blue gaze was fixed on her face with a half-dazed, half-wondering look.

Well! Jane thought, both amused and a little concerned. Perhaps there was some virtue in Lord Philip after all, if he were able to recognise Sophia's innate beauty and goodness at a single glance.

'Good God!' Lady Eleanor said suddenly and it was a measure of her shock that she used the phrase at all. 'It is your brother, Philip! Alex is here! I am sure...I have no recollection of him *ever* attending Almack's!'

The habitual sullen expression replaced the wondering look on Philip's face. 'Keeping an eye on me, no doubt, ma'am!' he said, with a tight smile. 'Miss Marchment—' he turned back to Sophia urgently '—will you grant me this next dance?'

'Of course, sir.' Sophia looked shy and confused. 'I should be honoured—'

Lord Philip had already drawn her away on to the floor before she could finish her sentence. Lady Verey, Lady Eleanor and Jane looked at each other with varying shades of surprise.

'Well!' Lady Eleanor said explosively, but Jane was no longer listening. All her attention was riveted on the tall figure of Alexander Delahaye as he came towards them across the ballroom. In full evening dress he looked magnificent, the black and white stark but elegant. As dark as Lord Philip was fair, his silky black hair gleamed in the light with the dark resonance of ebony. Jane dimly registered that her brother Simon and Lord Henry Marchnight flanked the Duke on either side and that their arrival was creating the biggest stir of the evening, bigger by far than that caused by Lord Philip and his friends.

'Alex!' Lady Eleanor had regained her *sangfroid* by the time they arrived. 'Must you create such a commotion wherever you go?' She turned to smile at Simon and Lord Henry. 'Gentlemen...allow me to congratulate you on turning an evening at Almack's into an event! If you are the cavalry you are sadly late, but fortunately there is no need of rescue! Philip has been before you and has done the pretty!'

The Duke raised his black brows. 'I saw that Ponsonby, Malters and Cheriton were expecting a show!' he said drily. 'I trust there were no problems, ma'am?'

Lady Eleanor smiled at him, in perfect understanding. 'Now, Alex, not even Philip would show such bad *ton* as to make a scene at Almack's!'

'I wish someone would tell me what all this is about!' Lady Verey said plaintively. 'I have heard nothing but veiled hints and mysterious remarks all evening!'

Simon cleared his throat. 'I'll go and find a drink, then, if the crisis is over! Harry? Alex? Can I fetch anything for you?'

Alex! Jane thought. It had not taken the Duke long to achieve a friendly footing with Simon! That did not augur well for her plans at all. She was aware that Henry Marchnight was looking at her thoughtfully and suddenly she felt rather hollow. Harry knew her well enough to guess at what she had done to get rid

of Lord Philip at Ambergate. Would he give her
away? Worse, Alex Delahaye was clearly no fool and
he was watching her with a mixture of amusement
and speculative consideration that was far more disturbing than Henry's friendly scrutiny. Suddenly Jane
felt as though all her difficulties had caught up with
her with a vengeance.

'Miss Verey.' Alex drew her to one side, speaking
softly. 'I hope that you are recovered from your accident earlier. It seems that you came to no lasting
harm, for you are in excellent looks this evening!'

Jane caught sight of Lady Eleanor looking absolutely stunned, her eyebrows almost disappearing into
her hairline. Evidently the Duke of Delahaye paid a
compliment as rarely as he attended Almack's, but
Jane did not flatter herself that he meant it. She had
a deep conviction that he was making the opening
moves in a game he was intent on playing with her.

'Yes, I thank you, your grace. I am much better
and I must thank you for your help.' Jane was glad
that she still sounded so composed when her heart
was racing.

The Duke shrugged negligently. 'I am glad that I
was able to be of service, Miss Verey. Now, I see
Lady Sefton approaching. May I ask her to grant you
permission to waltz with me?'

Even Lady Eleanor, for all her town bronze, gasped
at that one. Jane met the Duke's dark gaze and saw
the laughter lurking there. So she had been correct in
thinking that he was making a game of her! The temptation to respond was very strong, to show him that
she was no milk-and-water miss. However, that was
too dangerous. She would not play.

'I thank you, your Grace, but I do not waltz,' she said steadily.

She had the satisfaction of seeing the lazy amusement fade from his eyes, to be replaced by shrewd calculation. Lady Verey, unaware of the by-play, stepped in hastily to smooth over any awkwardness.

'Oh, Jane, you need have no concern as to that! It is perfectly proper for you to waltz if one of the patronesses of Almack's gives her permission—'

'Thank you, Mama.'

Jane, exasperated by her mother's well-meaning intervention, looked up to see the Duke's eyes still on her and, worse, that he had read her thoughts. The amusement was back. She knew that she had been checkmated.

'Lady Sefton,' Alex said clearly, turning to the approaching patroness, 'will you present me to Miss Jane Verey as a suitable partner for the waltz?'

Lady Sefton's good-natured agreement and Jane's acquiescence followed. It had to—she knew that he would brook no refusal. Meanwhile, across the ballroom another intriguing tableau was developing as Lady Jersey, not to be outdone, could be seen giving an eager Lord Philip her permission to waltz with Sophia.

Lady Verey, suddenly becoming aware that she had been neglecting Sophia in her concern for Jane, gave a little gasp. 'Oh, Eleanor, he has asked her for a second dance and immediately after the first! I am sure that Sophia knows how to go on, but I feel she should have a little more care! Besides...' her gaze swung back to Jane '...Lord Philip should surely be dancing with Jane!'

Jane dropped a neat curtsy. 'Oh no, Mama!' she

said sweetly. 'If I am favoured with the Duke's attention I can have no complaint!'

'Then come along, Miss Verey,' Alex said gently, in a tone that suggested he would have liked to call her a minx, 'for the music is starting!'

Jane took his hand, with a feeling that she was about to step right out of her depth. The gossip was deafening. Part of her was aware of the hum of discussion all around, but most of her senses were concentrating on the experience of being in Alex Delahaye's arms.

The sensation of closeness was intimate but in no way unpleasant, more intense than it had been that afternoon. One of Jane's hands rested lightly on his broad shoulder whilst the other was clasped in his. The touch of his fingers threatened to disturb her, for she found that she was very aware of him, and she tried to shut her mind to it. It would never do to make a fool of herself at Almack's!

Jane tried to concentrate on the steps of the waltz. She was a good dancer and it was easy to waltz with Alex because he, too, was so good at it. Besides, it gave her the excuse to stay silent and avoid looking up at him, which she was sure would unsettle her completely. Instead, she looked around at their fellow dancers, noticing that Sophia was whirling around and chattering nineteen to the dozen to Lord Philip. He was smiling and looked boyish and happy. It was an extraordinary transformation.

'It is not really so bad, is it?' the Duke said ironically, after they had circled the room twice in silence. 'I realise that, given a choice, you would not have danced with me, Miss Verey, despite your pretty little remark just now! You have a neat way of administering a set-down! It was a salutary experience for me!'

Jane raised her eyebrows, biting back a smile. The twinkle in his eyes was infectious. 'You surprise me, your grace! I would imagine your self-esteem to be much more resilient than that!'

Alex Delahaye smiled, looking suddenly as boyish as his younger brother. 'But appearances can be so deceptive, Miss Verey! Do you not find that?'

Jane was suddenly on her guard. There was no reason to read anything into his words and yet she was wary. He was too perceptive and she could not afford to trust him.

'I must allow that to be true sometimes, I suppose,' she said carefully. 'This is not a society where one sees much below the surface.'

She saw his smile broaden with real amusement. 'Indeed, Miss Verey! Yet sometimes it is the surface itself that is misleading! Take my brother's visit to Ambergate, for example!'

Jane felt herself jump in his arms and was sure that he had felt it too. She cast one swift glance up into his face and saw that the smile held a hint of challenge now.

'I have no notion as to your meaning, your Grace,' she said, with more composure than she was feeling, 'but I cannot regret the outcome of Lord Philip's visit. I am persuaded that he and I should not have suited at all!'

'Or was it that you took steps to ensure that you should not suit?' the Duke asked, his lazy gaze still watchful. 'As I say, I have the oddest suspicion, Miss Verey, that you have made a fool of my brother!'

'Oh, no, your Grace!' Jane avoided his gaze, her

eyes fixed on the swirling dancers. 'Whatever your brother has achieved has been on his own account!'

The Duke's arm tightened momentarily around her waist. He gave her a look of brilliant amusement. '*Touché*, Miss Verey! You are quite right that Philip's indiscreet descriptions of his visit have been most ill bred. But perhaps he was provoked? Perhaps you gave him a very different impression of Miss Jane Verey from the one that is on show tonight?'

Jane hesitated. She had no way of knowing how much he knew and what was mere guesswork. How she wished that she had never started this! In deception one could give oneself away so easily...

Whilst she hesitated, the Duke said blandly, 'Philip has already described your meeting, of course. Perhaps you would care to give me your version of events?'

Jane made up her mind. 'I think not, sir. That would be...embarrassing and unnecessary. You have seen that all has been forgiven and forgotten tonight!'

The Duke nodded. 'Of course,' he murmured, 'it may be better to let sleeping dogs lie. But indulge my curiosity, Miss Verey! How did you disguise yourself? You must be an accomplished amateur actress...'

The colour flooded Jane's cheeks as her guilty conscience, fully awake now, gave her a prod. He might as well have called her an accomplished liar!

'Please, your Grace, may we not change the subject?'

'I can see that it might not reflect well on you!' the Duke agreed. 'The disguise, the deceit...'

'Sir—'

'No, no,' the Duke murmured, 'say no more, Miss Verey! I would not wish to cause you mortification!'

Jane's eyes flashed with annoyance. 'But surely it was your intention to do precisely that, sir! And you have succeeded!'

'No, indeed!' Alex's expression of virtuous indignation was as good as anything Jane could have achieved. 'Surely you mistake, Miss Verey! It is never the lady who is at fault in these situations!'

Jane forced out a smile from between gritted teeth. Somehow—she was not at all sure how—Alex had managed to pin the blame on her neatly whilst turning the whole situation around to make it appear as though he was sympathising with her!

'I do believe that you are spoilt, your Grace,' she said unwisely. 'Surely the real cause of your ire is that you are so accustomed to people falling in with your plans that you cannot bear to be gainsaid!'

She saw Alex's eyes narrow in incredulous amusement, then he laughed. 'What an acute young lady you are, Miss Verey, and one who dares much! You have my measure—I have a great aversion to being thwarted! And unfortunately your astuteness only serves to convince me that you are exactly the right bride for my brother!' This time there was steel beneath the silky drawl. 'I intend the marriage to go ahead despite your best efforts to prevent it!'

Jane almost stumbled over the steps of the waltz. She had never contemplated that the Duke would still be of the same mind and insist that the match be made despite all that had happened. Surely she had made it clear by both her words and her actions that she would not marry Lord Philip? Yet it seemed that Alexander Delahaye had either not heard her or had disregarded her words. His final, patronising comments had suggested that he viewed her as no more than a precocious child who might be humoured a little but whose final obedience was taken for granted.

'I am sorry to hear you say that, your Grace,' Jane said slowly. 'I was in earnest when I said that Lord Philip and I should not suit and my mind is unlikely to change.'

'But you see,' the Duke continued softly, 'Philip needs a clever wife and you have proved yourself to be eminently suitable, Miss Verey! Where a man lacks certain...qualities himself, it is most beneficial if his life partner can supply what is missing! A perfect combination!'

Once again, Jane caught sight of Sophia and Philip, fair heads bent close, laughing at something Philip had just said. She felt a pang.

'Would it not be more beneficial for Lord Philip to choose his own bride, sir?' she said, a little desperately. 'He might feel a greater commitment to the match under those circumstances!'

'Happily, his wishes need not concern us,' the Duke said a little grimly. 'You are my choice, Miss Verey, and Philip knows it well! The financial rewards of such a marriage are his prime consideration!'

Jane could feel her temper slipping at his arrogance. 'But they need not be mine, I thank you, sir!'

The Duke laughed a little harshly. 'No, but there are other levers... I have immense social power, Miss Verey. A word here, a hint there... A reputation is so fragile. Think of the distress to your mother if doors were to be closed to you. I am persuaded that you would not want that. And Miss Marchment…she would be tainted by association, of course.'

Jane looked at him for a long time in silence. She could hear the music sweeping on in the background but it was as though she and Alex Delahaye were quite alone. His face was expressionless.

'I do believe that you are threatening me, sir,' she said slowly. 'Despite our differences I had considered you a man of integrity, but perhaps I mistake you. And I should warn you that I am not easily susceptible to coercion!'

'No, that was clumsy of me,' Alex agreed affably. 'I would not stoop so low, Miss Verey, and I beg your pardon. But perhaps you are more amenable to persuasion from your own family? Investment in Ambergate would be a great help to your brother. Were we to be related, I could assist him…'

Jane glared at him. 'I saw the ease with which you had gained his confidence! Simon does not deserve false friendship!'

The Duke's arm tightened about her waist. Jane felt quite breathless, as though the music was whirling faster and faster.

'Oh, my friendship would be offered in earnest,' he said pleasantly. 'I have the greatest respect for your brother and would never offer him Spanish coin! I only wished to point out to you that there are different ways to influence a situation! I must warn you to beware of crossing swords with me, Miss Verey. You cannot possibly win…'

Jane was rather afraid that he was correct. The combined wishes of the Duke and Lady Verey would be difficult to oppose, particularly if he enlisted the support of Lady Eleanor Fane and Simon as well.

Together they could chip away at her resistance, ignoring her wishes in their desire to achieve a mutually beneficial alliance. Jane caught sight of Lady Jersey's fascinated face as she watched them from the edge of the dance floor. She manufactured a dazzling smile. 'I shall bear your warning in mind, sir!'

'I am still curious, Miss Verey,' Alex said slowly. 'You seem most adamant in your refusal to wed. Can it be that your affections are already engaged?'

'No, sir,' Jane said steadily. 'They are not.'

'Then perhaps you are of a romantical disposition? A pity—I should have thought you much more practical than that! I did not expect sentiment from you!'

'I do not consider it sentimental to expect to make a match where mutual respect, if not love, is present,' Jane said hotly. She seemed to have stumbled from one conflict directly into another! Would this wretched dance never end? She could hardly walk off the floor in the middle of a waltz. 'Perhaps it is your Grace whose ideas of marriage are prejudiced! Your own experience, perhaps, has led you to reject romantic love out of hand!'

She knew that she had overstepped the mark even before the flash in those dark eyes suggested that she had hit a raw nerve. Madeline Delahaye and her notorious infidelities were common knowledge amongst the *ton*, but Jane knew it had been ill bred in the extreme to speak of it to the Duke. She closed her eyes briefly and awaited the set-down she knew that she deserved. It was one thing to engage in a spirited defence of her own ideals and behaviour, but quite another to touch on his personal tragedy.

'Perhaps you are right, Miss Verey,' the Duke of Delahaye said bitterly. His mouth was set in a tight, angry line, but Jane could read unhappiness in his face and felt a sudden uprush of misery. It had never occurred to her that he might have loved his wife so much that she still had the power to hurt him eight years after her death. And then that she had so carelessly raked up matters best left undisturbed…

'I am sorry—' She began, only to be harshly overruled in tones that held more passion than anything that had gone before.

'Do not be, Miss Verey! Do not seek to pity me! I do not require that from you!'

Jane felt close to tears. It was bad enough to be thought deceitful without Alex Delahaye believing that she had deliberately sought to hurt him. She would have tried to apologise once more, but there was something in his harsh, set expression that forbade it.

The music finished and Jane dropped a very deep curtsy. She found that she was shaking from their encounter, an explosive mix of anger and misery flooding through her. Part of her was burning with fury at Alex's high-handed behaviour and part was ashamed of what she had said to him. Yet her overriding feeling was shock at the sheer physical impact he had made on her. It was very distressing. Worse was the fact that she could not retire, could not escape the prying eyes and intrusive questions of her companions. Her dance card was full and she had to smile through the rest of the evening. She even had to smile when Lord Philip sulkily and belatedly presented himself for a country dance. By the end of the evening, Jane was wishing the entire Delahaye family to perdition along with the rest of polite society.

* * *

Alexander Delahaye, strolling back to Haye House in the early hours beneath an absurdly romantic full moon, found himself beset by various unfamiliar emotions. He had declined an invitation to return to Brooks with Simon and Henry, but had agreed to meet them there the following evening. Just now he was aware only of a need for solitude.

Miss Jane Verey… She had practically ignored him after their passage of arms during the waltz and he could not blame her for it. He was deeply ashamed of his behaviour towards her and considered it unforgivable. One did not go to Almack's in the expectation of threats and bullying. Miss Verey was young and inexperienced and, whatever she had done, she did not deserve to be treated so harshly.

The trouble was that she had read him all too well. It was true that he had been angry because she had overset his plans. Alex's calculations had not allowed for Jane's feelings at all, but now that he had met her he could ignore her no longer. Ignore her! He gave a mirthless laugh. There was no possibility of that!

Alex squared his shoulders. He was unaccustomed to being made to feel guilty. Miss Verey had done that and had made him question his own judgement into the bargain! Well, Philip had to marry; he was still resolved on that. The Verey match had been his grandfather's dearest wish and who better to manage Philip than a girl who had already shown her quick wit and devious ways? Besides, he was persuaded that Miss Jane Verey would soon relent. A spell in Town would make her realise that Philip was quite a good catch. All young ladies were anxious to marry well, after all, and why should Miss Verey be different? A show of reluctance was probably required for form's sake, but would be followed by meek acquiescence.

The matter was settled. Alex let out a long breath. He would continue to promote the betrothal, although perhaps in a more subtle way. Miss Verey would soon conform and then all this fuss could be forgotten. Alex frowned. The decision should have cleared his mind, but for some reason he still felt vaguely dissatisfied. This had to be Jane Verey's fault in some vague way that he could not specify. What a stubborn and opinionated chit! Who would have thought that the henwitted Clarissa Verey would have bred so unconventional a daughter?

He had reached the portico of Haye House and as he was about to start up the steps an extraordinary thing happened. He suddenly remembered with perfect clarity the softness of Jane Verey's body within his embrace, the translucent radiance of her skin and the dazzling challenge in those wide green eyes. His imagination, normally firmly subject to his reason, presented him with the further image of Jane held naked in his arms, her lips parted beneath his own. It was so vivid and shocking an impression that he stopped dead. The immediate ache in his body told him that the idea held instant appeal.

'Damn it all to hell,' Alex said forcibly, and raised his hand to knock with far more violence than was necessary.

'Oh, Jane!' Sophia curled up on the end of Jane's bed, leaning her chin on one hand. 'Was that not the most exciting evening you have spent in an age? And is not Lord Philip the most—' She broke off, blushing a little. 'I know that he left Ambergate with indecent haste,' she said in a rush, 'and he has admitted to me that his behaviour was not that of a gentleman, but…oh, surely he cannot be all bad! He seemed to me to be charming and lively and…oh, everything a high-spirited young man should be!'

Jane put down her hairbrush with a smile, looking at her friend in the mirror. 'I saw that you were enjoying his conversation,' she teased. 'I think that you had a better evening than I!'

Sophia's eyes sparkled in the candlelight. 'Yes, for you were obliged to be kind to that awesome Duke! Oh, but Lord Philip and I had a hundred-and-one things to talk about! It seemed as though we had known each other forever!' A slight frown entered her eyes. 'Dearest Jane, you do not mind, do you?'

Jane shook her head. 'No,' she said with perfect truth, 'I do not mind for myself. But…' she hesitated '…did Lord Philip tell you that his brother has plans for his future—very definite plans?'

'Yes—' Sophia hugged her knees '—but I am persuaded that I need have no concern over the Duke's plans to marry Lord Philip off! You see…' she looked suddenly shy '…Lord Philip can marry no one but me! Oh, Jane, he is the man I dreamed about all those years ago on St Agnes Eve! As soon as I saw him I recognised him at once!'

Chapter Four

Jane stared at her friend in stupefaction. 'Oh, no! Surely that was just a childish game!'

As soon as she had spoken she saw Sophia's face fall.

'But, Jane, I thought that you did not mind! You just said—'

'I know!' Jane put out a hasty hand to touch Sophia's. 'I do not mind for myself, dearest Sophia, for you know that Lord Philip and I would not suit! But the legend of the Eve of St Agnes is just that—a legend! It cannot be true!'

Sophia was looking distinctly obstinate. 'All I know is that I dreamed of Lord Philip that night and now I have met him! It seems quite simple to me!'

Jane knew that there was no arguing with her. Sophia was a sweet girl but she could be frighteningly stubborn at times. Besides, who was to say that it was not true? Sophia had dreamed of a handsome young man and now she thought that she had met him. She had certainly tumbled into love. What was more surprising was that Lord Philip appeared equally smitten. Jane, remembering the bad-tempered young man who had visited Ambergate, suddenly wondered whether it had been frustration and anger that had made Philip behave as he had. Certainly Alexander Delahaye was imperious enough to try the patience of a saint, as Jane herself had discovered, and if he had pushed Philip beyond endurance...

She moved over to give Sophia an impulsive hug. 'Oh, Sophy, I'm sorry! I did not mean to appear disbelieving! I am very happy for you!'

Sophia hugged her back, her spirits restored at once. 'Jane, it is so exciting! I am just sorry that you did not dream of your future husband that night! That would have been marvellous!'

Jane tried not to smile. 'Well, to tell the truth I did dream of a man that night, but—'

Sophia clutched her. 'Jane! Why did you not tell me? Who was he?'

Jane dropped her gaze. 'It was nothing, Sophy! I woke in the night and saw a man in the corridor and then I dreamed about him, but it turned out that he was just one of my parents' guests...'

Sophia's brow was furrowed. She focused on the one point of importance. 'Yes, but, Jane, who was he?'

'It was the Duke of Delahaye,' Jane said reluctantly.

Sophia squeaked and clapped her hand to her mouth. Above it, her eyes were huge and round. 'Jane! The Duke! But—'

'I told you that the legend could not be true!' Jane said urgently. 'Besides, I was awake when I saw him, and although I dreamed of him later I am sure that it does not count.'

Sophia was not so sure. She shook her head stubbornly. 'But you went to bed without supper? You did not look behind you?'

'No,' Jane admitted, wishing she had never mentioned it. 'It's true that I did those things, but—'

'Then it must be true!' Sophia's blue eyes widened even further. 'Oh, Jane, the Duke of Delahaye! Only think!'

Jane was thinking. With a shiver that was half-fear, half-pleasure, she remembered the curious attraction that Alex Delahaye held for her. Would it be so terrible to be married to him? Then she remembered that he wanted her to marry his brother and that he was still in love with his dead wife. How many reasons did she need to prove that it was all foolish superstition? She slid into her bed.

'It has to be nonsense, Sophy,' she said firmly. 'If Alexander Delahaye proves to be my future husband you may have that pair of silk gloves of mine that you so admire —yes, and the straw bonnet with the matching ribbons! That is how certain I am that it will never come true!'

It seemed that Sophia was as anxious to see Lord Philip again as Jane was to avoid him. Jane heard her friend humming at the breakfast table and noticed a distinctly dreamy look on Sophia's face as she picked at her buttered eggs. When the visitors started to arrive, Sophia's blue gaze was riveted on the door in much the same way as a dog watches for its master, her face falling as each new arrival proved not to be the man she wanted to see. A whole procession of sharp-eyed mamas and their hopeful daughters were filling up the pink drawing-room and still Lord Philip did not come.

The hum of conversation and clash of teacups grew ever louder. Several ladies noted Lord Philip's absence and teased Jane about it, their false smiles not quite reaching their eyes. A number of the daughters were casting a thoughtful eye over Simon, who had the look of a man wishing he could remember a pressing engagement elsewhere. More than one debutante was sighing soulfully over Alex Delahaye and his sad romantic history.

The door opened and Lord Philip came in. The assembled ladies cooed a little with pleasure. Jane moved unobtrusively across to a group of debutantes and inserted herself in the middle, making sure that there was nowhere for Lord Philip to sit. She saw Lady Verey glance over in her direction with a meaningful look, then turned her shoulder and pretended to be engrossed in the conversation. When she looked up again, Jane saw that Lord Philip had taken the seat by Sophia, who was pink with suppressed joy.

Lady Verey was not so pleased. When the drawing-room had emptied of their guests, she took her daughter firmly to task.

'Jane Verey, I do declare you can be the most provoking girl!' she chided. 'Lord Philip came here especially to see you! If you think to provoke his interest by appearing unconcerned, you are only being foolish! A gentleman needs some encouragement—a smile here, a soft word there. Try to be more pleasing!'

Jane bit back the retort that Lord Philip was receiving as much encouragement as he needed from a different source. Sophia had turned quite pale at Lady Verey's attack and was now trying to pretend that she could not hear. With a murmured word of excuse, she slipped out of the room. Lady Verey barely seemed to notice.

'Surely, Mama,' Jane said mildly, 'you can see that Lord Philip has no wish for my company—no more than I have for his! We are not suited.'

Lady Verey looked affronted. 'Not suited! What nonsense is this? It is my dearest wish that Lord Philip should renew his attentions! Now, he will be at Lady Winterstoke's dinner tomorrow and I expect to see an improvement in your manner towards him, Jane! Pray show him some partiality!'

'Excuse me, my lady.' Golding, the butler, had soft-footed into the room. 'There is a posy here for Miss Jane.' He snapped his fingers and the footman hurried forward, carrying a small but exquisite bouquet of tight pink roses.

Lady Verey's irritated face broke into a smile. 'From Lord Philip, no doubt! I expect he was too shy to present it himself, the foolish boy!'

Jane took the posy, wondering at her mother's championing of a man who had been so offensive to her only a month before. No doubt Lady Verey had conveniently ascribed Lord Philip's behaviour to a temporary aberration or boyish high spirits. She had to agree, however, that the flowers were beautiful, each tiny bud a deep pink colour and on the point of unfurling. She extracted the card and handed the flowers back to the footman to put in water. Much as she would like to send them back, it seemed a churlish gesture and Lady Verey would never permit it. She could not resist a certain curiosity to see the message. What could Lord Philip say to her that would not appear either rude or insincere?

The bold black writing had come from another pen,

however. It was not an apology, only a name: Alexander Delahaye.

Jane caught her breath and pressed the card to her chest in case her mother was about to snatch it from her. Lady Verey was still twittering on about Lord Philip and his thoughtful choice of flowers and Jane did not contradict her. She excused herself as quickly as possible and flew up the stairs to her bedroom. The posy was already on a side table by the window, its pink buds just tinged with gold. Jane hesitated. She could have torn the card into pieces and thrown it away, but instead she placed it carefully in a drawer, on a bed of silk ribbons.

The sensation at Lady Winterstoke's dinner was caused not by the presence of Lord Philip Delahaye but by that of his elder brother. For years the hostesses of the *ton* had tried to entice the Duke of Delahaye from his self-imposed seclusion, offering him the most tempting food and the best company. For years he had rejected all invitations. Yet that evening he arrived with Lord Philip in a convincing show of brotherly unity and caused Lady Winterstoke positively to crow with triumph.

Jane's heart had sunk when she saw them come in. It seemed that the Duke and his brother must be forever dogging her steps and spoiling things for her. After all, it was Alexander Delahaye's avowed intent to wear down her resistance until she capitulated and agreed to the marriage. She had spent much time thinking of the bouquet he had sent her and had come to the practical conclusion that it was an attempt to soften her feelings towards the match. Well—her pretty face set into lines of obstinate disapproval—it would not work! No matter how romantic it had seemed at first, in truth it was just another means by which Alex Delahaye hoped to manipulate her!

Accordingly, she was looking very severe when Lady Winterstoke brought the Duke and Lord Philip over to them as the guests assembled before dinner.

'I was about to inquire how you were enjoying yourself, Miss Verey,' Alex said lazily, once greetings had been exchanged, 'but you look so forbidding that I hardly dare! Can it be that Town does not agree with you?'

Jane checked to see whether her mother was listening. Fortunately Lady Verey was intent on engaging Lord Philip in innocuous conversation and deflecting his attention from Sophia. She gave the Duke a dazzling smile. 'Well, your Grace, it is not all bad, I suppose! The theatres and concerts are great fun but the company is sadly lacking—it seems to be the same people saying the same things to each other at the same events!'

Alex smiled. 'That's frank, Miss Verey! You are not afraid to blight your social position by appearing an eccentric? Young ladies are meant to be bowled over by the sophisticated charms of the Town, you know!'

'It seems to me that a lot of nonsense is talked about Society!' Jane said judiciously. 'If people enjoy the company and the entertainments then so be it, but if they prefer other pursuits then they should be allowed their choice!'

'How singular,' Alex said thoughtfully, 'and how true! You are quite fearless, are you not, Miss Verey? I know of no other lady who would express such a view even if they believed it!'

'Yet you yourself do not succumb to the charms of Society a great deal, if the stories are true,' Jane pointed out, feeling at the same time that her tongue was probably running away with her again. 'I had heard that the Duke of Delahaye chooses to immure himself in his northern stronghold with only his books for company!'

'And his faithful dogs,' Alex added. 'Do not forget the dogs, Miss Verey! What else do they say of me?'

'Oh, many things,' Jane said, plying her fan, 'but none of them appropriate for a young lady to repeat in company!'

They laughed together, stopped together and stood looking at each other in a silence that seemed curiously loaded. Only a foot away, Sophia was chattering to Philip and Lady Verey was gossiping with one of her acquaintances. Jane made an effort to break the silence.

'I must thank you for the flowers, sir. They were very beautiful.'

'They reminded me of you,' Alex said abruptly. 'Excuse me, Miss Verey.'

Jane was left feeling breathless and disconcerted. She had imagined him a man accustomed to paying light compliments, but his unexpected words and hasty departure had none of the polish that might have been expected. Frowning a little, she watched him cross the room, spare a word for a distinguished gentleman in uniform, then be artfully ambushed by a dashing blonde in a clinging scarlet silk dress. Jane felt a vague depression settle on her.

Excusing herself to her mother, Jane slipped away to the ladies' withdrawing room so that she should not be obliged to make stilted conversation with Lord

Philip. Whilst tweaking her curls back into place, she reflected that the Duke was likely to be one step ahead of her in arranging for his brother to escort her in to dinner. The seating would no doubt be in order of precedence but, at a word from Alex Delahaye, Lady Winterstoke would gladly rearrange her table plan. Peeking down the corridor to confirm that she was not being watched, Jane decided to detour via the dining-room and examine the place cards.

Her suspicions had been justified. Lord Philip's place was set beside hers and he was a long way away from Sophia for good measure. Jane made a little adjustment and was on her way back to the drawing-room when, in the doorway, she collided abruptly with a broad chest.

'Oh!'

'We meet again, Miss Verey,' the Duke of Delahaye said, in the deceptively soft tones that Jane had already come to distrust. 'Have you lost something?'

'No!' Jane knew that a guilty blush was staining her cheeks. 'That is—I lost my way!'

'I see. I had thought that your penchant for food had led you to try to steal a march on the rest of us!'

Jane looked surprised. 'Who told you that I enjoyed my food, sir?'

'Why, I believe that it was my aunt, Lady Eleanor. She commented that you had a sweet tooth.' Alex offered her his arm and they strolled back across the hall towards the drawing-room. 'No doubt it was ungallant in me to mention it, but I have to confess that you look very good on it, Miss Verey! Not all young ladies are fortunate enough to be able to eat as they choose and not look the worse for it!'

Jane, relieved that he had not discovered her activities in the dining-room and guilty at spinning another tale, started to colour once again. Alex was watching her with undisguised interest.

'I am not sure whether it is guilt or pleasure that makes you look so, Miss Verey! If only it were my poor compliments that put you to the blush!'

Jane found herself unable to resist responding in kind. 'I am sure that most young ladies would be overcome to be the object of your gallantry, your Grace!' she said sweetly.

'But not you, Miss Verey? No doubt that is your implication!'

'Alas, I have always been told that I am not like all the rest!' Jane said innocently. 'You said so yourself!' She dropped him a neat curtsy and went to join her mother, managing not to look back at him over her shoulder.

Alex watched her go. 'No, indeed,' he said softly, under his breath. 'You are not like anyone else, Miss Verey! I would venture to say that you are completely original!'

The butler arrived to announce that dinner was served. Jane was delighted to see Alex move away to attend to his duties as escort to a Dowager Countess in regal purple. She confidently expected that that would leave the field clear for her to exchange partners. Next, Lady Verey was claimed by an elderly baronet, who seemed flatteringly pleased at his good luck. That got rid of the final obstacle to Jane's plan. All it required now was for Lord Philip to be recalled to his duty as her escort. Unfortunately he seemed disinclined to leave Sophia's side. Jane wondered whether he meant to cut her anyway, and thought this would be rather funny after all the trouble she had gone to. But no, Sophia was gently encouraging her beau to relinquish her and escort her friend. As Lord Philip approached, Jane stepped forward to intercept him.

'I am so very sorry, my lord, but I fear that there has been a mistake,' she said, with a winning smile. 'I happened to see the table plan and I fear that Lady Winterstoke has made an error, for she has placed Miss Marchment by your side rather than myself.' She saw Lord Philip cast an incredulous glance in Sophia's direction and added, 'I am sure that we would not wish to embarrass our hostess, so the best thing would surely be for us to exchange escorts. I hope that Lord Blakeney could be prevailed upon to accompany me, if you would be so good as to offer Miss Marchment your arm.'

'Miss Marchment! Yes, of course!' Lord Philip had regained Sophia's side in less time than it had taken Jane to suggest it. She saw him speak earnestly in Sophia's ear, saw her friend look dubiously towards her and gave them a little smile and a nod of encouragement.

'I am so sorry, Lord Blakeney,' Jane said, turning to the young peer, 'you will have to make do with me rather than Miss Marchment! All in a good cause!'

It had indeed been Lady Winterstoke's intention that Lord Philip should escort Miss Verey in to dinner and she was mortified by the social disaster that had so nearly occurred.

When she saw Philip tenderly seating Sophia beside him, saw Jane with Blakeney and realised that the place cards were all in the wrong order, she could only bless the strange fate that had led the girls to accept the wrong escorts. No doubt the maids had jumbled the cards, which was irritating for she had given them the strictest instructions! Such social ineptitude would have been death to her reputation as a fashionable hostess!

Heaving a sigh of relief, Lady Winterstoke applied herself to the watercress soup. She cast a look at the Duke of Delahaye, bearing in mind that it had been his express wish that Lord Philip escort Miss Verey. She saw that Alex was also watching Jane Verey and there was a look of mingled exasperation and amusement on his face.

Jane was also aware of Alex's scrutiny. She knew that he had guessed that she had engineered the change of placements and had also exchanged escorts with Sophia. Thinking back, he would remember meeting her in the dining-room and immediately realise that she had told him yet another falsehood. The thought made her feel more miserable than she would have expected. She set her jaw firmly. She had warned him that she would do everything in her power to avoid Lord Philip. If the Duke thought badly of her, it would only reinforce his existing opinion that she was a liar and cheat.

After dinner there was impromptu dancing in the salon, which the older guests watched indulgently whilst the younger took part. Jane, whirling around the floor in Lord Blakeney's arms, decided that she had enjoyed the evening very much. A moment later she caught sight of the Duke of Delahaye talking to the elegant blonde woman again, and changed her mind. The evening had been a sad bore after all.

'Lady Francine Dennery,' Blakeney said, in answer to Jane's unspoken question. 'She's the widow of the

Eleventh Earl of Dennery and the scourge of the Twelfth Earl! He don't approve of his wicked stepmother! Not sure where she came from, but we can all guess where she's going! She aims to crown her career with ducal strawberry leaves!'

It seemed that Lady Dennery had her quarry well within her sights. Her blonde head was bent close to Alex Delahaye's dark one and there was a provocative little smile on her red lips. As Jane watched, Lady Dennery brushed her fingers swiftly across the Duke's hand, an intimate little gesture full of meaning. Jane hastily looked the other way.

The last dance of the evening was a quadrille and Jane had promised it to Henry Marchnight. She was not a little taken aback to find the Duke of Delahaye approaching her instead.

'Marchnight has asked me to present you his apologies and myself as a poor substitute,' Alex said, smiling at Lady Verey in a manner that Jane was annoyed to see made her poor mother melt completely. 'His sister has torn a flounce and twisted her ankle, and demands to be taken home at once! I promised him that I would try to make amends!'

'I am sure that Jane is greatly flattered, your Grace,' Lady Verey said, when Jane had singularly failed to provide any response of her own. 'Come, Jane,' she added sharply, 'thank the Duke for his condescension!'

Jane thought that she saw Alex wince. 'I assure you that the privilege is all mine, ma'am,' he murmured, 'but if Miss Verey does not care for my company…'

Jane met his eyes. She had been expecting to see mockery there and was taken aback that he was not even smiling. For some reason she felt a need to hurry in and reassure him. It seemed ridiculous—he was a Duke and had all the assurance that his fifteen years' seniority could give him. Surely he did not need a green girl to convince him that she appreciated his company! And yet...

'Thank you, sir,' she murmured. 'I should be very glad to dance with you.'

Alex took her hand and looked so genuinely pleased that Jane felt her heart leap. She almost drew back, appalled to find her pulse racing at his touch. It was shocking to feel so vulnerable to him, both mentally and physically, and she had no notion how to deal with her feelings. She only knew that she was becoming involved in something too complex to handle.

'The evening has been quite a triumph for you, has it not, Miss Verey?' Alex said quietly, so that only she could hear. 'I did appreciate your manoeuvre at dinner—a masterful piece of strategy! I find that I have to admire you for that!'

The figure of the dance separated them at that moment.

'Thank you, your Grace,' Jane said when they came back together again.

Alex gave her a broad smile that Jane found deeply disturbing. 'No pointless denials, Miss Verey? I admire that too!' The smile faded and his gaze became as brilliant as a sword thrust. 'You are ahead on points, I cannot deny it, but the game is not yet over! We shall see who triumphs in the end!'

Jane's heart skipped a beat but she gave him a look of limpid innocence. 'No doubt we shall be seeing a great deal of you then, sir.'

'I expect so.'

'Do you attend Lady Aston's masquerade on Thursday? I believe that your brother is invited!'

'A masquerade!' Alex looked quizzical. 'Such potential for dissembling, Miss Verey!'

The dance ended. Jane dropped a little curtsy. 'Indeed, sir! We are all looking forward to it! I have a pink domino that I am told is all the crack!'

Alex took her hand and kissed it, his eyes laughing at her. 'Giving secrets to the enemy, Miss Verey?'

'Perhaps so, perhaps not!' Jane withdrew her hand before he could feel it tremble and realise his effect on her. That was one secret she did not intend to give away. She was not at all sure why she had mentioned the masquerade, for it would have suited her plans better for Alex not to be present. Yet the urge to see him again had been a powerful one, a dangerous one. She did not like to examine the reasons for it too closely. As he escorted her back to Lady Verey's side, Jane saw Lady Dennery catch his eye with a significant little glance. At once, Jane felt young and naïve to have succumbed to the charm of a man who evidently preferred more sophisticated company. No doubt he would deliver her to her mother, then forget all about her. It was foolish to expect anything else and she had only herself to blame for being such a starry-eyed innocent.

Simon was alone in the Breakfast Parlour when Jane came down the following day. He was dressed for riding and was flicking through the *Morning Post*, but cast the paper aside with a smile when his sister slid into the seat opposite.

'Good morning, sis! How are you?'

He poured her some chocolate whilst Jane helped herself to a large portion of kidney and bacon.

'I am very well, I thank you.' Jane fixed him with a businesslike eye. 'Simon, I need to ask you something. How is it that you and the Duke of Delahaye are become such firm friends so quickly? It is particularly unfortunate, because I need your support against him in this ridiculous plan to marry me off to Lord Philip!'

A slight frown marred Simon's brow. He was accustomed to his sister's painful directness, although several years away from her company had lulled him into a false sense of security. He looked at her critically as she despatched her breakfast with an efficiency that argued a hearty appetite, if a certain lack of delicacy. He was forced to admit that Jane had grown into a strikingly attractive girl, with her jet black hair and the flyaway black brows that seemed only to emphasise the bright intelligence in those green eyes. Jane was no country mouse, nor could he imagine her playing the part just to find a husband in the marriage mart of *ton* Society. As for the suggestion that she make a marriage of convenience to Lord Philip, well, it seemed absurd. Except that he knew that his mother's heart was set on it and Alex Delahaye seemed insistent… He sighed unhappily.

The impatient drumming of Jane's slender fingers on the tablecloth reminded him that she was still awaiting his reply.

'Alex and I are not particular friends—' Simon prevaricated.

'Alex!' his sister interrupted, investing the word with scorn. 'You seem to be on first-name terms, at the very least!'

Simon sighed again. The martial light in Jane's eyes suggested that this was going to be difficult. 'Alex Delahaye is a friend of Harry Marchnight's,' he said carefully. 'He asked Harry to introduce us because he was concerned to avoid any… difficulties…that might have arisen as a result of Lord Philip's behaviour towards you. The trip to Ambergate and the rumours…' He could feel himself floundering.

'Difficulties?' Jane was momentarily distracted. 'Simon, what exactly did Lord Philip say about me?'

Simon shifted uncomfortably and avoided his sister's eye. He had no intention of stirring up the malicious gossip again. 'Why, nothing much to the purpose! It's better to forget it all now that everything is smoothed over! But Alex was anxious to avoid misunderstandings, or the possibility of me calling Philip out—as though I would waste my time on such a silly young cub!'

'I see.' Jane stirred her chocolate slowly. 'Then as you think him of so little account, you will understand my rejection of his suit! I may count on your support!'

Simon began to perceive that he had made a tactical mistake. Jane's mind was evidently more alert than his at ten in the morning. He smiled reluctantly.

'The trouble is…' He hesitated. He knew she was about to make mincemeat of him. 'The difficulty lies in a business transaction that is to be completed this very morning…' He watched Jane put her cup down and fix him with an unnervingly wide green stare. 'Knowing of my financial constraints at Ambergate, Alex has arranged to advance me a considerable sum on generous terms—'

'You sound like Pettishaw,' Jane said, with deceptive calm. 'Are you trying to tell me that you have sold me into marriage with Lord Philip in return for a loan to help you renovate Ambergate? I know the house is in sad need of repair, but surely your sister's happiness is too high a price to pay?'

'Dash it, Jane, you're running on like a novel from the circulating library!' Simon spluttered, his conscience pricking him. 'I mean no such thing! Of course you don't have to marry the man if you do not wish, but...' he risked a look at her face '...if you could just be nice to him for a few weeks it would help me immensely! Truth is, I'd never get the chance of such good terms from anywhere else and as Alex has seen fit to offer his help—'

'Yes, I wonder why that should be?' Jane marvelled in an innocent tone. Alex Delahaye's words to her at Almack's rang in her ears. *It would help your brother if there were investment in Ambergate... There is always a way...* 'Take care when you sign the agreement, Simon, or you may find your inheritance disappearing into the vast Delahaye estates!'

Simon looked affronted. 'What the devil has Alex done to deserve such opprobrium? You make him sound like a dashed moneylender! From all I hear he's as straight a man to do business with as one could wish!'

Jane shrugged, feeling a little ashamed of herself. She could hardly tell Simon of Alex's threats at Almack's and, as the Duke had seen fit to apologise, it seemed ungracious of her to continue to suspect him. And yet it made her uncomfortable. To think that he had an interest in Ambergate and a growing friendship with Simon brought him a little too close for comfort. It was almost enough to put her off her toast. She eyed the dish of butter with disfavour. This really was not to be borne! Alex Delahaye had achieved what no other man had ever done, and put her off her food!

After Simon had gone out, secretly relieved that his sister had not made more of a scene, Jane poured herself another cup of chocolate and sat back to consider matters She had believed the Duke entirely when he said that the game had only just begun. It would never do to underestimate him and, rather disconcertingly, she thought that he already had her measure. The patronising attitude he had assumed at Almack's had been replaced by something far more dangerous—the watchful respect a man might show a real adversary. The barriers seemed formidable. Ranged against her to a greater or lesser degree were her own family, who would be happy to see the match made with Lord Philip, as well as the Duke and Lady Eleanor. Worse, she would have to guard against her own wayward heart, which, despite her opposition to him, was inclined to consider Alexander Delahaye with far more warmth than was at all prudent for her peace of mind.

Chapter Five

'Oh Jane, is this not splendid?' Sophia said. Her eyes behind the mask were as bright as stars as she watched the dazzling company mingling in Lady Aston's ballroom. She smoothed her rose pink domino with excited fingers. 'I cannot wait for the Duke and Lord Philip to arrive! I have a wager with Lord Philip that he will never find me in this crush!'

Jane looked at her friend's radiant face and reflected that it would take Lord Philip all of two minutes to identify Sophia, for all that she was masked. There seemed to be some irresistible attraction that drew them directly to each other's side at every opportunity.

Their party was somewhat diminished that evening, for Lady Verey had suddenly succumbed to a sick headache, making it impossible for her to accompany them. Jane and Sophia had been consigned to the somewhat erratic care of her cousin, Mrs Brantledge. Mrs Brantledge had a daughter of her own to launch into society, a young lady who might unkindly have been considered to be firmly on the shelf at twenty-three. Fortunately a suitor had recently swum into view and both Miss Brantledge and her mother were hellbent on encouraging him. Simon Verey had been prevailed upon to accompany his sister, but had made a purposeful beeline for the cardroom and showed every sign of staying there all evening. This left Jane and Sophia very much to their own devices, which suited Jane admirably, since she was free to pursue her strategy without interference.

Sophia clutched Jane's arm. 'Jane! He is here! Lord Philip is here!'

Jane was amazed that Sophia could distinguish Lord Philip in the crowd about the door and yet her friend seemed quite certain. In a few moments, Sophia was proved correct as Lord Philip, dashing in a black domino, was beside them.

'Miss Verey?' he said cautiously, addressing himself to the pink domino. 'Will you do me the honour of dancing with me?'

'Happily, sir,' Sophia replied softly.

Lord Philip stiffened. His gaze went from the pink domino to Jane, in sapphire blue, who smiled encouragingly but did not speak. Lord Philip turned back to Sophia and his tone changed completely, softened. 'It is a great pleasure to see you again, ma'am. I trust that you are well? It has been too long since we last met!'

'I am very well, I thank you.' Sophia sounded as breathless and happy as he. 'But for shame, sir! It is all of a day since we were last together!'

'Does your brother accompany you tonight, sir?' Jane could not help asking. She convinced herself that she needed to know for strategic reasons, but felt her heart sink with disappointment as Lord Philip shook his head.

'I fear that Alex has cried off! Some party of Lady
Dennery's contriving, I believe. He tells me that a trip
to the opera is far more suitable for someone of his
years.' Lord Philip spread his arms out. 'He gave me
his domino and told me to dance with the beautiful
lady in the pink domino and I intend to take his advice!' He turned to Sophia and offered his arm, and
they moved away towards the dancing.

Jane sighed. The sharp pang of disappointment that
had assailed her when she heard of the Duke's absence was something that she did not care to think
about. She felt oddly flat, as though all the excitement
had already gone out of her evening. She frowned at
her own perversity. What could be better? Lady
Verey and the Duke were absent, Simon preoccupied
and no one there to notice that she and Sophia had
exchanged dominos!

On her left, Mrs Brantledge was chatting to another
chaperon, deeply engrossed.

'Such a suitable connection for my dear Evelyn!
Mr Coomberson's father made a vast fortune but he
is a man of both leisure and good education, with a
fine estate in Hertfordshire! I am persuaded that they
will make a match of it!' And she fell to discussing
Evelyn's prospects further.

It seemed to Jane that she was the only one without
a beau, a situation that would not have distressed her
unduly were it not for the irritating preoccupation she
appeared to have with the Duke of Delahaye. It was
inexplicable that her thoughts should centre on him,
for she had met several young men of good family
and unblemished reputation at her come out, and
many more men of a shadier sort, yet none of them
had interested her in the least. Whereas Alex Dela-

haye, far beyond her reach and completely uninterested, was constantly in her mind.

Still, there was always the food as consolation and she was already hungry... Excusing herself to Mrs Brantledge, Jane slipped out of the ballroom. A huge buffet supper was laid out on a long table in the next room, with small chairs dotted about so that the guests could gather in informal groups whilst they ate. The table was piled high with the most wonderful food and the smell was very appetising. Jane's mouth watered.

The room was completely empty. Jane tiptoed forward and reached tentatively for a slice of cold chicken pie. It was absolutely delicious, light and creamy with a flaky pastry crust. She licked her fingers, looking dubiously at the gap left on the plate where the slice should have been. Someone would be sure to notice the space.

'All alone, my lady?'

Jane jumped violently. She had not heard anyone approach, despite keeping a wary eye out for attentive servants. Yet the gentleman in the dark green domino was standing almost directly behind her.

The dark gaze behind the mask moved from Jane's guilty, flushed face to the pie dish. 'You could rearrange the remaining slices,' he suggested with a hint of a smile. 'I am sure that no one would notice. But only if you also removed this—' And he stretched out a hand and touched Jane's cheek. A crumb of pastry floated down to the floor.

He had not been wearing gloves and his touch seemed to burn Jane's skin. For a moment her startled gaze locked with his, then she took a hasty step back. She knew at once who he was, despite the disguise of the domino and mask. She had known as soon as he had touched her.

A footman and maid came in, bringing huge silver dishes of fruit, and the silence between them was broken.

'Perhaps I should escort you back to the ballroom,' the gentleman said gently, and there was a note in his voice that Jane did not understand. He offered her his arm and she took it without a word. She felt as though her whole body was tingling, alive to his touch. The recognition between them was not a matter of names or even faces, but something far deeper.

'You must tell me how I may address you,' the Duke said lazily, steering her purposefully along the colonnade that skirted the ballroom, and away from Mrs Brantledge's curious gaze. 'It is important to settle such matters early on at a masquerade, for you could equally be a Duchess or a milkmaid in disguise!'

Jane smiled a little, remembering the curious pleasure she had felt when he had called her 'my lady'. It seemed that they were to pretend to anonymity, which was, after all, the purpose of a masked ball. She had no objection, but she was certain that he had recognised her all the same. And she was wary. Why had he pretended to be engaged elsewhere and then attended the masquerade? What was his intention in seeking her out? And had he remembered that she should have been wearing a rose pink domino?

'Oh, I am nothing so exciting as either of those,' she said, with a smile, playing for time. 'I am only a young lady who has but recently come to Town!'

'Then it seems I must be formal, madam, if that is all the help you will give me.' Alex's gaze was warm with appreciation as it dwelt on her face. 'A young lady I could have guessed—a beautiful young lady, perhaps… Does your mama know how dangerous it is to allow you to wander unattended at a masquerade ball? There are plenty of gentlemen less scrupulous than I who would be eager to take advantage!'

Jane could see that this might well be true. Before they had arrived that night she had wondered at the appeal of a masked ball. Now she was experiencing it for herself. Freed by the disguise of a mask and domino, one might pretend to be whomever one pleased and flirt as one chose. It was strangely seductive, even to so level-headed a girl as Jane.

'I prefer to keep my name a secret, sir,' she said, 'just as you do yours, so you must call me what you will!'

'Ah…' she could see that he was smiling now '…but then I might offend you by having to call you sweetheart! Such endearments suit you well!'

'I thank you, sir, that is quite enough!' Jane realised that a strategic retreat was necessary already—he moved far too quickly. 'I said that I was a young *lady*—' she stressed the word '—and you must believe it, sir! No doubt my chaperon will be so good as to reinforce the point when you return me to her!'

The gentleman inclined his head. 'Your point is well made and well taken, ma'am! And that being the case, may I not keep you from her side a little longer? It is seldom one has the chance to match wits with a diamond of the first water!'

'A diamond, sir?'

'The sharpness, ma'am, as well as the beauty—do not tell me that you do not understand me. Diamonds cut diamonds, they say.'

Jane caught her breath. She could not deny that this was an intriguing skirmish, but it was hardly wise. She remembered her mama's strictures that ladies should never appear to be too clever, 'For you have a distressingly *mathematical* turn of mind, dear Jane, and I do beg you to dissemble it as much as possible. The gentlemen will not understand, nor wish to humour you…'

Yet the Duke of Delahaye had always expressed himself delighted to have the chance to pit his wit against hers, just as he was doing now.

'Have we met before, sir?' she asked innocently, testing how far he might take the pretence.

'No, indeed,' the Duke said smoothly, 'for I should not have forgotten!'

'How odd! I could have sworn… Then it is strange—'

'To feel such recognition, ma'am? I am flattered that you should think so!'

'I was about to say that it is strange that you should seem to presume on a longer acquaintance, sir!' Jane finished sweetly, and heard him laugh.

'Do you know, ma'am, I have the oddest feeling that the more time I spend in your company, the more I shall have to accustom myself to such set-downs!'

'Then pray do not put yourself through the experience, sir,' Jane concluded gently. 'My chaperon is just a few steps away and may take me off your hands!'

There was a silence. The pillars cast long shadows and Jane suddenly experienced the illusion that they were quite alone, rather than within feet of a ballroom full of four hundred people.

'Your suggestion holds little appeal, I fear, ma'am,' Alex said silkily. 'I would far rather dance with you!'

Jane opened her eyes wide. 'A most autocratic invitation, my lord!'

'You attribute a rank to me, ma'am?'

'A high one to suit your manner, sir!'

He laughed. 'Come and dance with me, if you please!'

The music was just striking up.

'A waltz!' Jane hung back.

'I collect that you must have danced at Almack's?' Jane realised that he was teasing her. Who would know that better than he?

'As you know, sir! But—' Jane was suddenly wary. It was too late. He had swept her on to the floor with an expertise that was very familiar.

There was also a difference between verbal fencing and this altogether more disturbing intimacy, Jane thought breathlessly. Clasped so close to the Duke, the dancers around them dipping and swirling, she felt frighteningly powerless. The awareness that was flooding her body was familiar and exciting, threatening to sweep her beyond common sense. The atmosphere of the masquerade, daring and raffish, could only encourage such abandonment.

'The supper dance is next,' Alex remarked, reclaiming Jane's attention from her wayward thoughts as the last strains of the waltz died away. 'You will not be wanting to miss that.'

'No, indeed.' Jane blushed at the memory of being caught with her mouth full of chicken pie. 'I am promised for that dance, sir. I must beg you to return me to my chaperon.'

'A pity. Remember to hurry into the supper room

at the end of the dance and you may be able to take another piece of pie before anyone notices,' her escort said smoothly. 'Otherwise there will be endless speculation on who the mystery eater could be—one of the servants may even be dismissed as a result!'

'You are unchivalrous to remind me, sir,' Jane murmured. She could see her partner for the supper dance approaching Mrs Brantledge. 'What could be more humiliating than being found stealing the food?'

'But it shows an interesting trait of character, perhaps...'

'That I like food?'

'That you will take risks to achieve what you want, ma'am.'

Their eyes met again, a quizzical expression in his. Jane wrenched her gaze away. What was this peculiar affinity that threatened her, this attraction that was like nothing she had ever experienced before? She had told herself that it was only common sense to try to keep out of his way, but the shaming truth was that she had no wish to do so. She was not at all certain of his next move. It was like an engrossing game of chess, but with an added edge of sensual awareness between the two of them. Jane frowned. His Grace of Delahaye might well be accustomed to playing such sophisticated games, but she was not at all sure that she would be able to carry it off!

'Lord Harvey is waiting for me, sir,' she said, a little at random. 'Please excuse me.'

He bowed. 'Certainly, ma'am. I shall see you later, perhaps.'

Jane, trembling inside, hoped that that was unlikely. Now that good sense had reasserted itself, she intended to do everything in her power to avoid him.

From the dance floor she watched the green domino skirt the edge of the room and take up a position by the door of the supper room, resting his broad shoulders against the wall as he watched her with undisguised interest. Jane shivered a little. She was becoming too entangled in this! Her feelings were hopelessly engaged and it seemed that Alex did not intend to allow her to withdraw.

Lord Harvey's bland presence was soothing. He made few conversational demands upon her and Jane began to relax as the country dance progressed, although Alex's continued scrutiny was unsettling. It was only as they progressed through the set that Jane realised that Philip and Sophia were also dancing, Sophia resplendent in the pink domino that should have been Jane's own. Jane risked another glance across at Alex and saw with a sinking heart that his gaze was also following Philip and Sophia. She knew that he would not be slow to put two and two together.

Jane realised that Simon had abandoned the card tables and was also dancing, his partner being a slender girl with very fair hair. Jane did not recognise her and wondered who she could be. There was a look on her brother's face that arrested her attention, for all that he had the protection of the mask. Jane sighed silently. So Simon was also succumbing to Cupid's arrow! It seemed that she was surrounded by romance and her own foolhardy heart had to choose an entirely inappropriate subject for its affections!

For once Jane did not enjoy supper, not because she was worrying about the piece of pie but because she was like a cat on hot bricks trying to locate the Duke of Delahaye. It seemed, however, that the green domino had vanished and, once fortified by food, Jane felt a little better. Her dance card was full and the rest of the evening fled, until Sophia touched her arm late on in the evening.

'Jane! It is only ten minutes to the unmasking! Are we to exchange dominoes?'

They slipped away to Lord Aston's study. There, the pink and the blue dominoes were hastily exchanged and Sophia hurried back to the ballroom to be blamelessly at Mrs Brantledge's side at the unmasking. Jane tarried a moment, so that they should not be seen returning together. She smiled a little, thinking of the neatness of her plan and how well it had worked in the end. Lady Verey knew that her daughter's domino had been pink and Sophia's blue. Now there would be plenty of people to report to her that Lord Philip had spent all evening dancing attendance on the pink domino... Her smile faded as she thought of the Duke of Delahaye. He too had known that her domino was supposed to be pink. That meant that either he had not recognised her earlier, and would flirt with any pretty girl he met, or that he was just playing along with her to see where the deception was leading, or that she had been mistaken and the green domino had not been the Duke at all... Jane gave up. It was a tangled web and she was becoming hopelessly confused.

She checked the clock and decided to give Sophia another minute before she followed her back to the ballroom. Lord Aston had a carved marble chess set on a round table before the window. Jane moved the Queen idly.

'All alone at the unmasking, Cinderella?'

She had not heard anyone come in. Whirling

around, her heart pounding, Jane caught her breath on a gasp.

'Oh, sir, you startled me! I was about to go back to the ballroom…'

The green domino's gaze fell on the chessmen.

'It is a fine set. Do you play?'

'Yes,' Jane said, 'my father taught me.' She put the Queen back in her appointed place.

'A game of cunning and strategy.'

'If played well…' Jane saw the glimmer in his eyes and smiled back in spite of herself. 'I make no claims to be a good player…'

'I am sure you are not doing yourself justice, ma'am! What other games do you play?'

'I do not gamble, sir, if that is what you mean…' Jane's breath caught a little. She knew exactly what he meant. Any moment now he would identify himself and upbraid her for her latest trick. He *must* know now that she had exchanged dominoes with Sophia and that it was Sophia, not she, who had spent the evening with Lord Philip.

'Excuse me, sir.' She was glad that her voice did not betray her. 'I think I should rejoin my party. They will be missing me…'

The long-case clock in the corner chimed the hour, making her jump.

'It is time for the unmasking,' the green domino said, his eyes intent on her face. 'Am I to be denied knowledge of the identity of so fascinating a companion? I assure you, it is the only reason I have lingered so long at the ball…'

He put out a hand to pull back the hood of Jane's domino, reaching for the ties to her mask.

She could feel his fingers amongst her tumbled

black curls and her whole body started to tremble. The mask came away and Jane felt as though she were naked. There was no chance of escape now. To play the innocent could be her only defence.

'You have the advantage of me, sir...' Her voice was husky. His hand brushed her cheek for a moment, sending more quivers of sensation along her nerve-endings. He pulled his own mask away with a quick, impatient gesture.

'Not so, Miss Verey. You have known my identity all evening, have you not?'

Jane cleared her throat. 'All evening, sir?'

Alex's dark eyes pinned her to the spot. 'Come now, Miss Verey, where is your much-vaunted honesty? Are you denying that you spent some time in my company earlier?'

Jane's wide green eyes met his virtuously. 'How could I know, sir? All the guests have been masked...'

She could see from his expression that he did not believe her and he looked to be torn between laughter and exasperation. He took a step forward and Jane's heart leaped into her throat. Her instinctive movement away caused the pale candlelight to shimmer for a moment on the rose pink domino; the shadows shifted and then Alex stood back suddenly, his voice changing abruptly.

'A pink domino, Miss Verey?'

'As you see, sir.'

'No doubt Miss Marchment is in blue?'

'Indeed she is.'

'But you were wearing the blue domino earlier this evening?'

'You might well have believed that, your Grace.'

Alex looked as though he was uncertain whether

to shake her or kiss her. For a moment Jane was held captive by the expression in his eyes, then he said,

'Oh, Miss Verey, I believe that it is not safe to let you from my sight!'

He sketched a slight bow and watched her positively run from the room. The oak door latched with a firm click behind her.

Alexander Delahaye slumped into an armchair, running a hand through his rumpled black hair. It was only with the greatest effort of will that he had made himself let Jane Verey go. His instinct, more powerful than anything he had felt in a very long time, had prompted him to crush her to him and kiss her until she could no longer stand.

As soon as he had met her in the supper room he had recognised her, blue domino or not. He remembered her references to wearing a pink domino and suspected that she had tricked him again. When he saw Philip paying court to the lady in pink, he had been certain.

Nevertheless, some impulse had led him to flirt with her, a whim that he barely understood but was forced to admit he had found deeply enjoyable. Jane's quick wit and willingness to cross swords with him were most stimulating. She was an intriguing conundrum, at once so daring and yet so innocent, risking a little then drawing back! Alex sighed. These were not the feelings he should be having for his brother's future bride! He stretched out his long legs and looked covetously at the decanter of brandy standing on Lord Aston's bureau. Suddenly he needed a drink.

Simon Verey was having a bad evening. He had lost the angelic beauty who had granted him one dance earlier in the evening and now his sister had disappeared as well. Belatedly remembering that he had promised his mother that he would look after Jane and Sophia, he started to search the ballroom for them.

A blue domino was visible in one of the alcoves, talking to a gentleman in black who looked completely besotted. Simon frowned. Had Jane been wearing pink or blue? Was that Sophia? Her face was turned away from him but the fair hair curling from beneath the hood certainly suggested that it could not be Jane.

Scowling, Simon ventured into the empty supper room and out into the conservatory. There were plenty of people strolling there, but none of them were Jane. Finally Simon stepped out into the garden, where the cool night air was refreshing after the humid atmosphere in the house. Giggles and rustling from behind the bushes suggested that the most amorous of the party-goers had decided to further their acquaintance in the relative privacy of the darkness. Simon did not for one moment believe that his sister would be amongst them, but he was almost ready to strangle her anyway. He retraced his steps to the terrace.

'I beg you, sir, to let me go! Your suggestions disgust me!'

Simon swung round abruptly. He knew that it was not Jane, but he recognised the voice. The shifting shadows of the terrace moved a little to show the slender shape of a girl struggling violently in the grip of a burly individual almost twice her size. There was a ripping sound and an exclamation from the man, who appeared to be bending her back against the parapet until it seemed she must break in half. Simon hurried forward and took him by the collar.

'You heard the lady, sirrah! Be off with you!'

The man was very drunk. He let go of the girl abruptly and swung his fist at Simon, making contact instead with the stone coping. With a howl of mingled rage and pain, he stormed off into the night. There was a silence. The girl smoothed down her torn domino, which was showing a dress of silvery gauze beneath.

'You're very kind, sir.' Her voice shook a little with agitation and Simon put out an instinctive hand.

'You must let me take you back to your chaperon,' he said gruffly. 'However appealing a breath of fresh air may be, it is not safe to be alone out here.'

He thought he saw her smile a little in the darkness. 'Oh, I have no chaperon to take care of me,' she said, with bitter amusement, 'but I thank you for your concern, sir.'

Simon stared at her through the darkness. Her words suggested that she was married or worse—better?—that she was a Cyprian who had attended the masquerade in the hope of attracting a rich protector. It was scarcely unknown, but Simon's whole being rejected the idea. She neither spoke nor acted like a courtesan and she had had every opportunity to try to engage his interest earlier, yet she had made no push to do so. Nor, indeed, had she encouraged the drunken overtures of Lord Hewetson, whom he had just seen off...

'Who are you?' Simon asked abruptly. 'You must be here as part of a party, you must have some protection! Let me escort you back inside—'

'I thank you, but no.' The girl's voice was low but firm. There was some kind of accent that gave it an added charm, elusive but very sweet. 'You misunderstand me, sir. I am quite alone, but I have no need of your escort. Please excuse me…' And she walked away, her footsteps fading away across the stone terrace.

Simon followed more slowly, determined to keep her within view and puzzling over what she had said. He had completely forgotten his intention of finding Jane and Sophia and escorting them home.

The girl could be seen hurrying along the edge of the ballroom towards the main door, her torn domino flapping behind her. She kept the hood up, held closely about her face, but her long silver-gilt hair streamed behind her. For the first time Simon reflected that she might have told him the literal truth when she had said that she was attending the ball alone. If so, she *had* to be a barque of frailty, for no respectable girl would ever attend a ball like this unescorted. And yet—

A scream pierced the air. Startled, Simon saw that the girl had checked in the doorway, restrained by the clutching hands of the Duchess of Merrion. The girl was pulling in one direction and the Duchess in the other, and they were making a comic spectacle of themselves. The Duchess was still screaming.

'My dress! She's wearing my dress!'

Everybody was staring. The Duchess had a very loud and penetrating voice. Simon tried to push his way through the gathering crowd.

'Dear ma'am, there must be some mistake—' he heard the girl say as she tried to prise herself free. Her hood had fallen back and strands of the silver fair hair tumbled over her shoulders. Her face was thin with high cheekbones, like a drawing from a fairy story. She still had her mask on and behind it her eyes shone with a blue fire. Simon stared, completely bewitched.

The old Duchess clung tighter. 'Mistake! I promised a fortune to Celestine for that dress! The only one, she said! It was to be delivered tomorrow! Where did you get it from? Who are you?'

With a gasp the girl wrenched herself free and ran into the hall. Her jade green domino slid from her shoulders and crumpled on the floor.

'Stop her, she's stealing my dress!' The Duchess shrieked, completely over-excited. For a moment no one moved, then a babble of conversation broke out, but no one made any move after the girl.

'Kitchen maid tricked up in her mistress' dress...' someone said.

'Dashed pretty girl...'

'Any old riff-raff at these events...'

People began to move away. Simon bent to pick up the discarded jade green domino. A faint sweet scent still clung to its folds, immediately evocative of its wearer. Simon was astonished to feel desire stirring in him. He knew that he had to find her. Whoever she was, he had to see her again.

Chapter Six

The trouble with the Season, Jane thought, as she prepared for yet another evening's entertainment, was that it gave one so little time to think and plan. She could well believe Miss Brantledge's smug assertion that she had attended fifty balls, twenty-six dinners and fourteen picnics the previous year. Miss Brantledge would be sure to have counted every one. And since the object of the entire exercise appeared to be to wear oneself to a thread as well as find a husband, Jane could see that it worked very well. However, the social demands gave her no chance to develop her scheme for avoiding the marriage with Lord Philip. Jane snapped her fan together sharply in frustration, causing one of the struts to splinter. That evening they were to be the guests of the Duke of Delahaye for a concert at Vauxhall Gardens. Jane's natural pleasure in visiting so exciting a place was tempered by the thought of close chaperonage and the embarrassment of being in Alex's company for the first time since the masquerade.

The memory of that evening a week ago was still disturbing to Jane. She had promised herself that she would think of it no more, but she could not help herself. There had been a moment, there in the darkened study, when Jane had been sure Alex was about to kiss her. The look in his eyes, compounded of exasperation and tenderness, had held her rooted to the spot. And she had wanted him to kiss her, had quite ached to be in his arms, with a desperation that puzzled and worried her. Surely it was not at all refined to be subject to such strong feelings? The mutual respect and comfort she had hoped to find one day in marriage were pale and cold in comparison.

Yet evidently Alex had not felt the same. He had had plenty of opportunities to seek her out in the past week—even if it was only to ring a peal over her for her conduct—and he had not chosen to do so. Clearly she had read far more into his behaviour than he had ever intended; the flirtation that she had found so exciting had no doubt seemed tame to him, a diversion quickly forgotten. It was shaming now to remember how his touch had stirred her senses and how much pleasure she had taken in his company.

Besides, Alex was now too occupied with the odious Lady Dennery to have a moment's thought for Jane. The whole of society was talking about them; they had been seen driving in the Park and Alex squired her to any number of events. Sighing, Jane tried to fix the splintered struts of her fan together again, then cast it away in exasperation. No doubt Lady Dennery would be there that evening and the prospect did not entice.

In one respect only were matters shaping quite well. Lord Philip and Sophia were clearly smitten with each other and therefore quite willing to give Jane as much tacit support as she needed. It only required for her to suggest that she and Sophia exchange partners for a dance, or escorts for a walk, and the substitution was accomplished. However, this could not be achieved as often as Jane would wish under Lady Verey's beady gaze. She was obliged to endure several tedious dances with Lord Philip during which he spoke in monosyllables, if at all. Jane decided that she would soon need to seek his more active participation in her plans.

They approached Vauxhall by river that evening and the gardens looked remarkably pretty in the fading dusk, with their lantern-lit walks and arbours. Jane thought that it looked very romantic and her sense of humour was tickled at the thought of their ill-assorted party. Lord Philip and Sophia were surely the only true romantics in the group and even if Lord Philip's intentions were of the purest, he could not declare them openly. Lady Dennery was hunting Alexander Delahaye with a single-minded concentration that had very little to do with romance, as far as Jane could see. Simon seemed forlorn and quiet, and she herself felt quite out of step with the brightly coloured illusion all around.

The concert and the supper were both excellent, despite Lady Dennery's somewhat sharp asides.

'What charming children!' she had said to Lady Verey when first introduced, for all the world, Jane thought, as though she and Sophia were still in leading-reins! Lady Dennery then took it upon herself to intersperse intimate little remarks to Alex with observations on the conduct of young ladies, until Jane was heartily sick of her.

'Why, Miss Verey, you have a most robust appetite!' she said archly, picking at her dessert and smiling at Alex. 'You will find that the gentlemen prefer young ladies who show less partiality for their food! No doubt Lord Philip will bear me out!'

Philip, who had been gazing soulfully at Sophia and had not heard the comment, grunted non-committally. Jane's cheeks flamed. Lady Dennery's laugh tinkled out as her sharp gaze appraised Jane's neat figure. 'Lud, Miss Verey, I think you should restrain yourself now! Over-indulgence at the table is often a sign of a sadly unsteady character! There is no knowing where such a lack of discipline will lead you later!'

Lady Verey and Lady Eleanor exchanged a horrified look at such vulgarity. Fortunately Jane and Sophia were both looking quite blank, for neither of them had taken her ladyship's coarse allusion. Simon, catching his mother's eye, got up and suggested a short stroll in the interval before the concert resumed. He offered his arm to Sophia and in short order Jane and Lord Philip had joined them. The others declined the exercise, making Jane almost burst as she tried to repress a remark on the benefits of activity for a healthy figure.

They admired the little pools and grottoes and sauntered amidst the crowds. All of them studiously avoided speaking of Lady Dennery and more particularly of the possibility that she might become the next Duchess of Delahaye.

Sophia and Philip paused to admire a group of marble statuary whilst Simon and Jane walked on ahead.

'Are you enjoying all this or do you miss Ambergate, Janey?' Simon asked suddenly, gesturing at the crowded gardens.

Jane smiled. 'A little of both, I suppose! I am enjoying the Season, but I shall not be sorry when it ends.' A shadow fell across her face as she realised that the matter of the marriage to Lord Philip would have to be resolved once and for all by then. In an effort to be cheerful she turned a smile on her brother.

'What about you, Simon? I suppose you'll be going home in a couple of months?'

'I'll spend some time at Ambergate,' Simon agreed, 'but Alex has invited me to Yorkshire for the shooting in August.'

'Has he!' Jane realised that she was out-of-proportion cross. The Duke of Delahaye seemed to interfere in everything! 'After you have helped him marry me off to his brother, I suppose!'

Simon flashed her an ironic glance. 'We shall have to be quick about it then, or else Philip will have eloped with Sophia!'

Jane sighed, sliding her hand through his arm. 'So you have noticed it! Yes, their affection is becoming a little too apparent! And whilst it would solve one problem, I suppose—'

'It would only cause another,' Simon finished grimly. 'Alex would be furious and matters would be off to a very bad start!'

'Yes…' Jane looked round to see if Sophia and Philip were within earshot. To her surprise they were nowhere to be seen. The empty walks stretched away on either side of the gravel path, dark with their high hedges.

'Oh! It is too bad! They should have more sense than to slip away together at a place like this! Sophia should be more careful of her reputation and if Lord Philip does not have honourable intentions—' Jane broke off, afflicted by a powerful guilt. She was all too aware that she had encouraged the couple to spend time together.

Simon was frowning as he scanned the crowds.

'They cannot have gone far. We may see them if we walk towards the pavilion—' He broke off suddenly, staring over the heads of the crowd. 'Well, I'll be...'

Jane saw that her brother was watching a slender blonde girl who was walking swiftly away from them. At her side, a portly man in a striped red and white waistcoat appeared to be talking to her urgently, almost running to keep up with her. Jane saw her shake her head once, decisively, then the man tried to catch her arm. The couple turned down one of the dark walks, and at the same time, Simon dropped Jane's arm and darted off after them without another word. Jane stared in stupefaction.

To have gone from being in a party of four to being alone seemed strange and vexatious, but Jane was a sensible girl and realised that she could find her way back to the rotunda with little trouble. There were plenty of people about and she felt quite safe. Far more provoking was Simon's erratic behaviour. Evidently he had recognised either the girl or her companion, but as to why he had rushed off without a word... Jane started to walk slowly back towards the rotunda. As she passed the pool with the statuary, she thought she saw Philip and Sophia just disappearing around the corner of one of the walks to the right of her. At the same time, Jane glimpsed the tall but unmistakable figure of the Duke of Delahaye coming towards her. She was not sure if he had seen her, but did not want to wait and find out. The first difficult explanation—why she was alone—was linked too closely to the second—where Sophia and Philip were. And if his Grace of Delahaye should come across Lord Philip with Sophia down one of the dark walks… Without further ado, Jane whisked around the hedge and hurried after the disappearing couple.

Although the crowds were thick only a few yards away, here between the high hedges it was dark and silent. Jane came to a crossroads, where a marble nymph reclined in a mossy bower. Looking around, she felt as though she had entered a maze. Any moment she would lose her sense of direction and become completely lost. She was about to abandon Sophia to her fate, turn around and retrace her steps, when she heard a faint noise.

Jane realised that the walk was not as deserted as she had at first thought. The portly gentleman she had seen earlier crossed her view briefly as he turned down a parallel path. The girl was no longer with him and he was skulking in the shadow of the hedge. For some reason Jane shrank back, praying that the gossamer white of her dress would not betray her. There was something so furtive in the man's behaviour that it made her deeply uneasy.

Then she froze. There was a summerhouse ahead of her at a point where five of the walks converged, and she had just noticed Alex's tall figure stride into the centre in order to scan the crowds thronging along the main walks. And she could also see the portly gentleman, stalking as quietly as a cat, up the shadowy edge of the nearby path. The moonlight glinted on the white stripes of his waistcoat and on the silver blade in his hand. It seemed ludicrous, yet there was a stealth about the man that was infinitely frightening, and each step took him closer to Alex's unsuspecting back.

Jane did not wait another moment. She flew down the walk, making as much noise as possible, raced up the steps and tumbled into Alex's arms. To her left she heard the rustle of leaves and saw the shadows move as the man slipped away as silently as he had come.

'Your Grace!'

'Miss Verey? I have been looking for you!' There was a lazy amusement in Alex's voice. 'Whatever can you have—?' His tone sharpened as he felt her knees give way and she sagged against him. He took her by the upper arms and shook her slightly.

'What has happened? Has somebody hurt you? Answer me!'

'No! Oh, you must come away…' Jane could hear her voice breaking shamefully. Now that the immediate danger was over she found that she was able to neither stand nor speak properly. Alex's face was very close to hers, his eyes blazing. If he had not held her, she knew she would have fallen.

'Jane? You must tell me what is wrong!'

Jane took a deep breath. 'You must come away from this place, your Grace! There is a man with a knife—'

Alex took a swift look around. 'A pickpocket—'

'No!' Jane said, beating her hands against his chest in her agitation. 'A murderer! He has a knife!'

'Very well. We will go at once.' Alex captured both her hands in his own, infinitely reassuring, grip. His voice was very calm. He saw that she was shaking and wrapped his cloak close about her, at the same time urging her forward and down the summerhouse steps towards the crowded paths.

'Can you manage to walk back to the others, Miss Verey? It is but a step and you are quite safe.'

With Alex's arm around her and one of her hands still resting in his, Jane managed to walk shakily back towards the main path. Once they had rejoined the press of people wandering back towards the rotunda, Alex let her go and offered her his arm in a more circumspect manner. Jane let out a huge shaky breath.

'Oh, thank goodness! What a horrid thing to happen!' She glanced up at Alex's face and saw that he was frowning. He drew her into one of the lit alcoves and helped her to a seat.

Seeing her look of surprise, he said quickly, 'We shall go back to the others directly. But first, Miss Verey, can you tell me what happened?'

He was so matter of fact that Jane was determined not to be missish. 'I saw the man earlier when I was walking with Simon,' she said, as calmly as possible. 'He was a fat man in a bulging waistcoat, not some ragged pickpocket. Then, just before I saw you in the summerhouse, I heard a noise and saw him creeping down the walk towards you. He had a knife in his hand! I saw it!'

Alex remained silent. His dark brows were drawn and he looked to be thinking of something far beyond the brightly lit pleasure gardens. Whatever his thoughts were, Jane could tell that they were not pleasant. She shivered.

'An opportunist thief,' Alex said easily, after a moment. 'It was foolish of me to step aside from the crowds, for Vauxhall is well known for its petty thieves and criminals. I am sorry that you should have had such a shocking experience, Miss Verey, but I beg you to forget it. The man missed his chance and will be long gone by now.'

Jane did not reply. Something in her wanted to protest that the man had been no simple thief, but what proof did she have? It was the most obvious explanation. After all, who would intentionally seek Alex out with murder in mind? The idea seemed ridiculous.

'I think,' Alex added, very deliberately, 'that we should not worry the others with this story, Miss Verey. The ladies, in particular, would be most distressed. Which reminds me to ask...' the frown deepened on his brow '...whatever were you doing alone in the dark walks?'

Jane hesitated. This was tricky, since she had no wish to cause trouble for the others. 'I became separated from the others by accident,' she said evasively, 'and was looking for them again when I saw you—and the thief.'

'I see,' Alex said drily. 'How very vague, Miss Verey! You *were* alone, I suppose?'

'What do you mean—?' Jane broke off and blushed. 'Your Grace!'

'Well?'

'Would it have been preferable for me to have been accompanied or alone in such a situation?' Jane asked spiritedly.

Alex raised an eyebrow. He got up and helped Jane to her feet. 'Ah, now I know that you are feeling more yourself, Miss Verey! And there you have me, for I am not at all sure!'

They walked back to the rotunda slowly. The music had already started again. Sophia and Philip were sitting several feet apart, looking on her part demure and on his suspiciously cheerful. Simon caught Jane's eye. His own expression was sheepish. Jane raised a cautionary finger to her lips and he kept obediently silent. She did not wish him to say anything that might contradict the sparse tale that she had already told Alex.

It was only as she was turning back to the orchestra that Jane realised that Alex had also seen her clandestine gesture and was watching her with a look that was both interested and deeply speculative.

Lady Eleanor Fane called at Haye House the following morning at a time that most members of the *ton* would have considered quite uncivilised. As she let the knocker fall she had a moment of doubt, for she had just remembered how much attention Alex had been lavishing on Lady Dennery the previous night. If she had managed to fix Alex's interest he would scarcely be receiving guests that morning... Lady Eleanor set her lips firmly as the door started to open. Too late!

Tredpole's impassive face gave nothing away.

'I will inquire if his Grace is at home,' the butler murmured, his stately progress across the hall suggesting that though the answer to his question might be in doubt, he would be equal to any eventuality. Left alone to wait in the drawing-room, Lady Eleanor peered critically into the mirror and fidgeted with her silver-topped stick.

Fortunately the Duke was receiving and did not keep her waiting long.

'His Grace begs you to join him in the library, my lady,' Tredpole murmured, preceding Lady Eleanor across the hall.

'Humph!' Lady Eleanor replied, secretly relieved not to have found her godson *in flagrante*.

Alex was sitting at his desk, slowly sipping a cup of coffee, the pungent fumes of which Lady Eleanor could smell across the room. She sniffed appreciatively.

'Tredpole, another cup, if you please!' Alex said with a grin, coming forward to kiss his aunt. 'What can bring you here so early, Aunt Eleanor? You might have found me otherwise occupied!'

Lady Eleanor fixed him with a repressive gaze. 'Perhaps that accounts for your deplorably high spirits, Alexander!' she said tartly. 'I shall not inquire!' Then, as her nephew's grin broadened, she added, 'It is another lady I have come to speak about—Miss Verey! I have been thinking that Philip's suit progresses very ill. According to Maria Winchester, Philip was spotted in the dark walks with Miss Marchment last night! I begged Maria to keep quiet for the sake of our friendship, but if Philip is pursuing other game... Meanwhile, the *on dit* is that Blakeney is hoping to fix his interest with Miss Verey, engagement or no! He has certainly been very attentive of late!'

Alex's smile faded. 'Blakeney? Are you sure, Aunt Eleanor?'

'What does it matter if it is Blakeney or some other gentleman?' Lady Eleanor demanded discontentedly. 'First the business at Lady Winterstoke's dinner and now this! Why, it seems to me that the little minx is running rings around you!'

Alex sat down on the corner of his desk, one leg swinging. 'Do you think so, Aunt Eleanor? It is early days yet, you know!'

Lady Eleanor took a reviving draught of the strong coffee. 'Decisive action is what is called for here, Alex, not shilly-shallying! Why, anyone would think that you enjoyed crossing swords with the chit!' She drained her cup, thereby missing her godson's fleetingly rueful expression. 'Whilst you are playing games, Philip is engaging the affections of another lady entirely! I should have thought that *that* would exercise your mind considerably!'

Alex did not seem either surprised or disturbed by this statement. 'I collect that by that you mean Miss Marchment? Philip has fallen in and out of love more times than I care to count, Aunt! You know that! It means nothing—he will marry where the money dictates!'

'Miss Marchment is no lightskirt to help Philip while away the time until he weds!' Lady Eleanor snapped. 'The girl has fallen head over ears in love with him and this time…this time, Alex, I do believe that Philip may feel the same!'

Alex was examining a paperweight, turning it over in his hands so that the light struck sparks off the deep blue interior. His head was bent and Lady Eleanor could not see his expression.

'I am certain that you must be mistaken,' he said levelly. 'Philip has never shown any sign of attaching himself to a respectable female!'

'Never before!' Lady Eleanor tapped her stick on the floor in her agitation. 'If you do not act quickly, Alex, the Verey match will be lost forever and then how will you square your promise to your grandfather with events?'

Alex looked up, the expression in his dark eyes quite unreadable. 'No doubt I should think of something...' he murmured. 'But I suspect that you had more in mind than to come here to berate me for my lack of action, did you not, ma'am? Unless I miss my guess, you have a plan!'

Lady Eleanor smiled reluctantly, soothed by both her nephew's teasing and the excellent coffee.

'Well, well...I thought to lend a helping hand! I had the idea of inviting the Vereys to Malladon!'

Alex put the paperweight down gently. 'You intend for me to open up Malladon for a house party? Now? In the middle of the Season?'

'Precisely!' Lady Eleanor leaned forward. 'It would not be a party Alex, only a few guests, and not for long! And I would act as hostess for you!'

'Good of you, ma'am!' her nephew murmured with irony.

Lady Eleanor was not to be deterred. 'I know it is the middle of the Season, but I thought that a few days in the country would be the very thing! The trouble with the Season is that too many people are milling around! It is easier to concentrate attention in a smaller group!'

'One of Miss Verey's tactics has been to employ others as a distraction,' Alex observed thoughtfully. 'It is true that she would find it less easy to be so evasive in so small a group. You realise, however, that Miss Marchment will have to be invited too? Courtesy demands that she should be included.'

'I suppose we cannot leave the wretched girl behind,' Lady Eleanor concurred, 'and really it is too bad of me to describe her thus, for she is the sweetest child, only a threat to your plans!'

'Plans can always be changed, ma'am,' Alex observed, but before his aunt could ask for further clarification, he continued. 'I am gratified to see, however, that you have come round to my way of thinking! Originally you were berating me for believing Miss Verey to be anything other than a witty and charming girl!'

Lady Eleanor smoothed her skirts. 'Well, I confess that at first I had difficulty in imagining Jane Verey as the artful schemer you described, Alex! But now I have seen the evidence with my own eyes! Oh, she is both witty and charming, I do not dispute that, but therein lies the problem! Girls these day,' Lady Eleanor said severely, 'can be too clever for their own good! A little feminine modesty would be more becoming!'

'Come now, Aunt Eleanor...' Alex straightened up and strolled over to the mantelpiece '...you are too harsh! Miss Verey is not precisely immodest! And she may be wilful but she is still beautiful and engaging—' He broke off as he saw the arrested expression on Lady Eleanor's face and finished a little hastily, 'The perfect wife for Philip, in fact!'

'For Philip! Of course!' Lady Eleanor's lips twitched a little as a certain truth made its presence felt. 'I am persuaded that Miss Verey will settle quickly enough once the match is made. I am anxious only to avoid a monstrous scandal if Philip takes it into his head to elope with Miss Marchment! That could not be borne, for although the girl is from an entirely respectable family, they have no estate or connections or fortune, and it could not be deemed suitable! So Philip—and Miss Verey—must be brought to the point as soon as may be!'

'Indeed!' Alex turned away. 'I believe that you are correct in thinking that the more intimate atmosphere of the house party might promote our cause. Besides, if the signs are not auspicious, we can always contrive to compromise Miss Verey sufficiently for a betrothal to follow!'

Lady Eleanor looked appalled. 'Alex! You would not! Your deceit—'

'Is matched only by that of Miss Verey, I assure you! If she can outwit me then I shall concede defeat gracefully. If not—well, we shall see who is the winner!'

Lady Eleanor said no more, but as she took her leave she found herself scanning once more her nephew's impervious features and wondering whether she had imagined the moment earlier when Alex had betrayed his own interest in Jane Verey. The way his voice had softened as he spoke of Jane's beauty and charm, and the indulgent note she had detected… Lady Eleanor suddenly remembered Alex's sharpened interest when she had mentioned Lord Blakeney paying court to Jane. She smiled a little as she stepped out in the direction of her home in Lower Brook Street. Perhaps she had dreamed it, but she did not think so. And if Alex was already aware of his own feelings, just what did he have in mind for Jane Verey? Certainly not marriage to his brother! The more she thought about it, the more equivocal some of Alex's remarks seemed, to the point where Lady Eleanor suddenly wondered just which of the Delahaye brothers Miss Jane Verey would be compromised into marrying.

Unaware of the unexpected invitation that was about to come their way, Jane, Sophia and Lady Verey spent the morning in Bond Street attending to

some essential shopping. Most improbably, Simon
had expressed a wish to accompany them. He had
murmured some excuse about needing a new hat and
Jane, unusually distracted by the purchase of a white
evening gown with an overdress of pale gold, did not
at first notice the piercing looks he was giving to all
the staff in the modiste's shop. It was only when her
brother had peered behind a curtain and startled a
shop assistant who was preparing to model a dress for
them that Jane had dragged him to one side.

'Simon! What on earth are you doing?' she whispered fiercely. 'You will have us all expelled from
the shop if you keep spying on models in their un-
dergarments!'

Her brother gave her a harassed look. 'This is Celestine's, isn't it, Jane?'

'Yes of course! That is Celestine herself over there
glaring at you! But what is that to the purpose?'

Simon glanced at his mother and Sophia, who were
chattering over a dress of pale green. 'Come outside
for a moment and I will tell you.'

The whole story of Simon's encounter at the masquerade came tumbling out, including how he had
danced with a girl then lost her for a while, only to
find her again out on the terrace in need of his help.

'She was the most beautiful girl I had ever seen,
Jane,' he said unselfconsciously. 'At first I thought
she was a Cyprian come to the masquerade to—'
Simon broke off, grinning at his sister's rapt expression. 'Anyway, she ain't. I could tell. So then I
thought she might be a maid, tricked out in her mistress' dress for the ball, but...' he wrinkled up his
nose '...she was no servant. I could tell that too.'

Jane stepped to one side to allow a couple to squeeze past them on the pavement.

'Yet she would not give you her name?'

'No, only that she had come alone to the ball. She ran away from me,' Simon finished. 'After I'd saved her from Hewetson she simply walked off. Her domino was torn in the struggle and the old Duchess of Merrion spotted her, and thought she recognised the dress underneath. It was extraordinary, Jane! The Duchess was ranting and raving, swearing that the girl had stolen the dress because Celestine had promised her that there had been only one, then the girl just turned on her heel and left, and everyone was speculating about her identity... Can't think how you missed it!' He frowned. 'Where were you, anyway?'

Jane, realising that she had been closeted in the study with the Duke of Delahaye whilst this drama had been unfolding, chose to ignore this question. It would involve too many difficult explanations and also involve an examination of her own feelings. She shrugged, trying to look vague.

'Goodness knows... But what size was she, Simon?'

Simon looked confused. 'Size? Who? The Duchess of Merrion?'

'No, of course not! Your wits have gone a-begging along with your heart!' Jane said severely. 'I refer to your young lady! If she was small and slender then a dress made for the Duchess might well have fitted her. The Duchess of Merrion is a short woman, after all! But if she was taller then it is unlikely that it was the same dress, in which case the Duchess might well have made a mistake!'

Simon looked totally baffled. 'Don't know what the

deuce you're talking about, Jane! All I know is that I must find her again! Last night—'

'Yes!' Jane said wrathfully, remembering that she had not yet had the chance to take him to task for deserting her at Vauxhall. 'What did you mean by leaving me all alone like that? Why, anything might have happened!'

Simon looked self-conscious. 'Yes, I do apologise, Janey! I thought I saw her again, you see, so I had no thought but to rush after her! Anyway, it was no good, for she had disappeared. But you must see that I have to find her!'

'Why?' Jane asked bluntly. 'Have you truly thought about this, Simon? You say she was no servant, but how do you know? She might be a governess or a confectioner's assistant or—'

Simon blushed bright red. 'Never put you down as a snob, Jane!'

'Oh, don't be so foolish! That was not what I meant!' Jane frowned at him. 'Think about this, Simon—what would such a girl believe, if a peer of the realm came to find her and tell her that he wished to pursue an acquaintance with her?'

'Why, that—' Simon stopped dead.

'Exactly,' his sister said drily.

'Then I should persuade her of my good intentions—'

'Intentions? Then you wish to marry her?'

Simon thrust a hand through his fair hair. 'Devil take it, Jane, I don't know! All I know is that I need to find her! I—' He broke off, realising that he was about to say that he loved her. It seemed so extraordinary. He had seen the girl twice, for such a brief time. He did not even know her name, and yet...

'I suppose you think me run quite mad,' he finished glumly.

Jane looked a little rueful. Privately she thought that her own feelings for Alex made her ill-equipped to judge anyone else. 'Not really, Simon. I can only respect your feelings. So I shall go and ask Celestine if she can help us. Wait here for me!'

Presently Jane, Sophia and Lady Verey all came out of the modiste's talking nineteen to the dozen. As they strolled slowly up the pavement in the sunshine, Jane caught her brother's eye and fell back a little. She took his arm as Lady Verey and Sophia walked on ahead.

'Well?' Simon could scarcely contain himself.

'I spoke to Celestine,' Jane said softly. 'There is a girl—her name is Thérèse.' She felt his arm jerk under her hand, as though she had shocked him. 'Try to look as though we are talking of something inconsequential,' she added humorously, 'unless you wish to acquaint Mama of your plans at this early stage! I hope we are speaking of the same person,' she added. 'Slender and very fair?'

Simon nodded speechlessly.

'Celestine says that she did piece work for her. Bits and pieces of sewing,' Jane added, seeing that her brother was looking puzzled. 'It is cheaper for the modiste to employ people only when she needs them. She says that Thérèse was a very good seamstress but that she had to dismiss her because of a complaint from the Duchess of Merrion. Apparently Thérèse borrowed the Duchess's gown for a masquerade and the Duchess threatened to take all her custom elsewhere...'

They walked on a little in silence.

'Thérèse…' Simon said slowly, '…is she French?'

'Yes, an *émigrée*, Celestine said. She knows little more about her,' Jane warned. 'She said that Thérèse kept very much to herself and told no one of her circumstances.'

'But did she have an address for her? Surely she must…'

Jane gave him an old-fashioned look. 'You think that she would be anxious to part with such information? She was already deeply suspicious of me and your peering into cupboards and around doors hardly helped! For all that I told her that Thérèse had been recommended to me and I wished her to do some work for me, I believe she thought me a procuress!'

'Jane!'

Jane delved into her reticule. 'This is the address she gave me. Do not be surprised if she has already sent to warn her—'

Simon grabbed the paper and held it triumphantly high. 'Thank you, Jane!' He kissed her cheek and dashed off down the street.

Lady Verey and Sophia turned to look at Jane in astonishment.

'Simon has forgotten the hat he wanted,' Jane said foolishly, grasping at the first excuse that came into her head. 'He has the details written on the piece of paper. He will join us later for luncheon.' And he may bring you your new daughter-in-law, she added silently, looking at her mother's unsuspecting face and wondering a little apprehensively what on earth would happen if he did.

Chapter Seven

In the event, Simon did not reappear for the whole day. Jane was left torn by speculation and worry. She would have warned her brother to be prepared for disappointment, but she knew that he would not have heeded her words. Simon had been alight with excitement and anticipation, and nothing she could say would have touched him. Of more serious concern to Jane was Simon's assertion that he had seen Thérèse at Vauxhall the previous night. If she had been the girl with Alex's assailant, Simon could be getting himself into more trouble than he bargained for. Jane's mind fretted away at the problem and she was so quiet that Lady Verey asked if she was feeling unwell.

In the afternoon Jane accompanied her mother on a series of visits to friends and on their return prepared for the musical soirée they were all promised for in the evening. As her maid helped her into the new white and gold dress, Jane caught herself wondering whether Alex would be at the soirée. What did it matter if he was—no doubt Lady Dennery would be hanging on his arm! Whilst Cassie brushed her hair the regulation hundred strokes, Jane viewed her despondent face in the mirror. Every so often she would forget that the Duke of Delahaye intended her to be his brother's wife, and when she remembered, the depression of spirits was greater than she had ever experienced before.

Simon was waiting with Lady Verey and Sophia when Jane joined them in the hall. He looked flushed and not particularly happy. Jane's heart sank further. That must mean that his trip had not met with success and worse, he appeared to have been drowning his sorrows as a result. The smell of alcohol hung about him and Lady Verey pointedly opened the carriage window and gave her a son a look of deep disapproval.

As they all entered Mrs Wingate's drawing-room, Jane caught her brother's arm. He almost over-balanced.

'Simon! What happened to you this afternoon?' Jane demanded. 'Are you foxed?'

'Devil a bit,' her brother muttered. He slipped into the seat next to hers. 'One or two li'l drinks at White's…met Harry Marchnight—'

Jane's lips tightened. 'I would have hoped Harry would keep you out of trouble!' she whispered crossly, trying to hold a clandestine conversation and make it look as though she was not doing so. 'What happened? Did you not find Thérèse?'

'I went to the address,' Simon muttered. 'It was dreadful, Jane—such a poor and dirty street, and—' He broke off. 'This is hardly the time… At any rate, she was not there. An old crone opened the door and denied that she knew anyone called Thérèse, but I did not believe her.' He drove his hands into his pockets and scowled. 'I know she lives there!'

'How do you know?' Jane asked, wondering whether her brother was just blindly refusing to admit defeat.

'Because as I was about to go, someone from within called out in French and the crone shut the door in my face,' Simon said with dogged logic. 'So you see it must be an *émigré* household.' He stumbled a little over the word *émigré*. 'I will go back—again and again if I must, until she agrees to see me! It's just so damned—dashed—frustrating, Jane!'

'Which was where the drink came in, I suppose! Do try to sober up!' Jane said, still cross, waving away a servant who was trying to press some wine on them. 'Really, Simon! I thought that you had more self-control! Reeking of drink is hardly the way to a young lady's heart!'

Simon looked crushed. 'I know! I just felt so miserable…'

Jane glanced round, but no one appeared to be attending to them. The musicians were tuning up in a corner and the Duke of Delahaye was just ushering the striking Lady Dennery into a seat in the front row of the audience. Jane thought sourly that her ladyship was set upon making a show. Her blonde hair was dressed high with diamonds and her plunging blue gown left little to the imagination. She was trailed by a crowd of admirers and gossiping cronies, all intent on drawing as much attention to themselves as possible. Jane shrank in her seat and reflected bitterly that she need hardly have wasted her time thinking about Alex. He evidently had more on his mind than an ingenuous schoolroom miss!

Mrs Wingate came forward to announce the start of the recital and the chatterers were obliged to hush. The music was very good and once or twice the pathos of the arias brought a lump to Jane's throat and made the tears tickle behind her eyes. In contrast, Simon disgraced himself by falling asleep and had to be nudged by Jane when he snored in the quiet parts.

'The Duke and Lady Dennery look very intimate, do they not,' Sophia murmured in Jane's ear as the interval was announced and the gossip and chit chat broke out again. 'But, oh, Jane, did you ever see anything like that dress! I am sure she has damped it, and for a small musical soirée!'

'Very bad *ton*!' Lady Verey said, overhearing. 'I am glad Lady Eleanor is not here tonight! I cannot believe that she would wish for such a connection for the Delahayes!'

Lord Philip was also missing that evening and Sophia was noticeably less cheerful as a result. Jane, with her downcast friend on one side and her morose brother on the other, began to feel trapped under her own small rain cloud. Worse, Lady Dennery was directly in view and, having despatched the Duke to fetch her some syllabub from the refreshment room, was engrossed in flirtation with another gentleman.

Jane got up, excused herself to the others, and made a beeline for the food. The thought that it was her only solace restored her spirits a little. It was better than resorting to drink, as Simon had done!

'Good evening, Miss Verey. Are you enjoying the music?'

Jane had been hesitating between the ice cream and the fruit pudding when the Duke of Delahaye paused by her side. His query seemed no more than mere politeness—indeed, she could see his gaze straying over her head to where Lady Dennery sparkled as brightly as her diamonds. Jane castigated herself for spending even a moment thinking about him when it was clear that the Duke had barely given her one moment's attention.

'Good evening, your Grace,' she said coldly. 'The music is very pretty, is it not? Or perhaps you have not noticed?'

Alex's gaze came back from Lady Dennery and focussed on Jane's face with sudden intentness. He gave her a glimmer of a smile that set her heartbeat awry despite her intention to resist his charm.

'Oh, I have noticed several things, Miss Verey! More, perhaps, than you might think! I have observed that your brother is not himself tonight, that Miss Marchment appears to have lost some of her sparkle and that you are cross about something—would you care to enlighten me?'

'No, thank you!' Jane said smartly, secretly taken aback at his perspicacity. She allowed her own gaze to drift back to Lady Dennery, who was laughing as she allowed one of her admirers to feed her with grapes. 'Would that we were as perceptive of our own circumstances as you are of other people's, your Grace!'

'Ah, true!' Alex smiled whimsically, not one whit put out. 'It is always so difficult to see the beam in one's own eye, is it not, Miss Verey! Now, lest I forget, I believe that Lady Eleanor will be calling on you tomorrow to deliver an invitation to my home at Malladon. We had a sudden urge to escape the pleasures of Town and seek some country quiet!'

Jane eyed him suspiciously. This sudden invitation

seemed most questionable. She had a horrid misgiving that the net was closing in around her; that Alex had tired of her resistance to the match with Philip and was now planning to put an end to her games. He had allowed her some latitude, had even played along to a certain extent, but now he had lost patience. She looked at him through her lashes. He was smiling blandly, but there was a hint of challenge in his gaze that only confirmed her doubts. Clearly there was some plan that hinged on Malladon.

'I am not certain that Mama would wish to leave Town whilst the Season is in progress,' she said cautiously, testing the water. Despite her words, she knew that it was very unlikely that Lady Verey would refuse. She would be too flattered, too grateful for such a sign of Lady Eleanor's regard.

Alex's smile grew. 'Oh, I am persuaded that she will accept the invitation!' he said easily. 'And it will only be for a short while! The benefits outweigh the drawbacks, you know, for I am sure your mama's main purpose in bringing you to Town is to see you suitably settled by the end of the Season! In that she and I are as one!'

Jane's feeling of entrapment pressed closer about her. He had summed up Lady Verey's reactions so accurately! Jane knew that her mama had never made any secret that she wished to revive the Delahaye match and such a sign of encouragement and approval from the Duke and Lady Eleanor could not be rejected. The three of them were united in the attempt to wear down Jane and Lord Philip until they capitulated.

'I am sorry that you are not more enthusiastic, Miss Verey,' the Duke said mockingly. His gaze had not left her face once and now Jane felt so frustrated she was sure that it must show. Vexed, she bit her lip.

'Checkmate, Miss Verey?' Alex added softly. 'You know that you must concede soon! We are all ranged against you!'

Jane's stormy hazel eyes locked with his.

'Check, perhaps, but not checkmate, sir! Beware that your complacency does not catch you out!'

Alex laughed. 'How stimulating it is to cross swords with you, Miss Verey! I never knew an opponent who could look defeat in the face and yet persist in opposing me!'

He bowed and sauntered back to Lady Dennery, insinuating himself at her side and displacing several of his rivals with what seemed the greatest of ease. It made Jane feel even more annoyed. He obviously did not care that he had to share Lady Dennery's affections with so many others! It was all a little too sophisticated for Jane to either understand or appreciate.

The music was starting again. She slipped back into her seat beside Sophia and observed the droop of her friend's mouth as she contemplated the rest of the evening without Lord Philip. With a further spasm of despair Jane realised that the success of the Duke's plan would mean the death of all Sophia's hopes. She set her chin. She needed some allies now and she was already starting to plan her next strategy.

Jane had intended to plan her next move once she was in bed that night, but in the event she fell asleep almost as soon as her head touched the pillow. She awoke again, suddenly, and for no apparent reason, and lay in the dark, wondering what it was that had disturbed her.

Then there was the sound of gravel spattering against the window and a whisper, 'Jane? Jane, are you there?'

Jane slipped from the bed and leaned out, the curtains billowing behind her.

'Who's there? Harry? What on earth—'

Lord Henry Marchnight was in the street below, supporting another figure whom Jane recognised with deep foreboding as Simon.

'Harry? Is Simon hurt?'

'Of course not,' Henry said tersely. 'Come down and open the door, there's a good girl! I don't want to wake the whole house!'

Obscurely reassured, Jane dragged on a robe and sped downstairs. A single light burned in the hall, and from behind the door leading down to the servants' hall she could hear the low murmur of voices. She slid the bolts back softly.

'Thank God!'

Henry was already outside the door and strode in to deposit his burden in the hall with scant concern for Simon's welfare. Jane recoiled from the smell of drink as her brother lurched towards the stairs, missing the handrail and slumping on to the bottom step. She had thought that Simon had recovered his sobriety during the soirée that evening, but evidently he had made up for it immediately afterwards with a trip to his club.

'Good heavens! He's three parts disguised!'

'Just be grateful you didn't have to bring him all the way home as we did,' Henry said bitterly.

The door closed and Jane spun around with a gasp. She had thought Henry was alone, but the tall figure emerging from the shadows was as familiar as it was unexpected.

'Can you get him upstairs on your own?' the Duke of Delahaye was asking Henry. He cast Jane one single dark glance. 'I need to have a word with Miss Verey.'

'I can call Simon's valet to help—' Jane said. She had already stretched out a hand towards the servants' door when Alex's fingers closed around her wrist.

'No,' he said, and there was such a note of authority in his voice that Jane fell silent. For the first time, her gaze moved from Henry to Alex, noting their extraordinary appearance. Gone were the gentlemen of *ton* Society, and in their place were two rather disreputable characters in shabby black and white. Henry, with his tumbled fair hair and billowing white shirt, looked rather like a poet fallen on hard times, whilst Alex's sinister black cloak made him look like the archetypal highwayman. Jane had to press a hand to her mouth to stop herself laughing. Above it her eyes were bright.

'Oh, dear! You look—'

'Thank you,' Alex said drily. 'Your face says it all, Miss Verey! Henry, please—before we wake the whole house—'

But it was already too late. The door from below stairs opened and Cassie stepped into the hall, holding her candle high. She gave a muted squeak.

'Lord save us! Miss Jane! And the young master! Foxed again! George,' she shouted back down the stairs, 'come and help the young master to bed! He's as tight as an owl!'

Jane realised that Alex was still holding her wrist. In the ensuing confusion he pulled her round to face him. Suddenly she saw that for all their comical appearance their business was deadly serious. Alex was looking both grim and determined.

'Miss Verey—may we speak in private?'

Jane's eyes widened. 'Now? We cannot!'

A hint of a smile lightened the grimness of Alex's expression. 'I fear we must! I assure you, you are quite safe with me! I simply need to ask you a few questions!'

Jane's startled gaze searched his face. 'Surely it can wait until the morning—'

'I am afraid not,' Alex said, very definitely.

'Best do as he asks, Janey,' Harry Marchnight said soberly. He was helping the servants to manoeuvre Simon up the staircase and suddenly Jane and Alex were alone in the shadowed hall. Alex dropped her wrist and stood back to allow her to precede him into the drawing room, picking up the candelabra as he followed her in. The door shut with an unnerving click.

'Your Grace, this is very improper...' Jane said faintly, curling up in an armchair and drawing her robe more closely about her.

'I know.' Alex smiled with sudden and devastating charm. 'Needs must, Miss Verey! I shall not keep you long and this is very important.' He took the chair opposite and sat forward, fixing her with a stern look that almost made her shiver. 'Is Simon in some kind of trouble?'

Jane met his eyes very directly. 'I am not aware of it, your Grace. What kind of trouble?'

Alex shifted a little. 'We found Simon far from his usual haunts, in circumstances that suggested foul play. He was slumped in the gutter, in severe danger of having his pockets picked—or worse! He is not in the habit of getting blind drunk and hanging around street corners in Spitalfields, so—' He broke off, his eyes narrowing on Jane's face. 'Do you know anything about this, Miss Verey?'

Jane knew that her expression had given her away. She had assumed that Simon had over-indulged at his club, but as soon as Alex mentioned Spitalfields, she realised that Simon must have returned to look for Thérèse, just as he had sworn he would. As she hesitated, Alex said drily:

'I see that you do know, Miss Verey! You have the most expressive face! So what is this all about?'

Jane resented his high-handed tone. 'What business is it of yours, your Grace? Forgive me, but you and Harry Marchnight are the ones who have been creeping around London like Mohawks!'

Alex gave her a reluctant smile. *'Touché,* Miss Verey! I can see that our behaviour must look suspicious! However, have you considered that your own actions are also most questionable?'

'Mine!' Jane looked incredulous. 'I have no notion what you mean—'

'No?' Alex was not smiling any longer. His face looked as cold and carved as stone. 'Consider the circumstances. I find you skulking in the dark walks alone last night at Vauxhall. You tell me a very thin tale to explain the situation. When you are reunited with your brother, you give him a sign to say nothing. I had already seen him in very dubious company last night and tonight he is found dead drunk in a low neighbourhood. And I believe that you know what is going on.' He brought his clenched fist down with heavy emphasis. 'This seems most suspicious to me, Miss Verey!'

Jane's head was spinning. 'I assure you, there was nothing remotely suspect about my behaviour last night! I only gestured to Simon to keep quiet because—' She broke off, suddenly aware that any explanation would incriminate Sophia and Philip in some way. Alex was waiting patiently, his dark gaze riveted on her face.

'You appear to be in some difficulty, Miss Verey,' he said after a moment. 'The natural consequences of chicanery, I fear! And can you be surprised at my distrust? You have, after all, proved yourself adept at deception!'

Jane gasped. 'How dare you, sir! I have done no such thing!'

'No?' Alex said again. 'What about the exchange of partners at Lady Winterstoke's dinner, the change of dominoes at the masquerade... I do not believe that you are to be trusted, Miss Verey!'

Jane found that she was on her feet with no real idea of how she got there. She reached for the door handle, but Alex was before her, resting one hand against the panels and blocking her path.

'Oh, no, you don't,' he said pleasantly. 'Not until you have told me what I need to know!'

'This is outrageous!' Jane realised that her voice was shaking. 'You cannot behave in this high-handed manner, sir! How dare you accuse me of deception when all I have done is oppose your plan to marry me off to your brother!'

'Perhaps we may discuss that on another occasion, Miss Verey,' Alex said smoothly. 'Just now it is very important that I know what it going on. The company your brother is keeping is dangerous—'

'I know that!' Jane glared at him. 'I told you that that man was trying to kill you!' She stopped suddenly, seeing the flash in his eyes and realising that she had been provoked into saying rather more than she had intended. She bit her lip.

'And just how much do you know about that, Miss Verey?' Alex said, very softly.

Suddenly Jane was frightened. There had always been something exciting about crossing swords with Alexander Delahaye, but now she realised that she was completely out of her depth. This was real, and dangerous and threatening. She thought of the way in which he had casually referred to her deceit, the fact that he did not trust her, and the tears stung her eyes.

Alex stood back with an ironic bow, gesturing to her to sit down again. Jane sat without a word, curling up as tight as she could for both warmth and comfort.

'Shall we start again, Miss Verey?' Alex said.

There was a little silence. The candle flame flickered. Jane capitulated.

'Very well! There is no mystery! It is misfortunes in love rather than anything else that trouble Simon.'

'Indeed. What matter of the heart could take him to Spitalfields?'

Jane's eyes flashed at his disbelieving tone. 'Something far less dubious than your own activities, I am sure, your Grace! Simon is looking for a young lady by the name of Thérèse, who apparently lives there. He wishes to marry her.'

There was a sharp silence. 'Does he, by God!' For the first time, Alex seemed startled. 'Mademoiselle Thérèse de Beaurain?'

'Mademoiselle—' Jane broke off. 'Is that her other name? You know her?'

'I know of her,' Alex admitted. 'She is the daughter of the late Vicomte de Beaurain, who lost his head in the Revolution. Her mother fled to England with her daughter when the child was very young. I imagine that she must be about twenty years of age now. Her mother is an invalid and Mademoiselle de Beaurain supports both of them on a pittance from sewing. How did Simon meet her?'

'She was at the masquerade ball,' Jane said, in a small voice. Suddenly Simon's Thérèse had become a real person and had taken on her own character. Jane looked at Alex, troubled.

'Simon saw her again at Vauxhall last night, and rushed off to try to speak to her. She was with the man in the striped waistcoat, the one who—' She broke off. 'Oh, I do hope that Simon knows what he is doing... I would not like to think that Miss de Beaurain is involved in something criminal...'

'Do not worry,' Alex spoke quietly. 'As far as I know, Mademoiselle de Beaurain is quite innocent. She has nothing to reproach herself for except a stubborn pride which I understand has led to a rupture with the English branch of the family!'

'Oh, how unfortunate!' Jane's sympathies were already thoroughly engaged with the young *émigrée* girl who had to struggle so hard to care for herself and her parent. 'You mean that she has relatives who might help them?'

'Yes, indeed, very respectable ones! Her mother is a distant cousin of General Sir John Huntington, who heard of their plight several years ago and summoned Thérèse de Beaurain to offer them a home.' Alex smiled. 'I only know of this because I heard him telling all and sundry of his kind condescension in offering a home to destitute relatives! Truth to tell, he was so patronising that I can only imagine he offended the girl mortally. Anyway, the whole *ton* was later regaled with the story of how he had had his generosity spurned and that the family could rot in hell for all he cared! Not a pretty tale!'

Jane shivered. 'So they have been left to make shift as best they can? How cruel!'

'It seems very harsh, certainly. But if Simon can rescue her from all that—' Alex shrugged. 'But we are becoming distracted from the main point. I am relieved to know that there is so innocuous an explanation for tonight's escapade, although I suppose finding Simon drunk outside his beloved's house is a sign that his suit is not prospering!'

'No,' Jane said cautiously, 'I believe that it is not!' She took her courage in both hands. 'But Simon's misfortunes are not the main concern, are they, your Grace? It was only coincidence that brought him into contact with the man in the striped waistcoat—oh, I wish I knew his name, for to refer to him as such sounds so foolish! But he is clearly the one who is dangerous!'

'His name is Samways,' Alex said, stirring the fire to a fresh blaze, 'and he is, as you have surmised, Miss Verey, a dangerous man. I do not know what led you to disbelieve my excuse that he was merely a common pickpocket. I thought I was a better liar than that!'

Jane smiled faintly. 'I am not really sure why I did not believe you, but—it was his demeanour, I suppose, and the fact that he did not look as though he intended to rob, but to kill.' She shivered convulsively, despite the warmth of the fire. Looking up, she found that Alex was watching her with a thoughtful regard.

'I suppose that you cannot tell me what this is all about,' she finished, a little forlornly.

'You suppose correctly, Miss Verey.' Alex gave her a slight smile. 'It really is safer that you do not know! Take comfort from the fact that Simon's Thérèse is innocent and that her association with Samways is not a close one!' He sighed. 'It seems unfortunate that Simon should choose this of all times to visit Spitalfields! It is not a healthy place to be!'

Jane had other fears. 'Upon my word,' she burst out, 'you do not seem very concerned that someone wishes to murder you! One might almost believe that you encounter such situations every day!'

Alex grinned. He got to his feet and stretched. Jane hastily averted her gaze.

'You would be surprised, Miss Verey!' he said easily. 'Thank you for your help tonight. I regret that I cannot enlighten you on the reason for my interest and once again I must beg you to keep quiet about this. One day, perhaps, I will tell you why...'

His gaze travelled over her, lingering on the soft hair tumbling about her shoulders and the slender curves of her body beneath the thin robe. Jane, who had been about to uncurl from the chair and stand up, kept very still. Suddenly there was an expression on Alex's face that she did not understand, but it turned her throat dry and started her heart racing.

'I must also thank you for your concern,' Alex said slowly. His voice had dropped several tones. 'I do believe that you are genuinely upset at the thought of someone sticking a knife in me!'

'Of course it concerns me!' Jane's voice had risen, anxiety overriding her natural reticence. 'A strange creature I should be if I took pleasure in thinking you stabbed to death by some dangerous criminal!'

Alex put out a hand and pulled her to her feet. His touch lit something inside of Jane, something that made her tremble. They were standing very close and she could not tear her gaze away from his.

'Even though we are in opposition?' Alex queried softly. 'You would still wish me no harm?'

Jane cleared her throat. For some reason she was finding it very difficult to breathe. 'I have never had any wish to be in opposition to you, your Grace.'

Alex's voice was caressing. 'I do believe that we could be in the most perfect accord, Miss Verey.'

His mouth was only inches away from her own and he was still holding her lightly, but with a touch that burned her blood with sensuous awareness. Yet only ten minutes before he had spoken of her in terms of the deepest scorn, called her deceitful and untrustworthy, and Jane was not about to forget that.

She stepped back.

'I collect that you mean we are both accomplished in dissimulation,' she said coolly, covering the turbulence of her emotions with a strategic withdrawal. 'I think that you should leave now, sir.'

Jane opened the door and pointedly stood holding it for Alex to leave. He did not move. She felt his gaze, as powerful as a physical touch, searching her face.

'Well,' he said ruefully after a moment, 'I suppose

that I deserved that! I can only apologise for my remarks. I said it mainly to provoke you—'

'Oh! That makes it much more acceptable then, sir!'

Alex laughed, conceding the point. 'We'll talk about this again! Good night, Miss Verey.'

The clock struck two. Jane took the candelabra in one hand almost as though it was a shield. By its flickering light she could see that Henry Marchnight was loitering in the hall, but otherwise the house was dark and silent. Conscious of Henry's thoughtful look resting on her still-pink face, Jane avoided his eyes and made a business of shepherding them towards the door. The night was fine and the moon hung low in the sky. Jane shivered a little.

'Go back inside,' Alex said, abruptly. 'Harry and I will make all secure.'

Henry bent forward and kissed her cheek and after a moment Alex followed suit, taking her hand and drawing her to him as his lips brushed her skin in the lightest of caresses. Jane, scurrying back to the sanctuary of her room with one hand unconsciously pressed to her cheek, reflected wryly that she would be the most envied girl in London if anyone found out. To have been kissed by both Harry Marchnight and the Duke of Delahaye! It was enough to make one swoon, and all in one evening, too! As she slipped between the chilled sheets, Jane paused long enough before sleep to wonder why one salutation had left her totally unmoved whilst the other felt as though it had been branded on her skin with fire.

Chapter Eight

It was Henry Marchnight, not Alex Delahaye, who called first in Portman Square on the following morning. Simon had not yet risen from his bed but the ladies were assembled in the parlour, Sophia and Lady Verey sewing placidly and Jane watching the clock and wondering at what hour any visitors would call. She jumped when the bell rang and her disappointment on seeing Henry rather than Alex was acute. Henry, a twinkle in his eye, came across to sit by her.

'Your servant, Miss Verey. I hope that you are recovered from last night!'

'Oh. Lord Henry, I daresay that I should not mention it, but I must thank you for your help in bringing Simon home,' Lady Verey said eagerly. 'A most unfortunate occurrence, but gentlemen must be allowed, I suppose...'

Henry stretched out his long legs and gave her the smile that always worked on Dowagers. 'A small transgression and very rarely committed, Lady Verey...'

Lady Verey fluttered. 'Of course! And he would come to no harm at his club—'

'At his club!' Henry's gaze touched Jane's innocent face briefly. 'Of course!'

'So good of you and Alexander Delahaye,' Lady Verey burbled. 'Such good friends!'

'Yes, ma'am, but I beg you not to mention it to Delahaye—he is rather a reticent fellow!'

Henry smiled at Jane again. 'I see you have been singing our praises, Miss Verey!'

Jane cast her eyes down modestly. 'There was some speculation about last night's activities, sir… I simply did my best to quash it. How fortunate that I heard the hack draw up and came down to see what was happening!'

'Fortunate, indeed!' Henry murmured. Under the cover of the refreshments being served he added, 'I see you have no need of me to concoct a story, Miss Verey!'

The door opened again and Alex Delahaye came in. Jane saw the infinitesimal nod that Henry gave him before Alex came across with easy grace to bow over Lady Verey's hand and inquire of her health.

'I am here to bring your formal invitation to Malladon,' he said, with a smile. 'Lady Eleanor had hoped to call herself, but she is slightly incommoded with a cold in the head. Oh, not enough to spoil your visit,' he added, seeing Lady Verey's look of concern. 'I am sure she will be better directly! But as we were planning to travel on the morrow I did not wish to delay any longer. You will, I hope, be able to accept?'

Jane saw that Lady Verey was fluttering and recognised it for a bad sign. Her mother was flustered, which meant that she was inordinately flattered by the invitation and would not dream of refusing.

'Oh, your Grace...such condescension, we should be delighted...tomorrow, you say? Well, I dare say it can be arranged...'

Alex's eyes met Jane's and she saw the wicked twinkle in them that said that her plans had been foiled. 'I am so glad,' he murmured.

Jane had, in fact, almost forgotten the invitation to Malladon in the mystery that had happened the previous night. She had been too tired to consider it when she had got back to bed, but that morning she had lain awake for quite some time puzzling over the nature of the business that could have taken Henry and Alex to Spitalfields. Clearly they had been involved in something that they preferred to keep secret, but the thought that they might be entangled in criminal activities seemed ludicrous. It was far more likely, Jane thought as she sipped her tea, that they were working to foil some illegal enterprise. She had known for years in a vague sort of way that Henry Marchnight worked for the government, which led logically to the idea that Alex might too...

'Will it still be convenient for your Grace to spare the time to host us at Malladon?' she asked limpidly, her eyes innocent.

'Oh, certainly, Miss Verey,' Alex responded, the laughter lines deepening about his eyes. 'I should not miss it for the world! Do not forget that Philip will also be there to squire you about!'

This was another unwelcome reminder for Jane and she saw that Sophia, who had been very quiet that morning, looked flushed and unhappy. All in all, it was not going to be a comfortable trip.

* * *

Malladon was only half a day's drive from London, set in the lush Hertfordshire countryside. It was the least favoured of the Duke of Delahaye's estates, for he considered it too close to the capital and the countryside too bland for his tastes.

'Philip tells me that his brother prefers Hayenham to all his other establishments,' Sophia had reported shyly to Jane as they packed their bags for the unexpected trip to the country. 'It is a medieval castle on a wild northern cliff, Philip says, and the Duke locks himself up in there for months at a time! Only fancy!' Sophia shivered with enjoyable fear. 'It sounds quite Gothic! What a very odd man he is!'

Jane, looking out of the carriage window as the verdant scenery sped past, reflected that it seemed very much in keeping with Alexander Delahaye's character that he should prefer the untamed reaches of the North to more gentle climes. There was something about him that suggested, for all his eminent title and position, that he scorned the conventions of polite society. The elements of danger and restlessness were well hidden behind the veneer of authority and sophistication, but they were there nevertheless. Like Sophia, Jane shivered a little. She knew that she had pitted her wits against an opponent worthy of the name and that this unexpected invitation, seized on with such excitement by Lady Verey, had been the Duke's way of raising the stakes in their game.

Lady Verey had fallen asleep, lulled by the movement of the coach. Ahead of them, Lord Philip was driving Lady Eleanor with exemplary skill and care, whilst the Duke's own phaeton headed the expedition, the fair Lady Dennery at his side. No one had had the indelicacy to refer to Lady Dennery's presence in the party, but it had been an unwelcome one for all that. Lady Eleanor had set her lips tight in clear disapproval when the Duke had bowled up with his companion, and Lady Verey had worn the anxious look of a chaperon who knows that her innocent chicks are in danger. Jane's own predominant feeling was one of jealousy, which she both despised and despaired of. It seemed that Alexander Delahaye was bringing out the worst in her in more ways than one.

It was an oddly assorted party, Jane reflected. Simon had declined to join them, preferring to stay in Town and, she suspected, pursue his quest for Thérèse. Lady Eleanor had bemoaned the lack of a young man for Sophia, making Jane horribly aware that the intention was to throw herself and Philip together as much as possible. She had noticed that both Lady Eleanor and Lady Verey had started to bracket their names together as though it were the most natural thing imaginable. Sophia had also noticed and was looking ever more strained and upset, although she had not reproached her friend for the circumstance. Oh, dear, Jane thought, as they rumbled through a picturesque village and turned into a long driveway, this is not going to be at all pleasant!

The others had just arrived as their carriage drew up on the gravel sweep, and Lady Dennery was intent on giving instruction to the harassed servants over the care of her luggage.

'You, there! Take this portmanteau! No, not like that, like this, you dolt!'

Lord Philip was standing watching with a look akin to horror on his face and Jane, who still remembered his own churlish behaviour at Ambergate, was surprised to feel a certain sympathy. Unquestionably Lord Philip did not welcome this potential sister-in-law!

Matters did not improve at dinner. There were only seven of them around the imposing polished table and Jane had been firmly placed next to Lord Philip whilst Sophia was acres away, next to the Duke. So cowed was she by his magnificent presence that she barely said two words and Jane noticed how Lady Dennery, on the Duke's other side, took no more notice of Sophia than to bend a patronising smile on her every so often. Lady Dennery was saving all her attention for Alex, touching his sleeve with intimate little gestures, smiling into his eyes and hanging on his every word. It made Jane feel so sick that she was barely able to do justice to the excellent dinner. At her side, Lord Philip chewed moodily, spoke little and gazed fixedly at Sophia.

Jane was up betimes the following morning. She had excused herself to bed immediately after dinner in order to avoid Lord Philip's unwilling company and by the morning she was feeling very restless. It was a beautiful day. Throwing back the shutters, Jane could see the green parkland shimmering in the early sun and the glitter of a lake in the distance. She resolved on an early morning stroll.

The house seemed silent as she slipped outside. It was a very pretty building, small but elegant, red-brick and foursquare. Jane stood on the drive to admire it, before taking a well-mown grassy track that cut across the park towards the lake.

It seemed that she was not the only one up and about early that morning. As she emerged from the shadow of the trees on to the gravel path that circled the water, Jane saw a figure standing in the shade of the summer pavilion. Another moment helped her to identify it as Lord Philip Delahaye. This was surprising. It was very early and Lord Philip was renowned as a late riser, never up before midday. As Jane hesitated, he turned his head and saw her. For a second she saw the expression of unhappiness on his face, clear in the bright sunlight, before he schooled his features to indifference.

'Good morning, Miss Verey.'

It seemed he was about to pass her without another word, but Jane put out a hand.

'A moment, if you please, sir!'

Lord Philip paused. 'Madam?'

'I need to speak to you, sir,' Jane said clearly, determined not to lose her nerve. 'It is a matter of extreme importance!' She saw that he was about to refuse and added, 'Please!'

Lord Philip gestured to her to fall into step with him on the gravel path, but his expression was not encouraging, nor were his words. 'Well, Miss Verey?'

'It concerns our projected marriage, my lord,' Jane said, fixing her gaze firmly on the plane trees in the far distance. 'I do not wish to marry you and I have observed that you do not wish to marry me, so I propose that we join forces to avert a horrid fate!'

There was a startled silence.

'Are you always so outspoken, Miss Verey?' Lord Philip said, tight-lipped. He cast her a quick sideways glance, which she met with a blithe smile.

'Always! I find it is much better to be honest, or one might find oneself married to the wrong person! I have been quick to notice that you have a certain

admiration for Miss Marchment, a regard which
might lead you to wish *me* in Hades!'

Lord Philip swallowed convulsively. They had
reached the summerhouse and he paused, turning to
look at Jane properly for the first time.

'Has Miss Marchment…? That is…did she say that
she—' He broke off, looking suddenly boyish and
eager. 'She is the most delightful creature, Miss
Verey! A veritable angel! When she smiled on me
that night at Almack's I believe I counted myself the
most fortunate man in the room!' A shadow fell
across his face as he realised the absurdity of addressing such sentiments to his intended bride. 'I beg your
pardon,' he muttered. 'You are most fortunate in your
friends, Miss Verey!'

'Pray do not apologise!' Jane said sweetly. 'I am
very fond of Sophia! She is the dearest girl imaginable and I wish to see her happy. Which is why I
wanted to talk to you, sir! Let us sit down together
and put all to rights!'

They sat on the seat in the shade of the summerhouse veranda. 'Let us be straight with one another,
sir,' Jane said practically. 'Neither of us wish to be
joined in matrimony with the other, but we need not
repine. If we work together we may be able to thwart
your brother's plans for us!'

Lord Philip's face had brightened, only to fall
again. 'I appreciate your plain-speaking, Miss Verey,
but if I may be equally blunt, it is a matter of money!
Alex will only pay my debts if I marry you!'

He drove his hands into his jacket pockets. 'It is
not that I am extravagant, precisely, although I do find
that Alex keeps me on a ridiculously tight allowance,
but…' he frowned a little '…the matter cannot be

avoided. For whatever reason, he favours this match and no other. I fear we are doomed!'

It was at that exact moment that Jane looked up to see the Duke of Delahaye, magnificent on a raking chestnut hunter, approaching them down the ride. He sat the horse with negligent skill. He had not seen them yet, but Jane knew that it was only a matter of time.

'If we can persuade your brother that all looks set fair for a match between us, we have the advantage,' Jane pressed. 'Trust me, sir, I will think of a scheme to avoid the marriage *and* to pay your debts! Then you may marry Miss Marchment and we shall all be happy!'

Lord Philip was looking slightly stunned at this *force majeure*. 'Can you contrive such a plan?' he asked weakly.

'Indeed! Look how easily I hoodwinked you!'

Lord Philip tried to look disapproving, but could not prevent a smile. Jane realised that she was warming to him.

'Yes,' he said reluctantly, 'you took me in magnificently, Miss Verey, and by rights I should be out of charity with you for such a shabby trick!' He cleared his throat. 'I have a bad conscience about that night, however. I know I behaved churlishly, but I was so angry with Alex for forcing me into the situation! I did not mean to denigrate your home and hospitality, or—'

He broke off and flushed bright red.

'I heard the maid come up to your room,' Jane said helpfully. 'Let us not speak of it, nor of the unfortunate rumours about me which circulated about Town after your visit…'

Lord Philip looked mortified. 'Miss Verey...' He was positively stammering, 'I did not mean... how did you...?'

'Forgive me, I know I should not have mentioned it.' Jane was trying not to laugh. She was starting to feel a real affection for Lord Philip, who reminded her of nothing so much as an overgrown schoolboy. 'Let us start afresh,' she added, in kindly fashion. 'I can understand that your brother must be a sore trial to you!'

'Oh, Alex is a good enough fellow,' Philip said grudgingly. 'It's just that he can be rather forceful at times! Perhaps you have observed it, Miss Verey!'

Jane could see the Duke approaching now. She smiled blindingly. 'Perhaps his Grace is not accustomed to polite society,' she agreed sweetly. 'His address certainly lacks polish!'

Philip gave a crack of laughter. 'Well, that's the first time I've heard Alex criticised for his skills in the petticoat line, Miss Verey!'

They were still laughing together when the Duke reined in beside them.

Philip turned to his brother with a grin. 'Morning, Alex! Lady Dennery not riding with you?'

'Her ladyship does not care to ride,' Alex said, unsmiling. 'Good morning, Miss Verey. Are you walking unaccompanied?'

'Obviously not, Alex! Miss Verey is walking with me!' Philip said with a grin, throwing himself into the part of Jane's beau with convincing alacrity. 'We are becoming better acquainted! Don't spoil sport, I beg you! Miss Verey and I wish to converse alone!' He saw his brother's lips tighten angrily and added, 'It is all perfectly respectable!'

Jane was aware that Alex Delahaye's penetrating gaze had hardly wavered from her even when he was speaking to his brother. There was something disturbing about such single-minded attention, nor could she understand why he was bestowing it on her. Did he suspect of them of play-acting? She had to admit that it was a rather sudden turnabout, but since this was precisely the outcome the Duke wished for, she could not understand why he was looking so furious!

'Forgive me,' he said through his teeth. 'I had no intention of interrupting a romance! I will see you at breakfast if you can tear yourselves away from the beauties of nature! Good day!'

'Well, we brushed through that rather well,' Lord Philip said, seemingly unaware of his brother's anger as the Duke galloped away. He stood up and held out a hand to help Jane rise, giving her a look of genuine admiration. 'What a capital girl you are, Miss Verey! I had no idea!'

Alex Delahaye was able to work off much of his bad temper on a gallop across the parkland, but as he trotted into the stableyard in more decorous fashion he was aware that a niggling irritation still troubled him. He slid from the horse, patted its heaving flank with appreciation and handed it over to the groom with a word of thanks, before turning towards the house. Lady Eleanor was waiting for him at the top of the wide terrace steps and her eyes were alight with satisfaction and a certain complacent self-congratulation.

'I told you so!' she said in greeting. 'I knew that a week in the country would do the trick! Miss Verey and Philip are out walking together and looking absolutely *épris*! I told you!'

'You did indeed!' Alex said wryly, feeling all his bad temper return with a rush. He could see his brother and Jane Verey wandering slowly up the path from the lake and appearing to be engrossed in each other's company. Jane's hand was tucked through Philip's arm in a way that seemed positively confiding and their laughter was for themselves alone. Alex felt a pang of something that was uncommonly like jealousy…or possibly pain.

He had felt nothing akin to it since the terrible time, years before, when his wife had told him that his unsophisticated ways bored her and she had taken a lover to provide some entertainment. He could still remember the look in her eyes: the hard cruelty, daring him to reproach her, goading him to lose his temper. It had seemed inconceivable to him that matters between them had altered so desperately. They had been entwined in love when they had married, Madeline eighteen, he twenty, but the pursuits and entertainments of Town had undermined that love. Madeline was weak and easily led; soon she became a spendthrift, complaining when Alex had tried to reason with her and finally scorning him publicly as an old-fashioned and tedious husband, old before his time. He might have come to accept that they shared no interests, but her taunts had hurt and the blow of her infidelity had destroyed Alex's still-cherished belief that all might be saved. If only they had never gone up to London, if only he had taken her back to Hayenham before it was too late, if he had been stronger…

Alex followed Lady Eleanor back into the salon,

allowing the door to slam behind him with unwonted ferocity. At least Francine Dennery would not rise for another couple of hours—that was one irritation that he was spared! Lady Dennery's increasingly unsubtle hints about their relationship had aroused nothing but indifference in him and he was already regretting the impulse that had led him to invite her to Malladon. Lady Eleanor had implied that it was tantamount to a declaration and Alex was annoyed to think that she might almost be correct. It was a complication he would rather do without. For a moment his imagination compared the slender but devastatingly desirable curves of Jane Verey with the overblown charms that Lady Dennery was trying to place at his disposal. Jane would be so soft and sweet, innocent but waiting to be awakened. He felt himself suffused with so potent an desire that he had to turn away.

The door opened again to admit Jane and Lord Philip. With curiously sharpened observation, Alex noted the pink colour in Jane's cheeks, whipped up by the breeze, the way that one windswept black curl rested in the hollow of her throat, the brightness of laughter in her eyes. His fists clenched as some nameless emotion clutched him by the throat. It was just that she had disappointed him, he told himself. She was like all the other debutantes after all, a little wilful, perhaps, but ready to see the benefits of a good match in the end. Lady Eleanor had been right when she had predicted that Jane Verey would settle down and accept the betrothal. Alex had just not believed that it would be so easy.

He told himself that his disappointment stemmed from the fact that the game was over before it had really started. He had expected that Jane Verey would

been made of sterner stuff and he felt obscurely discontented to have been proved wrong. He knew that
he was lying to himself. The problem was that he had
already started to consider an alternative plan for Miss
Jane Verey, and now apparently it would not be
needed. He would have to treat her as a sister-in-law
after all. Ironic, when he had promoted the Verey
match so actively, but that had been before he had
realised that he wanted something else—

Lady Dennery's fluting voice suddenly impinged
on his notice.

'God damn it!' Alex said violently under his breath
and, before any of his startled relatives could utter a
word, he had turned on his heel and walked straight
out of the door again. They did not see him again
until dinner.

'You are perfectly sure that you are happy about
this, Sophia?' Jane asked, as they reined in their
horses at the top of the hill and looked down on the
roof of Malladon nestling in the valley below. 'You
do not feel uncomfortable with Lord Philip apparently
paying open court to me? For if you do, you have
only to say the word and we will stop at once!'

Sophia threw back her head and laughed. Her face
was flushed and her blue eyes sparkling. She was in
excellent looks and Jane was surprised that no one
else had spotted the improvement in her friend's spirits, but then she could only be grateful that it was so.
To rouse the suspicions of Lady Eleanor—or worse,
the Duke—would defeat her plan utterly.

They had been three days in Hertfordshire and matters were progressing precisely as Jane had intended.
Lord Philip was playing her devoted suitor to the top

of his bent in company and, whilst ostensibly monop-
olising his attention, Jane had in fact been engineering
opportunities for him to court Sophia. Lady Verey
and Lady Eleanor were lulled and off their guard, and
with Jane drawing all the attention, Sophia's actions
went almost unnoticed. Lady Dennery had also
proved a staunch if unknowing ally, for she had kept
the Duke occupied throughout.

Jane smiled contentedly. She could see Lord Philip
galloping towards them up the hill, having set off for
a ride before them with the intention of meeting up
once out of sight of the house. Lady Verey had felt
reasonably at ease in allowing the girls to go riding
together within the estate, for both Jane and Sophia
were country-bred and unlikely to come to harm so
near to home.

Lord Philip drew up beside them and raised his
whip in salutation. He smiled at Jane before turning
to Sophia and engaging her in conversation. The
horses walked on slowly, with Philip and Sophia a
little ahead and Jane careful to stay out of earshot.
She was well pleased with her strategy, for it had the
additional benefit of keeping Lord Philip in a very
good mood indeed and with both him and Sophia as
allies, Jane felt immeasurably stronger. The only
problem was not getting caught out…

'I saw Alex driving Lady Dennery over to Moreton
Hall,' Philip said over his shoulder, with a grin for
Jane. 'He looked in a very black mood, but he only
has himself to blame for foisting that creature's company on to us! A more ill-bred, rapacious woman
would be difficult to find!'

Sophia hushed him reprovingly. 'Philip! At the
very least we may be grateful to her for keeping your

brother occupied!' She shivered. 'It frightens me to think that he might find us out!'

'I'll protect you, my love,' Philip said cheerfully, and Jane saw Sophia blush becomingly at the endearment. Once again she felt a moment's concern as she watched them ride on ahead together down the track between the beech trees. It would be a dreadful thing to be conspiring in the romance if Lord Philip was not in earnest! But surely she could not have mistaken his sincerity? Jane frowned. She was certain that it was only the need for secrecy that held Lord Philip silent and that as soon as he could he would make Sophia a declaration...

The Duke had returned in time to witness the three of them riding into the yard together at the end of their expedition, with Lord Philip very firmly at Jane's side by this time. Alex had been leaning over the stable door and chatting to the head groom, and he straightened up as they clattered past, a frown descending on his brow. Jane noticed it and reflected that he seemed to have frowned far more since she had reached an understanding with his brother. He had been noticeably better tempered when they were at odds!

Dinner that evening was a far from comfortable meal. Lady Dennery had evidently indulged in some disagreement with the Duke and vented her spleen through sharp comments on how slow the country was and how poor the company. Alex barely bothered to respond to her barbs and, with such a lack of amity between them, the others fell quiet and ate in almost total silence. When the ladies withdrew, Jane thankfully took the opportunity to slip away to the library for a little peace. She selected a tattered copy of *Tom*

Jones and Maria Elizabeth Jackson's *Botanical Dialogues* from the shelves and curled up on a window seat.

It was a good hour and a half before the sound of footsteps recalled her from the pages and then a dry voice said,

'Escaping into literature, Miss Verey? No doubt you find it more congenial than the atmosphere in the drawing-room!'

Alex Delahaye was standing before her, a quizzical lift to his black brows as he assessed her choice of reading matter.

'Are you a student of botany, Miss Verey? There have been some interesting studies in recent years.'

Jane nodded. 'I have read a few of the books and done a little studying at Ambergate,' she admitted.

'It is certainly an interesting contrast to *Tom Jones*,' Alex observed. 'I scarcely think that your mama would approve, Miss Verey!'

Jane put her book to one side with reluctance. 'No, indeed she would not! She particularly told me that I should not read it before I married! But—' She broke off, on the edge of giving herself away by saying that she believed she would never marry. That would never do, given her supposed affection for Lord Philip! She had a sudden conviction that Alex could accurately follow her every thought process and see right through the deception. A guilty blush stole into her cheeks and she stood up hastily.

'Excuse me, your Grace. I should rejoin the ladies.'

She was about to slip past him, when he put hand on her arm. 'A moment, Miss Verey. I will escort you back, but there is something I would like you to see first.'

He drew her across the room, to where a huge oil painting hung in a recessed alcove. Jane had noticed it when she had first entered the room but it had been wreathed in shadows and she had not paused to study it. Now, as Alex moved a lamp so that more light fell on the picture, she stood still and considered it.

The subject was a lady, fair and delicate, dressed in the high fashion of a decade before. She looked very young. She was reclining with languid grace on a chaise-longue, one white hand resting on the collar of a small dog that was gazing up at her with undisguised adoration in its eyes. Jane considered it a poor painting, studied and artificial, and yet there was something compelling about the beauty of the sitter and the sweetness of her expression. So this was Madeline Delahaye! No wonder the Duke was still so attached to the memory of so gentle and gracious a lady. Looking at the vacant, painted face, Jane wondered what had happened to change so unspoilt a girl into the selfish pleasure-seeker who had apparently betrayed her husband with such blatant disregard for his feelings and public opinion. Remembering Alex's bitterness when they spoke at Almack's, Jane thought she understood. Evidently he had chosen to ignore his wife's infidelity and concentrate on the happier times they had experienced when first married. The fact that he had kept this early portrait in so prominent a position seemed to underline his attachment to her and his determination to keep her memory alive.

A sort of anger took possession of Jane that Madeline Delahaye could have taken Alex's love and treated it with such contempt. If she had had the love of such a man... The painting shimmered in a sudden wash of tears. All Jane's feelings locked in a tight pain in her throat. It was so unfair that Alex should still have such strong feelings for his dead wife, for how could anyone else ever compare? With a smothered sob she pulled her arm from his grasp and ran from the library.

She heard Alex say, 'Jane, wait!' but her pride would not permit him to see her tears.

Later, as she sat dry-eyed in her room and acknowledged to herself for the first time that she loved him, she thought bitterly that pride was indeed all that she had now.

Chapter Nine

'Is this not fun!' Lady Eleanor Fane said, a twinkle of repressed mirth in her eyes as she surveyed her ill-assorted guests as they sat on picnic rugs and under parasols.

There was Lady Dennery, a little worn and over-dressed in the unkind light of day, picking petulantly at her food. Beside her sat Alex Delahaye looking, Lady Eleanor thought, decidedly bored and moody. Oddly, it was as though he had reversed roles with his brother, for Lord Philip seemed happy and at ease as he laughed and talked with Jane Verey. A little distance from them sat Sophia, being charming to Lord Blakeney and apparently enjoying herself immensely. Lady Verey, a contented smile on her face, dozed in the sun.

Well! Lady Eleanor thought now, with secret amusement, if Miss Verey does not like Philip she is making a very good pretence at it! All seems set fair! And the Marchment girl, whom Philip seemed so taken with before, does not appear concerned! I wonder... Her gaze slid to Alex, who was leaning forward to attend to something Francine Dennery was saying.

If Alex allows himself to be caught by her, then more fool him, Lady Eleanor thought astringently. Yet there was very little of the lover in Alex's demeanour and every so often his gaze would rest on Jane Verey in a completely unfathomable regard.

The arrival of Lord Blakeney had been most opportune. He had called at Malladon on the fourth day of their stay, after visiting a rich old uncle in the neighbourhood and hearing that the Duke was in residence nearby. Philip, conscious of a certain constraint in the party, had pressed him to join them and Blakeney had taken little persuading.

'Whole countryside's buzzing with the news,' he had confided to Jane, on the first evening. 'Delahaye never comes to Malladon; now he's not only here but he's brought a party as well!'

Jane considered that it had been a decidedly odd week. On the surface, all had been delightful. There had been riding in the countryside and walks in the park and visits to friends and neighbours. There had even been an informal dinner and dancing in the evening, but now Alex Delahaye had signalled his intention to return to Town and the picnic was the last event before they all drove back the following day.

Beneath the surface matters had not been quite so straightforward. Jane, made hopelessly self-conscious by her behaviour in the library and the discovery of her feelings for Alex, had gone out of her way to avoid him. He had seemed preoccupied by estate matters and plagued by Lady Dennery's increasingly broad hints about the future, and scarcely seemed to notice her anyway. Lady Verey had been dropping broad hints of her own, and Jane had suddenly awoken to the fact that her mother was expecting to announce the betrothal to Lord Philip as soon as they returned to Town. Meanwhile, Sophia and Lord Philip were moving inexorably towards their own conclusion, which Jane devoutly hoped entailed an engagement of their own. Suddenly it all seemed intolerably complicated and bereft of hope and enjoyment.

Jane swotted an eager wasp that was attacking her lemonade and tilted the broad brim of her hat forward a little to shade her face. She had also become aware of the unsettling nature of Alex's gaze as it drifted over her. Certainly he could object to nothing in her manner, for she was behaving towards Philip with the greatest cordiality and he was responding effortlessly. Yet she sensed that there was something angering Alex, something she could not comprehend. It was very puzzling and she had been aware of it for almost the whole week.

She looked up and caught Philip's eye. They had already agreed that Jane should manufacture a reason for a stroll and that Sophia and Blakeney should help distract attention. Sighing inwardly, Jane got to her feet and dusted the crumbs off her skirt.

'Gracious, I feel quite in need of some exercise to walk off the effects of all that delicious food! Would anyone care to join me for a turn about the park?'

Lord Philip, taking his cue, scrambled up with alacrity. 'I should be glad to, Miss Verey! Miss Marchment, Blakeney, do you care to come?'

'Oh, yes, that would be delightful!' Sophia agreed eagerly. She allowed Lord Blakeney to help her up and adjusted the ribbons on her bonnet. Jane took her shawl from Lord Philip with a pretty word of thanks. Lady Verey smiled indulgently to see such harmony.

'You may discount me, my love,' she said sleepily.

'I am happy dozing here in the sun and I do not doubt
that Lady Eleanor will keep me company. But perhaps the others...'

Jane saw that the Duke was frowning quite darkly.
Some imp of perversity prompted her to extend the
invitation as her mother had suggested.

'Would you like to join us, your Grace? Lady Dennery?'

She saw Philip looking quite appalled and tried not
to laugh. It seemed a safe gamble, for Lady Dennery
was looking quite horrified. 'Oh, no, I do not care to
walk at all!' she said as though Jane had suggested
some activity in bad taste. 'I am persuaded that Alex
will stay here with me, for we may have a delightful
coze together!'

Jane smiled brilliantly. 'Just as you wish, my lady!'
She did not dare to look at the Duke for his reaction.

'You run along, my dears,' Lady Eleanor said comfortably. 'We older folk will do very well here in the
peace and quiet!'

Lady Dennery was now looking quite affronted to
be classified with the ancients and the Duke's frown
had not lifted. He looked almost murderous. Jane
dropped a mischievous curtsy.

'Thank you, ma'am!'

The four of them wandered off, chatting happily
amongst themselves.

'Oh, I shall not be sad to return to Town,' Sophia
sighed. 'The country is all very well, but it has not
the same excitement! I believe Lady Jersey is hosting
a ball next week that promises to be the highlight of
the Season!'

'Heard about that myself,' Blakeney confirmed.
'Word is that the theme will be classical myths and

legends! The talk in the clubs was that Francine Dennery intends to appear in little more than a sheet!'

'Won't be the first time!' Lord Philip guffawed, then caught Sophia's look of innocent bewilderment and cleared his throat loudly.

Jane stopped abruptly, turning to Lord Blakeney urgently.

'Oh, no! I have left my parasol behind and Mama will be furious with me if I catch the sun! She considers freckles most unladylike! Lord Blakeney, would you be so good as to run back and fetch it? I should be so grateful...'

Lord Blakeney was as amiable as he was undiscerning. Expressing himself honoured to be of service, he trotted obediently back in the direction from which they had come. Jane watched him go, then turned to her companions with a smile.

'Pray walk on ahead! There is no sense in all of us waiting here! Lord Blakeney will only be a moment and we will follow you when he returns!'

Sophia and Philip needed no second bidding. Jane, moving into the shadow of a group of trees, saw them stroll away slowly, deep in conversation. She smiled in spite of herself. She would do a great deal to secure Sophia's happiness and it was a joy to see her strategies working so effectively. Splitting up the group meant that Sophia and Lord Philip were, to all intents and purposes, alone, yet within view and perfectly respectable. Lord Blakeney would be back shortly, but Jane would ensure that she did not walk quickly enough for them to catch the others up. Really, she felt that she had the tactics to match any of the King's generals!

Jane frowned a little as she contemplated the next

stage of the plan. Matters were likely to become decidedly tricky from now on. For a start, she knew that Lady Verey intended the announcement of her betrothal to Lord Philip to be sent to the *Morning Post* as soon as they returned to Town. That had to be avoided at all costs. Then a way had to be found to solve Lord Philip's financial difficulties and promote the match with Sophia. Jane was forced to admit that she did not have any ideas at present...

At that point her musings were interrupted by a completely unforeseen hitch.

A figure was striding towards her across the grass brandishing her parasol in his hand like an avenging angel. It was not the slightly corpulent Lord Blakeney, but the altogether more impressive figure of the Duke of Delahaye. In a sudden panic, Jane turned round and plunged deeper into the trees, heedless of the sudden slope and the muddy ground beneath her feet. She was not sure whether she was intending to run away or to hide; she only knew that she was about to be caught out and that she did not appear to be able to think quickly enough to explain herself.

In the event she was able to neither run nor hide, for Alex caught up with her with unnerving speed.

'Miss Verey! What is this nonsense about a lost parasol? And where are my brother and Miss Marchment?'

Jane was at something of a disadvantage. The hem of her skirt was an inch deep in mud and her bonnet had slipped to one side, making her look like a dowager who had taken rather too much port. She was out of breath and flushed, and Alex's proximity and the altogether furious look on his face increased the fluttering nervousness inside her.

'There is no nonsense, your Grace,' she said with more composure than she was feeling. 'Why, you have the parasol there in your hand! Be careful that you do not attack that branch!'

She watched the grim expression on Alex's face ease slightly as he lowered his arm and handed the offending parasol to her.

'And my brother and Miss Marchment?' he asked, with a dangerous calm.

Jane gave him a winning smile. 'I suggested that they strolled on ahead. There was no point in all of us waiting! Indeed, I was expecting to catch them up when Lord Blakeney returned!' Her tone managed to convey reproach that it was he, and not Lord Blakeney, who had appeared. 'I expect they are back with the others by now!'

'I am surprised that Philip could bear to be from your side,' Alex said drily. 'He has stuck like a burr all week!'

'Yes, is it not delightful?' Jane said blithely. 'You must be so pleased that your brother and I have reached an understanding!'

'It is the nature of the understanding that concerns me,' Alex said affably. 'You had me fooled for quite a little while this time, Miss Verey, but not any more!'

'I have no notion what you mean, sir!' Jane said, managing to preserve her air of injured innocence.

Alex caught her arm and swung her round to face him. 'Oh, come now, Miss Verey! I used to admire your honesty! The truth is that you have managed to enlist the support of my disgraceful brother—and Miss Marchment, no doubt—in your scheme to thwart the marriage plans! It was so obvious,' Alex mused, a smile starting to curl the corners of his mouth, 'I cannot think why I did not see it before! To think that I believed that you had meekly accepted the plans made for you! My wits must have gone a-begging!'

There was a long silence. Jane's intellect, which had served her so well up to that point, suddenly seemed to have deserted her, banished by the insistent pressure of Alex's touch. Worse, although her mind was frighteningly blank, her senses seemed unusually sharp. She was conscious of the plaintive sweetness of the birdsong, the rustle of the leaves and the cool caress of the breeze on her hot cheeks. Her gaze was held by his and no power on earth could have broken the contact.

Jane saw the amusement fade from Alex's eyes, to be replaced by an expression that made her shiver.

'Am I to test my theory and the strength of your feeling for my brother?' he asked softly. 'It is irresistible, I fear...'

Jane had plenty of time to move away from him and she knew that he would not have tried to stop her had she done so. She could not have said what it was that held her captive, unless it was that fatal curiosity of hers; it had prompted her to wonder secretly what it would be like to be kissed by Alex, and now she wanted to know the answer. Whatever the reason, she stayed quite still, and Alex leant forward and kissed her.

The touch of his lips on hers was deceptively light, almost casual, were it not for an undercurrent of sensuality that sprang shockingly to life as soon as they touched, elemental as sheet lightning. Jane felt a surge of sensation wash over her, leaving her weak with a most delicious pleasure. She knew a moment when she was sure that Alex was about to sweep her into his arms, then, to her great disappointment, he released her and stepped back.

'My apologies, Miss Verey,' Alex said expressionlessly. 'I fear I succumbed to an impulse that has been troubling me for some time.'

Jane took a deep breath. She was dizzy with the memory of taste and touch of him, torn by disappointment that he had let her go.

'Well!' she said, with incurable honesty. 'I do not see that it is at all the thing to kiss your brother's intended bride, your Grace!'

'No…' Alex slanted a glance down at her '…I agree that it would not be at all appropriate—were you to be that bride, Miss Verey! Now, permit me to escort you back to the others before anything else befalls you!'

After a moment's hesitation, Jane took his proffered arm and they walked slowly through the dappled shade towards the edge of the copse. Her shaken nerves were beginning to settle again, but she was still acutely aware of Alex's physical presence. She reflected a little ruefully that Alex himself seemed quite unmoved, almost as though he had forgotten what had passed only a moment before. In fact he suddenly seemed a great deal more cheerful than he had for the entire week.

'So,' he said conversationally, 'will you concede the truth? It is all a scheme, is it not?'

Not even Jane found herself brass-faced enough to tell a direct lie. 'It was all working so well!' she said a little plaintively. 'You said yourself that you had been taken in!'

'Yes, I must have been very slow,' Alex agreed

pleasantly. 'In truth, I thought I knew you far too well to be deceived again!'

Jane cleared her throat. For some reason his words and tone had disturbed something in her. They created a feeling of intimacy that stirred emotions already aroused by their encounter. For some reason he did not sound accusatory—there was too much warmth in his voice.

'You have said before that you knew I was untrustworthy,' she began, a little bitterly, but Alex stopped and turned to face her properly.

'I did say that, and I am sorry for it. I said it only to provoke you at the time and the fact that it worked does not make it any more admirable! The truth is, Miss Verey—' his tone dropped '—I have long admired your strategies and your determination not to give in!'

There was a silence broken only by the chatter of the birds and the running of the brook. Jane felt the colour sting her cheeks and dropped her gaze, and Alex, sensing her discomfort, started to walk again.

'Tell me, what did you plan to do next?' he asked. 'Your plan was a good one in the short term, but dangerous as well! You must realise that your mother in particular is planning an announcement as soon as we reach Town!'

'Yes…' Jane was glad to be distracted from her own complicated feelings '…I own that was a problem! I had not quite fathomed how to avoid the formal engagement!'

'No doubt you would have thought of something,' Alex said, so consolingly that Jane looked up sharply to see if he was teasing her. He was smiling at her, but without mockery.

'I expect so,' Jane said dolefully, 'but now that you know the truth—'

'Yes, we shall have to think of something else!'

'I only wanted Sophia to be happy,' Jane said, still following her own train of thought. 'That is,' she added scrupulously, 'I did not wish to marry Lord Philip, but when it became apparent that Sophia *did*, I hoped for a happy outcome! Do you think—' she glanced at Alex hopefully '—that you might permit...?'

Alex was looking preoccupied. 'I shall have to think about it, Miss Verey,' he said.

Jane left it at that. She wanted to make a push for Sophia's future, but knew full well that Alex was hardly a man who could be pestered into agreement. Besides, she wanted to escape the leafy shade, for being alone with him was making her nervous. The strength of his arm beneath her fingers, the brush of his body against hers...she was very aware of him and had no wish to betray her feelings.

They stepped out into the bright sunshine and Jane nearly gasped with relief.

'I see Miss Marchment and my brother ahead,' Alex said, matter of factly. 'As you predicted, Miss Verey, they are almost back with the others!'

'Oh, by all means let us hurry to catch them up!' Jane said thankfully. She had no wish to prolong this unsettling encounter. Alex, however, appeared to have other ideas.

'Oh, let us not rush back,' he said lazily, with an amused look down at her. 'It would not do for you to go hurrying about in the full sun!'

'I have my parasol now,' Jane said pertly, unfurling the lacy white material, 'and I am no fragile flower!'

'No, indeed, a most resilient root, Miss Verey, although that is scarcely a flattering description of you! I would never underestimate your resourcefulness!'

Jane tilted her head to look at him. 'You are speaking in riddles, your Grace!' she said bluntly. 'It is most disconcerting!'

Alex gave her a smile that was even more disturbing. 'Forgive me! I thought, perhaps, that you would understand me, being so accomplished in strategy! I simply meant that though I have seen through your current plan, I would not put it past you to devise another! I must beg you not to do so. You see, I already have one of my own in the devising, and though it will take a little time to sort out, I have high hopes that it will come to fruition!'

'I hope that it is not along the lines of your other tactics, sir,' Jane said tightly and not entirely truthfully. 'I consider them indefensible!'

'If you mean the kiss, it was not an intentional part of my plan,' Alex admitted, still smiling, 'but now that I have found it so effective and enjoyable I may have to employ it again! Now, Miss Verey, tell me if you would protest! *That* is an interesting test of your honesty!'

Jane's stormy gaze locked with his but she was not able to respond because of the proximity of the others. She did not like to imagine what they might have read into her expression. The picnic had been neatly packed away and Lord Philip was assisting Lady Verey and Lady Eleanor up into the gig that was to convey them back to the house. Lady Dennery, her face as thunderous as it had been earlier, was standing a little apart from the others and tapping her parasol angrily on the grass.

Lord Philip hailed his brother with a deeply suspicious innocence. 'Alex! We had all but given up hope of you and imagined that you had spirited Miss Verey away!'

'Tempting,' Alex said under his breath, with a limpid look for Jane. He raised his voice. 'Is everybody ready to go back?'

'I have been ready this past hour!' Lady Dennery snapped. 'Have you no thought for others, Alexander?' Her contemptuous gaze raked Jane. 'Or perhaps you were lost in your pastoral idyll with that little—?'

'Have a care, Francine!' The Duke's tone was soft but with an undertone that made Jane jump. For a moment she saw a flash of some vivid emotion in his eyes, before he turned to her with scrupulous courtesy.

'Miss Verey, do you care to walk back or would you prefer to drive?'

Before Jane could reply, Lady Dennery made a rude and derisive noise and stormed off in the direction of the house.

'Shocking *ton*!' Lady Eleanor was trying not to smile at Lady Dennery's downfall. 'I fear it is about to rain, Alex—perhaps you should go to her aid?'

The Duke raised one eyebrow. 'I am persuaded that Lady Dennery will find her own way home,' he said easily. 'No doubt she prefers to be alone!' He turned back to Jane and his smile was dazzling in its warmth. 'Miss Verey?'

'I will drive, I thank you, sir,' Jane said hastily, although she would indeed have enjoyed the walk through the parkland. She allowed him to help her up into the second gig and squeezed in next to Sophia.

'Oh, Jane,' her friend whispered, 'did you see the look that the Duke gave you? I do believe…and Lady Dennery clearly thinks you a rival! Oh Jane, I do believe that the Duke of Delahaye is developing a *tendre* for you!'

'Poor Lady Dennery,' Sophia said the following morning, as the summer dust settled on the drive behind her ladyship's coach, 'she had such high hopes and finds them all dashed! It must be very hard for her—'

'To be a rich widow?' Jane asked, a little waspishly. 'She may not have managed to attach the Duke, but there will be plenty of other suitors!'

She came away from the bedroom window and moved rather restlessly across to the portmanteaux that her maid had already packed. They were all returning to Town that morning, but Lady Dennery would not be accompanying them, for she had been invited to stay with friends in Buckinghamshire and had high hopes of a certain elderly Marquis who would be of the company. Jane felt that the journey back would be rather more comfortable without her ladyship, but it was only a small relief amongst the other matters that preoccupied her.

Sophia was looking at her friend with concern. 'Are you quite well, Jane? You seem sadly out of sorts today!'

Jane sighed, unpacking half of the clothes that Cassie had already put away as she rummaged for a favourite pair of gloves. 'I'm sorry, Sophy! You are right in thinking me like a bear with a sore head! It is just all so difficult…'

She sat down and Sophia came to sit beside her on the bed.

'Tell me what is troubling you,' she urged. 'Is it that Lady Verey plans the betrothal announcement for as soon as we return to Town? I'll allow that it is a little difficult...'

Jane made a sound that was halfway between a sob and a laugh. 'Oh, Sophy, you have such a talent for understatement! The truth is that my mother wishes to promote my engagement to a man who should by rights be marrying you! I have come up with no plan to solve Lord Philip's financial difficulties and can see no solution to the whole problem other than that you elope with him!'

Sophia had paled a little. 'Oh, Jane, I do not think that a very comfortable solution! Why, the Duke would cut Philip off altogether and then everyone would be unhappy!'

Jane got to her feet and moved restlessly across the window. 'The Duke knows that my apparent affection for Lord Philip is all assumed!' she said over her shoulder. 'That is the worst part of the situation! He challenged me about it only yesterday and warned me to make no more plans! There is nothing to be gained by further deception!'

'He is a most perceptive man,' Sophia said with a shiver. 'All the time that I was smiling on Blakeney, I was convinced that he knew the truth!'

'A guilty conscience!' Jane said bluntly. 'The Duke had no notion until he took Blakeney's place and brought me the parasol yesterday. Then, when he saw that you and Lord Philip had walked on together— *then* he knew the truth! I tried to persuade him to look upon the two of you with kindness, but—' She broke off, not wishing to raise Sophia's hopes unnecessarily. After all, Alex had told her that he had a plan, but it might not be one that would make everyone happy.

'But perhaps—' Sophia avoided Jane's eye '—the whole matter may be solved if the Duke has feelings for you, Jane—' She broke off and looked hopeful, bursting out, 'Oh, if he were to love you then he would no longer wish you to marry Philip and his heart might be softened towards us—'

But Jane was shaking her head. 'No, Sophy, I fear you have it all wrong! I know that you thought yesterday that the Duke had developed something of a *tendre* for me, but I am certain that you are mistaken!'

Sophia looked stubborn. Jane realised that this was because she so desperately wanted it to be true. It would solve the whole problem of the projected marriage to Lord Philip and they might all live happily ever after... Jane made a wry grimace.

'I am sorry, Sophy, but it really isn't true.'

'But I saw the way that he was looking at you, Jane! And when Lady Dennery made her ill-bred remarks he gave her the set-down she deserved for slighting you! Surely—'

Jane took a deep breath. There was only one way to convince Sophia.

'I know it cannot be true for the Duke kissed me yesterday and thought so little of it that he had forgotten it the next second!'

Sophia gave a little squeak. 'I beg your pardon, Jane?'

'He kissed me,' Jane repeated, with a hint of irritation.

'Oh, Jane!' Sophia's eyes were huge. 'Was it truly dreadful?'

'No,' Jane said slowly, 'it was not. I am obliged to admit that it was rather nice!' She smiled suddenly, against her will. 'Which is very confusing, but progresses our situation not at all!'

'Oh, Jane!' Sophia said again, breathlessly. 'But if he kissed you—'

'It was only part of the game!' Jane said, the light dying out of her face. 'I told you—he was completely unmoved by it! It is all a game to him!'

Sophia was looking at her with blank incomprehension. 'A game?'

Jane decided that she could not begin to explain the complicated steps in the encounter between herself and Alexander Delahaye. Pitting her wits against his had been amusing at first, a challenge that had had an underlying current of excitement. She had never dreamed that it would ever have the power to hurt her. Yet now...

She decided to opt for the easier explanation.

'I believe that the Duke of Delahaye is still in love with his wife,' she said, 'and that is why no other lady would have the chance of engaging his affections. He showed me a picture of her, Sophia—she was very beautiful and the picture is displayed so prominently that I think it must be a sign of the regard he still has for her.' She turned away, closing the portmanteau lid and struggling with the straps in order to hide her confusion. Her feelings were currently too raw to allow her to confide.

'Oh, Jane,' Sophia said, and there was pity in her

voice, as though she has guessed Jane's state, 'what are you going to do?'

'Avoid him, I should think,' Jane said bleakly. 'I will not marry Lord Philip, but nor shall I have any further dealings with his brother!'

Chapter Ten

Alex's opposition to this plan became apparent almost immediately. Whilst Jane was intending to avoid him, he seemed to seek her out deliberately. When they met in the entrance hall for the journey home that afternoon, he expressed the aim of taking Jane up in his phaeton whilst Philip drove Sophia and the ladies of more mature years travelled in the carriage. This was sufficiently improper for Lady Eleanor to raise an eyebrow, but no one contradicted him. Lady Verey was too much in awe of him, whilst Jane saw no point in arguing only to be overruled. Sophia and Philip both looked a little stunned by this public sign of approval and as Sophia went out onto the carriage sweep she gave Jane a look of mingled doubt and pleasure. Interpreting this correctly, Jane thought that Sophia was now convinced of Alex's partiality and would quiz her mercilessly about it later.

They bowled down the drive and out on to the road in the wake of the carriage. It was very pleasant to be driven so expertly. The phaeton was very well sprung, the view enjoyable and day fair. Jane was relieved to discover that they could chat inconsequentially on various topics as wide-ranging as her child-hood at Ambergate, her interest in botany and many other subjects of mutual interest.

'I hope that you have enjoyed your stay, Miss Verey,' Alex said a little formally, after an hour or so and for some reason it felt as though they had moved from impartial to more personal subjects.

'Yes, thank you,' Jane said cautiously. 'It has been pleasant to be in the country again and Malladon is a fine house.'

Alex laughed softly. He cast her a sideways glance. 'No mention of the entertainments or the company, Miss Verey?'

Jane shifted a little uncomfortably. 'I find it diffi-cult to spend any length of time in the same com-pany,' she admitted. 'Everyone seems to live in each other's pocket! I believe that there must be some fault in me that makes me intolerant of the society of oth-ers!'

'Why do you suppose I spend so much time at Hayenham?' Alex said, with a crooked smile. 'I am the least sociable of creatures, Miss Verey, and find the demands of the Season or the houseparty a severe trial! Perhaps we are kindred spirits, you and I!'

Jane did not trust herself to answer directly. 'I cer-tainly find the country preferable to London. I fear I must be a sad trial to my mother, for all that she tried to turn me into a perfect young lady!'

'Well, don't change!' Alex said abruptly. 'Indepen-dence of mind is a quality seldom found in a young lady, let alone valued as it ought to be! I lose count of the number of vapid, feather-brained girls one meets every Season and it appals me that they are encouraged to act so!'

'You are very ungallant!' Jane said severely. 'What do you suppose is their opinion of you, your Grace?'

Alex looked startled. 'A good question! Apart from as a rich Duke in need of a wife?'

'Upon my word! But then, I suppose there are some young women who will tolerate any number of faults for a title and a fortune!'

Alex smiled as the point went home, but he did not rise to her comment. 'You would not count yourself amongst them, Miss Verey?'

'No, indeed! You have not answered my question,' Jane pointed out. 'Perhaps you are so quelling that all the young ladies you meet are over-awed by you!'

'Then it is fortunate that I do not ask them to bear with me,' Alex said laconically. 'Though you, Miss Verey—' He broke off with an exclamation.

Following his gaze, Jane saw that the wheel of the carriage in front was wobbling wildly and even as Alex shouted a warning to the coachman, there was the sound of rending wood and the vehicle lurched violently to one side. The wheel rolled off into the ditch and the carriage sat marooned like a fat dowager in the middle of the road.

Philip, whose phaeton was at the front of the procession, reined in and turned back hastily. By the time that Alex and Jane had drawn level, Lady Eleanor had already been helped down and Sophia was comforting her by the roadside whilst Philip and the groom tried to aid Lady Verey.

It quickly became apparent that Lady Verey had fallen awkwardly when the coach had tipped up and seemed to have sprained her wrist. She had fainted from pain and shock, and as she was no lightweight the two men were having some difficulty in extracting her from the carriage. Eventually they managed to pull her out, by which time Alex had sent his own groom to fetch a physician and had driven to the nearest inn to alert them to the accident. They laid the invalid on the travelling rugs at the side of the road and stood around a little helplessly as they waited for her to return to consciousness.

'Hartshorn!' Lady Eleanor said triumphantly, after rummaging in her reticule. 'My poor Clarissa! She looks as white as a sheet!'

Jane suspected that Lady Verey was better off unconscious, at least until the doctor arrived to have a look at the injured arm. Fortunately Alex returned at that moment, bringing a makeshift stretcher made out of a tavern bench. They wrapped Lady Verey up and carried her to the inn.

It seemed to Jane, watching with anxiety tinged with amusement, that Alex's presence seemed to smooth all possible obstacles. In the space of a few minutes, Lady Verey was carried to a bedchamber, a parlour and refreshments were bespoken for the other guests and the physician arrived to set the broken limb. The damaged carriage was brought in and a wheelwright set to work whilst the ostlers attended the horses. It was all achieved with maximum speed and minimum fuss. Jane sat with her mother whilst the doctor was busy and presently went down to the parlour where the others were waiting, standing around a little awkwardly as they awaited some news.

'My mother is much better now that her arm is bandaged,' she confirmed in response to Lady Eleanor's anxious enquiry. 'She is sleeping now, for she is quite worn out, but declares that she will be quite well enough to return home tomorrow. Perhaps—' she turned instinctively to Alex '—you would be so good as to give my brother a message when you return to Town, sir? If he could come to fetch us tomorrow we shall do very well, and need not delay your departure any further.'

Her words were met with a storm of protest. 'We cannot leave you here alone, child!' Lady Eleanor said astringently. 'No, indeed, we must all stay!'

Sophia added her own concerns. 'Oh, Jane, it is impossible that you should stay here! Why, everyone knows that inns are most dangerous places! You would be ravished in your bed!'

'It is natural that Miss Verey would wish to remain to look after her mother,' Alex said smoothly, stifling a smile. 'I have already spoken to the landlord and they have only three rooms altogether, so it is clearly impossible for all of us to stay. It would be better for you to return to London, Aunt Eleanor, for I am assured that the carriage wheel has been mended already. Philip can escort you and Miss Marchment. She will need to stay with you tonight, for she cannot return to Portman Square and be alone with Lord Verey! I shall stay here with Miss Verey and her mother.'

Jane opened her mouth to object at the arrogant way in which Alex had taken charge. She closed it again as he shot her a quelling look. Lady Eleanor looked affronted. 'Well, upon my word, I see that you have it all worked out, Alex!'

'Yes, Aunt Eleanor,' Alex agreed, shepherding her towards the door, 'but it really is all for the best! There is little we can do for Lady Verey until tomorrow and there is Miss Marchment to consider as well. Philip—' his brother came forward with alacrity

'—please take Lady Eleanor and Miss Marchment out to the carriage. And let Simon Verey know what's happened, there's a good chap…'

Jane escaped upstairs. Alex's high-handedness had evidently won the day and for the moment she did not wish to confront him. She was certain that he had manoeuvred matters so that they would be alone together and she was tempted to spend the rest of the day in Lady Verey's chamber in order to avoid him.

Lady Verey was asleep, showing none of the signs of incipient fever that the doctor had warned against. Jane sat with her for a few hours until night fell outside and Jane's stomach began to rumble and remind her that she had not eaten for a number of hours. Whilst she was hesitating over whether or not to venture down to bespeak supper, there was a knock at the door. The landlord's daughter poked her head in.

'His Grace's compliments, miss, and will you join him for dinner in the parlour? I am happy to sit with your mother whilst you are away.'

Jane was tempted to refuse but it seemed that Alex had already removed the most obvious excuse by engaging the girl to sit with Lady Verey. She washed her face and hands slowly, and made her way downstairs.

The parlour was cheerful with a small fire burning in the grate and an enticing smell of food. Jane's spirits began to revive a little. Alex was standing before the fire and came forward at once to hold a chair for her and to ask after Lady Verey. Jane realised that she felt nervous; the strangeness, intimacy even, of their situation, suddenly struck her. He passed her a glass of madeira and, after a moment's hesitation, Jane took a sip.

'You are very quiet, Miss Verey,' Alex observed, after she had made no effort to speak during the entire first course. 'I hope that the distress over your mother's accident has not overset you?'

'Oh, no!' Jane tried to pull herself together. 'That is…I am very sorry for Mama, for it was a dreadfully unlucky thing to happen, but I believe that she will recover well. I must thank you for your help, sir. You have eased our difficulties considerably.'

'Even if the price is having to accept my company?' Alex said, with an unrepentant smile. 'I saw that you disapproved of my high-handedness, Miss Verey!'

Jane bit back an answering smile. 'You are very frank, sir.'

'I deal straight, as you do, Miss Verey. Perhaps you would have preferred to stay here alone, facing whatever dangers Miss Marchment feels lurk in such places?'

'I do not believe that I would have been in any great peril,' Jane said judiciously. 'However, your Grace evidently felt it necessary to provide protection, for which, no doubt, I should also thank you!'

'It was nothing. I have my own reasons.'

'I do not doubt it,' Jane said, a little crossly. 'Does everyone always fall in with your plans, sir?'

'Almost always!' Alex said cheerfully. 'Except for you, Miss Verey! You are the one notable exception and it has been a salutary experience for me!'

Jane met his eyes squarely. 'I collect that you refer to my refusal of your brother's suit? If you thought to spend your time this evening persuading me, I should warn you now that it would be a waste of time! I am still of the same mind!'

Alex considered the deep ruby red of his wine. 'Oddly enough, Miss Verey, that was not my intention.' He looked up suddenly and Jane's heart did a little flip as their eyes met. 'Though I should be gratified to know why you are so adamantly against the match.'

Jane looked away. 'It is simply that marriage is a very serious business, your Grace. I esteem your brother—we are fast friends—but we have little in common on which to base a life together.' She blushed. 'Must we speak of this? I have no wish to prolong the subject!'

Alex inclined his head. 'Then we will not do so. It would be ungallant of me to persist with a topic you find distressing.' He paused. 'However, your reluctance did lead me to wonder whether your feelings were already engaged. I asked you before, of course, but now that we know each other better you might be willing to confide...'

Jane stared at him, her pie congealing on the plate in front of her. Of course! Why had she not thought of that for herself? It would have been the obvious delaying tactic! She could not believe that it had not occurred to her to invent a secret fiancé, or indeed to plead guilty to an affection that was not returned! There was only one problem—the identity of her secret love...

'Harry Marchnight, for instance,' Alex was saying, carefully expressionless. 'I have observed that you are very fond of him, but perhaps your feelings are of a deeper nature than mere affection...'

Dark eyes and hazel met and held. Jane trembled on the edge of committing herself. Henry was a perfect candidate for her unrequited love, handsome, dashing... Yet there was something in Alex's gaze that compelled her honesty.

'Oh, I have known Harry for an age,' she said, as carelessly as she was able, 'and I love him like a brother! I wish I could claim that you are right, sir, but it is not true and I shall not pretend otherwise.'

She thought she saw Alex relax infinitesimally, but could not imagine why. The silence between them suddenly seemed oddly significant.

'Let us speak of other matters,' she said impulsively. 'Tell me about Hayenham, sir. I have heard that you spend most of your time there.'

Alex's description of his Yorkshire home took most of the rest of the meal and by the end Jane could almost taste the sea spray and feel the wind in the heather.

'I can tell that you love it very much,' she said, a little wistfully. 'It sounds so very beautiful! Yet I would have thought that a man like you would still need other employment...some sort of gainful activity—' She broke off and flushed at the look he gave her. 'I beg your pardon, sir. I was thinking aloud.'

Alex was smiling. 'So you do not think that my estates provide sufficient interest or occupation, Miss Verey?'

Jane blushed all the more. 'I did not intend... I suppose that I see you as needing more of a challenge...forgive me,' she finished hastily. 'I am tired, I think, and should retire.'

Alex put out a hand to detain her. 'A moment. This is interesting—an interesting insight. What would you see me doing, Miss Verey?'

Jane made a vague gesture. 'Well, take Harry Marchnight as an example—'

'Must we? I am fast becoming tired of his name!'

'Nonsense! Harry is the perfect example! He gives the impression of being a rake and a gamester and yet he is nothing of the sort!'

Alex's gaze was suddenly very intent. 'What do you mean, Miss Verey?'

'Why, that Harry is forever disappearing on mysterious errands and pretending that he is nothing but a pleasure-seeker, but anyone who knows him must realise he is no dilettante! It is obvious that he must be engaged upon secret government business. Just as you—'

Jane broke off and blushed scarlet. 'Excuse me, sir. I have said too much. My imagination runs away with me.'

Alex leant forward. 'What does your imagination see for me, Miss Verey? A self-proclaimed recluse using his somewhat eccentric reputation to cover—what?'

Jane shrugged. 'I know not, sir. I promised that I would keep quiet about that night at Vauxhall—and about your activities in Spitalfields—and I have kept my word! But I do not have to be a bluestocking to calculate that there is some strange business afoot! Only...' she frowned, aware that her glass was empty and her mind slightly fuzzy from drink and tiredness '...I do believe that you should be careful, sir. It cannot be right that someone is stalking you armed with a knife!'

'I will take your advice, Miss Verey,' Alex said gravely. 'I do take it. And once again I am touched at your concern for me. What does that betoken, I wonder?'

Jane suddenly realised how very tired she did feel.

The food, the warmth of the fire and most of all the wine, had filled her with a sudden lassitude. She stood up. It seemed very late. The shadowed room was far too intimate for comfort and Alex was coming far too close to the truth. It was best to retire before she gave away all her secrets.

'I hope that my mother may stand as chaperon even though she is asleep in bed,' Jane said doubtfully. 'I do not think that this is at all respectable, your Grace!'

Alex smiled. 'Perhaps you are right! Certainly I could argue that you are hopelessly compromised!'

Jane blinked at him a little owlishly. 'Surely it is your brother who has the rake's reputation!'

Alex's gaze was bright with mockery. 'Perhaps,' he said again, 'but you have had the proof that I am not safe, have you not, Miss Verey?'

The room suddenly seemed far too small. Jane edged towards the door. Alex stood up and stretched with a lazy grace. 'Allow me to escort you to your room…'

Jane started to protest, but to her horror she found that she was so tired she could not be bothered to form the words. She grasped the back of a chair to steady herself.

'Oh, dear…'

'It is just a reaction to all the events of the day,' Alex said practically, and before Jane could object, he had swept her up into his arms. 'I will take you upstairs.'

'Oh, no!' Jane's eyes opened wide, sobriety suddenly restored. 'You cannot do that!'

He was laughing openly at her, the mocking tone still very much in evidence. 'You are quite safe, Miss

Verey! I have never had to stoop to seducing young ladies in alehouses…'

'No, but…' The effort of argument was almost too much for Jane, whose eyes seemed to be closing of their own volition. 'If somebody saw us—'

'Then you would have to marry me. It is a perfectly simple solution.'

Suddenly it all seemed perfectly simple to Jane also. Various pieces seemed to slot together in her mind. 'Yes,' she said sleepily, 'because that is the real reason that I cannot marry your brother, sir…'

She opened her eyes. Alex's face was very close above her own, his eyes so dark she imagined that she might drown in them. The firelight cast its shadow along the hard line of his jaw, his mouth…

'Why is that, Miss Verey?'

'Because it is you that I…'

Jane's eyes closed. Her head rested against his shoulder. She thought she heard him say, 'You stopped at the most interesting moment, Miss Verey!' Then he was holding her even closer and she felt his mouth brush her hair with the lightest of touches. She could not protest, could not even open her eyes. She felt warm and safe and by the time he had carried her up to her room, Jane was fast asleep.

It was very late when Jane awoke the following day. The sounds of the voices upraised in the kitchen floated up to her room mingled with the rumble of wheels on the cobbles of the yard. Jane stretched. She felt warm and content—until she remembered the events of the previous evening. She had been very sleepy…what had she said? She must have fallen asleep in the parlour and Alex… She was in her shift!

With growing horror, Jane saw that her clothes were neatly folded over the back of a wooden chair by the window. She closed her eyes in dread. Certainly she could not ask...

'Miss Verey!' The landlord's daughter had knocked briskly at the door and stuck her head inside. 'Your mother is asking for you and your brother is already arrived! Do you care for some breakfast, madam?'

When Jane reached her mother's chamber it was to find Lady Verey was up and dressed, partaking of breakfast and in a surprisingly buoyant mood.

'I am very well, my love,' she said in answer to Jane's inquiry, 'though the arm pains me a little. Of all the foolish accidents! Your brother is come to take me back to Town and the Duke has graciously agreed to drive you—'

Jane flushed bright red. 'Oh, no, Mama! I am persuaded that it would be better for me to accompany you and Simon to tend to your comfort—'

'Your mother will be more comfortable with the additional space in the carriage,' a smooth voice said from the doorway behind her. 'Lady Verey, your servant, ma'am! I can scarce believe I find you looking so well!'

Lady Verey fluttered becomingly. 'Oh, your Grace! So unfortunate an accident, but I thank you for all your help...'

'It was nothing,' Alex said easily, smiling at her. His gaze travelled to Jane and lingered. 'Good morning, Miss Verey. I believe you were just evincing a desire to be rid of my company?'

Jane dropped a slight curtsy. She did not choose to

be diplomatic that morning. It was so very frustrating to find that he was ahead of her at every turn!

'Just so, your Grace. Excuse me, I must go and greet my brother.' Before Lady Verey could reprove her she had slipped from the room.

When the time came to leave, it seemed that her feelings were not to be taken into account. Lady Verey and Simon took the carriage whilst Alex handed Jane up into his phaeton as though she had never expressed any disinclination for his company. Jane found herself so annoyed by this that she was uncharacteristically cross and silent. Her feelings were already rubbed raw by a self-consciousness in Alex's presence and her mind was worrying over the events of the previous night. Had he...? No, surely it was impossible... The memory of the pile of neatly folded clothes came back to haunt her. No one would know, least of all herself...

'I do believe that you are quite out of charity with me this morning, Miss Verey!' Alex said cheerfully, observing her stony face. 'You must allow that it is better for Lady Verey to have plenty of space. She needs a cushion for her arm, you see—'

'I am perfectly aware that my mother requires not to be squashed!' Jane snapped. 'It is simply—'

'That you did not wish to travel with me. I am aware. What can I have done to have given you so strong a dislike for me?'

Jane turned her face away and gazed unseeingly at the passing countryside. Her tormentor was not silenced.

'Perhaps you are regretting the things you said last night,' he said softly. 'Such an avowal of affection...'

Jane turned to him, her hazel eyes huge and stricken. Oh, why could she not remember? 'I made no such avowal!' she said hotly. 'How dare you, sir!'

'Oh, but indeed you did!' Alex took his eyes off the road to consider her flushed and furious face. 'You said that you could not marry my brother because—'

'I beg you,' Jane said hastily, in a fierce tone that belied her words, 'not to put me to the blush, your Grace! I swear you are no gentleman!'

He shot her a smile. 'Gentleman enough to leave you to the tender mercies of the landlord's daughter rather than acting as lady's maid myself! Though the temptation—'

Relief and anger washed through Jane in equal measure. Why did he have to be so provoking? And how could this laughing man be the same austere Duke of Delahaye whom everyone described as cold and remote?

'Your Grace!' she began stormily. 'Pray show a little decorum!'

'Very well.' Alex lowered his voice. 'We shall talk about it another time.'

'I have no ambition for it,' Jane said, turning her shoulder. Her hands were shaking and she pressed them together to still them. It was with the most profound relief that she realised they were already driving through the outskirts of London and she did not speak again until they were in Portman Square.

'I wondered if I might call on you tomorrow,' Alex was saying, effortlessly casual, as he helped her down from the phaeton. 'Would ten o'clock be convenient? It is early, I know, but then my business is urgent.'

'I...yes, of course.' Jane tried to think of an excuse

and totally failed to do so. More than half of her wanted to see him, but the timid part of her was still urging her to withdraw before it was too late. 'That would be quite convenient.'

'Good.' Alex smiled at her and the glimmer of humour in his dark eyes set her pulse awry. He kissed her hand. 'Until tomorrow, then, Miss Verey.'

It was good to be home again. Whilst the servants fussed over Lady Verey and led her away to rest, Jane cornered Simon over a cup of chocolate in the drawing-room. She had thought that her brother looked strained and tired in the brief time she had seen him before their departure from the inn. Now she was shocked as the harsh morning light showed just how hollow-eyed he had become.

'How did you fare whilst we were away, Simon?' she asked lightly, only the expression in her eyes betraying her concern.

'Very ill, Janey.' Simon's smile and his use of the childhood diminutive confirmed her worst fears.

'Have you seen her?'

Simon turned away, making a pretence of scanning the *Morning Post*. 'I collect that you mean Thérèse? No, I have not seen her. She would not see me!' He turned back sharply and his face was full of so much misery that Jane could feel his unhappiness. 'For the first three days they continued to deny that she lived there, then they said that she would not see me and finally she told me to take my foolish flowers and leave her alone!'

'You sent her flowers?'

'By the barrowful,' Simon confirmed grimly, casting the paper aside. 'She didn't want them, nor the food I sent, nor any of the things I could offer...' His mouth tightened. 'So in the end I thought, what's the point? She don't want me but there must be hundreds who would! So I thought to throw myself into the party spirit—'

'Oh, Simon!'

'—and I've been entertaining myself ever since! Plenty of pretty girls out this season, and ladies of another sort for other sport—' He caught himself up. 'Sorry, Janey, feeling a bit rough...'

'Go and sleep it off,' his sister advised unsympathetically. 'And you need a shave!'

'No time!' Simon said, with an attempt at a jaunty grin. 'I'm engaged to take the divine Miss Shearsby driving!'

Jane sighed. She was hardly fooled by Simon's assumed insouciance and knew it hid a deeper pain. It seemed that Thérèse de Beaurain simply did not wish to know and, Jane thought, there was no possible way to make her care for Simon if she did not.

'What about you?' her brother asked, pausing in the doorway. 'Am I addressing the future Lady Jane Delahaye?'

Jane looked affronted. 'No, Simon! I have *told* you that I will not marry Lord Philip! I have told everyone and no one is listening!'

'Thought that was the point of your trip to the country,' Simon said, tactlessly but with truth. 'Mama seemed to think that it would bring matters to a head! She and Lady Eleanor were banking on it!'

'Well, they will have to accept it! Philip is to marry Sophia—I have it all planned!'

Simon raised an eyebrow. 'Then you may solve the problem by marrying Alex,' he said easily. He eyed his sister's sudden blush with frank interest. 'Oh, dear, it seems I have struck a nerve there, Janey! Well, you have my blessing! I should like above all things to have Alex as a brother-in-law!'

'Oh, go away!' Jane hustled her brother out of the room, suddenly anxious to see the back of him. Simon knew her well enough to suspect the truth and she did not want him to realise just how much his suggestion had appealed to her. 'Go and devastate poor, unsuspecting Miss Shearsby! Though why she would wish to be seen with so disreputable a character defeats me!'

Alex Delahaye was not at Lady Sefton's ball that night. Sophia Marchment and Philip Delahaye danced with each other three times, to the delight of the gossips. Simon Verey behaved quite scandalously, flirting with any lady who glanced in his direction, and Jane Verey sat quietly in a corner, wondering what on earth the Duke was going to say to her the following morning.

Chapter Eleven

The following day was bright but cooler than previously and Jane was glad of the warmth of her red riding habit when she and the Duke of Delahaye rode out. She had been awake for hours, but in the event, Alex was early and he brought with him a horse from the livery stables.

'We can take the phaeton if you prefer, Miss Verey, but I wondered if you would like to ride,' he said. 'You seemed to enjoy your country rides so much at Malladon that I took the liberty of bringing what I hope is a suitable mount for you!'

He had chosen a horse that was sufficiently spirited to keep Jane occupied through the busy streets and they did not speak much until they reached the quieter environs of the Park. It was still very early and there were few people about. Jane noticed that Alex had instructed the groom to ride a long way back, where there was no danger of them being overheard.

The cool, green expanse was very welcoming and Jane had to curb a sudden urge to gallop away.

'Thank you for thinking of this, sir!' she said spontaneously. 'It was a delightful idea!'

Alex smiled. 'I thought that you might enjoy it, Miss Verey. It is not quite the same as being in the country, but nevertheless...'

'Nevertheless, it brings a sense of freedom that one seldom finds in Town,' Jane allowed, her eyes sparkling. 'It is very pleasant to escape sometimes!'

'The country has, perhaps, fewer diversions?'

'Just different ones, I think,' Jane said, smiling a little.

'Some might argue that Town is more exciting.'

'That,' Jane said serenely, 'depends on one's interests. If excitement is derived from creeping through the streets cloaked in black and carrying a pistol—'

Alex burst out laughing. 'You will not let me forget that, will you, Miss Verey?'

Jane looked at him. Today he was in black again, but with a very different appearance from the disreputable and sinister figure of that strange night. His jacket was cut by a master and fitted without a wrinkle. His linen was a pristine white and his boots had a high polish.

Jane privately thought that he looked devastatingly handsome.

'How is Simon?' Alex was asking. 'Did his suit prosper whilst we were away?'

Jane shook her head. 'No, indeed, it goes very ill for him. Mademoiselle de Beaurain has told him to take his attentions elsewhere!'

'I am sorry to hear that. I imagine it must have made him very unhappy.'

Jane looked resigned. 'Oh, he pretends that he does not care and, indeed, to see him at Lady Sefton's ball last night one would have believed it! However I think that he feels it very keenly... It is too bad! Everyone is in love with the wrong person!'

Alex cast her a sideways glance. 'Everyone, Miss Verey?'

'Oh, Simon with Thérèse and Philip with Sophia!' Jane said, greatly daring. 'Matters so seldom progress in the way one would wish!'

'Very true. And what of yourself, Miss Verey?'

Jane, who had steeled herself to answer this question suddenly found it more difficult than she had imagined.

'I?'

'Who are you in love with?'

Jane blushed and hated herself for it. 'I am in love with no one, sir. I told you when we—I told you that night at the inn...'

'Of course,' Alex said smoothly. 'I remember! This touches on the matter I wished to discuss with you, Miss Verey. Would you care to dismount? I will ask Dick to walk the horses.'

Jane looked dubious. 'I am not at all sure that we should. We have been away some time. Mama will be worrying—'

'I will square matters with her later. I must crave your indulgence, Miss Verey. This is important.' There was an imperative note in Alex's voice. He had already dismounted, summoning the laggardly groom with a wave of the hand. As the man took the horse's bridle, Alex helped Jane down.

'Walk the horses for a while, would you, Dick? Thank you...'

He offered Jane his arm and they walked slowly along one of the winding paths. There was no sound but for the clop of the horses' hooves, growing more distant as the groom led them away.

'I no longer wish to promote the match between Philip and yourself, Miss Verey,' Alex said abruptly. 'You mentioned Philip's affection for Miss Marchment and indeed, I have seen you promoting that romance most zealously! So...' He shrugged. 'I am not entirely heartless! I realise that you and my scapegrace brother are very amicable, but scarcely romantically inclined! Whereas Philip behaves as though Miss Marchment is the very pattern of perfection! So I will give the match my blessing!'

Jane felt as though her breath had been taken away. To have connived and schemed for just such an outcome and then to have it put so suddenly into her hands... It was scarcely to be believed.

'Sophia is indeed the sweetest girl,' Jane said warmly, 'and if you are to allow them to wed then I must give you credit for greater sensibility than I had previously thought, your Grace! I am quite overwhelmed!'

'Thank you,' Alex said gravely. He was smiling a little. 'You have not, however, heard the second part of my proposal.'

'There is more?'

'Indeed. In permitting Philip to wed Miss Marchment I am no longer able to honour the commitment I made to my grandfather. Would you permit me to explain a little of the background, explain why I wished for the match at all?'

'Of course,' Jane said, feeling a little at sea. If Alex was no longer interested in the Verey-Delahaye alliance, why should he need to explain? She was suddenly uncertain where this was leading.

Alex squared his shoulders. 'I believe that it was our paternal grandfathers who formed the idea that an union between the two families would be beneficial. They were both in the diplomatic service and met in Vienna. Did you know that they had formed a friendship?'

Jane shook her head. 'My father's father died when I was but young, sir. I had no idea he planned a grand family alliance!'

'Unfortunately there was no one appropriate in our parents' generation,' Alex said drily. 'My own mother and father were already married and I believe the other children were either promised or unsuitable in some way! Nevertheless, the grandfathers were not deterred!'

'They planned to skip a generation?'

Alex smiled. 'Precisely, Miss Verey! My grandfather summoned me before he died and acquainted me with his plan. I was already married but Philip was still a bachelor and already giving cause for concern with his wild antics. My grandfather knew that your parents had married late and that you were still in the schoolroom. Nevertheless, he suggested that it might be a good match. So I went to Ambergate to find out whether your father liked the idea.'

'I know.' Jane said. 'I saw you.'

Alex looked startled. 'You *saw* me? At Ambergate?'

'Four years ago,' Jane said. 'I saw you one night going along the corridor past my room.'

For a moment the memory of the night came back to her: the dancing candle flame, the dark stranger, the legend… Jane felt suddenly resentful, all her bitterness over the arrangement with her father flooding back, reminding her that Alex had sought to use her as a pawn to further his own ends.

'I suppose you had come to look me over and negotiate with my father as though I were some commodity!' she said sharply.

Alex winced. He drove his hands into his jacket pockets. 'I concede that the plan was ill conceived. I was trying to honour my grandfather's wishes and find a solution to Philip's wildness. I did not think—' He broke off, to resume:

'I must be honest and admit that I thought nothing of your hopes and wishes! Oh, it was old-fashioned of me to wish to arrange a match, but I had the best of intentions. I really thought that it would be the making of Philip!'

'And so it will be,' Jane said stoutly, 'immeasurably more so now that he has been allowed to choose his own bride!'

'Yes.' Alex slanted a look down at her. 'I suppose my reasoning was at fault in thinking that marriage was the means to compel Philip to settle down. He would no more accept a forced match than he would reform of his own accord! Yet now that he has attached himself sincerely to a young lady, he is a changed character!' Alex shook his head ruefully. 'I admit that I have made some bad mistakes in this business.'

Jane was prey to mixed feelings. It seemed from Alex's words that matters were now settled. Philip and Sophia would be permitted to marry and Jane would no longer be obliged to scheme and plan to avoid her fate. She could return to Ambergate, perhaps, and then she would never need to see the Duke of Delahaye again...

'Of course,' Alex was continuing, 'that leaves me with the difficulty of resolving my pledge to my grandfather. Then I thought that if one plan could not suffice, another might.'

Jane realised that they had stopped walking. They were in the shadow of a huge clump of cedars and the figure of the groom seemed suddenly far away. There was no one else in sight. Her throat had gone dry. She could read his intentions in his face...

'Oh, no...'

Alex gave her a whimsical smile. 'Is it so horrifying a prospect, Miss Verey? You must be quite honest, as I know you can be! You do not wish to marry me? It is such a neat solution!'

The breeze caressed Jane's hot cheeks. Her mind was racing.

'Oh, I could not! I am...you are so—' She stopped before she could say anything she regretted. She was not entirely sure what she had meant to say. For all her feelings and half-formed wishes, the whole idea was so shocking, so sudden, that she could not comprehend it. Yet Alex was looking quite composed, almost lazily amused, as though her confusion pleased him.

'Oh!' Jane burst out. 'This is so like you! To replace one outrageous suggestion with one even more monstrous! After all the trouble I went to—'

'To thwart me?' Alex was laughing openly now and it only added to Jane's distraction. 'But surely you did not wish to marry Philip?'

'No, but—' Jane almost stamped her foot with frustration. 'Nor did I plan to have to reject you, your Grace!'

'Then do not...' Alex had taken her gloved hand

in his and his touch was almost too much for Jane to bear. She realised that something strange was happening to her. The combined shock and the heady influence of Alex's presence threatened to sweep away her good sense. It would be thrilling to give in to her instincts and accept him. For a moment she revelled in the idea, before sanity intervened.

There were so many reasons to refuse him. He had admitted that he had proposed in order to fulfil the pledge to his grandfather. Then there had been his bitterness when he had spoken of his dead wife. Alex must have loved her very much, and who could compete with a ghost? Surely not a naïve girl of nineteen! And then there was Francine Dennery...

'What of Lady Dennery?' she said, suddenly forlorn, remembering the Beauty's flagrant charms.

Alex raised his black brows. 'You need not concern yourself over her,' he said cryptically. 'Lady Dennery will not be surprised at our betrothal.'

He was moving much too fast for Jane. Betrothal... She frowned a little at his presumption.

'I do not find that particularly reassuring, sir,' she said candidly. 'Do you imply that Lady Dennery would accept the situation and carry on as before, or that your association with her would be at an end?'

Alex gave her a wicked grin. 'Straight to the point, Miss Verey! Do *you* imply that Lady Dennery is my mistress?'

'I have no wish to discuss your precise relationship!' Jane snapped, fast losing her temper. 'My point was that I would not marry a man who would be unfaithful to me!'

Alex inclined his head. 'I respect your views and

you need have no concern on that score. I do not intend to be unfaithful to my wife!'

His wife… Jane realised that her question had given the false impression that she would accept. Drawing away a little, she turned to look at him. She had to put a stop to this now, before she became further entangled. Alex had viewed the marriage as a neat solution, and on that basis she had to decline. The balance would be too unequal otherwise—she loved him, but he saw her as a way out of a problem…

'I am sorry,' she said formally. 'I cannot accept you, your Grace.'

Alex's face was very still. Jane found herself studying him closely, committing to memory the strong lines of his face, the dark eyes that could lighten so easily to unexpected laughter… Her throat ached with tears as an intense love swept over her. Oh, if only he had said that he loved her!

'May I ask why you have refused?' he said at length, very quietly.

'Because…' Jane cleared her throat '…I understand that it would only be a match of convenience—'

'A match of convenience! What extraordinary ideas you do have, Miss Verey!' Alex stepped closer. 'Surely you must realise that I find you prodigiously attractive?'

Jane gave a despairing squeak. That was not what she had meant at all and now matters were taking a decidedly difficult turn. 'Oh, no, your Grace, that cannot be so! You are funning me! Please do not say any more!'

'Pray do not distress yourself, Miss Verey,' Alex murmured. 'Let me convince you of my good faith!'

Jane was aware that the situation was slipping from her grasp. She had witnessed Alex's potent charm on many an occasion but never imagined that there would be a serious need to defend herself against it. She put out her left hand to ward him off—he appeared to already have possession of her right—but he simply captured it in his and pulled her closer.

She knew that he would release her at once if she appeared truly distressed and yet she discovered that she had not real inclination to pull away from him.

He freed her hands only to draw her more closely into his arms and Jane found that, instead of pushing him away, she was leaning confidingly against his chest. His cheek grazed hers, rough against the softness of her skin and Jane gave a pleasurable shiver, breathing the delicious male scent. She had a sudden urge to turn her face against his neck and inhale deeply until she was intoxicated with the essence of him, but Alex was kissing her already and this time it was very different from at Malladon. Gone was the gentleness, to be replaced with a real urgency that was both exciting and a little bit frightening at the same time.

The stretch of parkland, the tall trees and the cool breeze all receded from Jane's consciousness. She was aware of nothing beyond the powerful circle of Alex's arms and the melting warmth that was invading her body.

Her lips parted instinctively beneath the skilful pressure of his own and Jane felt herself tremble in response. Nor did Alex seem unaffected by the embrace as she had thought him at Malladon, for she could feel the racing of his heart where her hand still rested against his chest. She slid her arms up around his neck and felt him draw her all the closer until she was resting against the whole length of his hard, muscular body. The kiss deepened into a dizzying spiral of desire, easing after an immeasurable time only as Alex let her go a little to catch his breath.

Jane swayed a little within his arms, aware that she would have fallen without his support. She was still trembling and her blood was alight with a strange mixture of heat and ice-cold excitement.

Jane struggled to free herself, suddenly overcome with emotions she could not understand.

'Oh, please—'

Alex let her go at once. He was pale and breathing hard, and for a moment Jane saw the reflection of an emotion in his eyes that she found deeply disturbing.

'I am sorry,' he said expressionlessly. 'I forgot that—' He broke off. 'I did not intend to frighten you, Jane.'

'I was not frightened precisely,' Jane said, incurably truthful, 'only a little shocked to know how it felt. I am told that young ladies should not be subject to violent emotions…' She looked away, too shy to admit that she had found the encounter as enjoyable as it was disturbing.

Alex tucked her hand through his arm and steered them back towards the path. 'I have heard that said too, and thought it so much nonsense!' he said cheerfully. 'I should feel flattered and more encouraged were you to admit to taking pleasure in the experience!'

'Oh!' Jane cast a dubious look at him. 'More encouraged?'

There was a wicked glint in Alex's eyes. 'My dear Jane, I wish to repeat my actions on plenty of future occasions, but will not do so if you hold them in strong dislike! However, I cherish a hope that my advances were not entirely unwelcome, and as your fiancé—'

Jane felt her spirits sink a little. The delicious pleasure of Alex's embrace had helped her to forget temporarily that he had other motives for the marriage, motives that had little to do with love. She frowned a little. For a moment she hesitated on the edge of confiding her concerns in him, then there was a spattering of gravel and she realised that the groom had returned with the horses. A carriage crossed her line of vision, then two ladies on horseback. The Park was beginning to wake up.

'Have you changed your mind?' Alex asked quietly, as they turned the horses towards the gate. 'Will you marry me?'

Jane's troubled green gaze searched his face. 'I do not know…I am not sure…there are reasons…'

She saw the shadow that touched his eyes, before he said with constraint, 'Is that a definite refusal, Miss Verey?'

'No, I—' Jane knew instinctively that she had hurt him, although Alex's dark face was carefully expressionless.

'I am sorry,' she said wretchedly. 'I need to think. If you could allow me a little time…'

'Of course,' Alex said with a scrupulous courtesy that was somehow chilling.

They rode back to Portman Square in silence.

'I have business to attend to,' Alex said, still with the same cool civility, after he had helped Jane down and the groom had set off back to the stables, 'but I shall hope to see you tomorrow night, Miss Verey.

Perhaps you will be able to give me an indication of how long you need to consider my offer.'

Jane's face crumpled as she tried to hold back the tears that threatened to ambush her. Somehow this had all gone wrong and she felt dreadful, as though she had casually inflicted some great hurt on Alex and had damaged for ever the relationship between them. She could not understand how it had happened.

She put an instinctive hand on his sleeve. 'Wait!'

'Yes, Miss Verey?' Alex said, with the same distant politeness.

'I...that is...please be careful,' Jane said, her words coming out in a rush. 'If your business is part of what has gone before, you could be in danger and—' She knew she was making a wretched mess of this and felt even more desolate.

Surprisingly, Alex's grim expression had lightened considerably. One gloved hand covered Jane's briefly as it rested on his sleeve.

'Thank you for giving me hope, Miss Verey,' he said very softly. Before Jane could even guess his intention, his arms had gone around her and he had kissed her hard on the mouth.

She was released, breathless and ruffled. 'Oh! For shame! In the street!'

Jane had seen the stealthy movement behind at least half a dozen curtains, including the ones of Lady Verey's drawing-room.

'Yes,' Alex said, his good humour apparently restored, 'you will have to marry me now, Miss Verey! Think about it! I will see you tomorrow!'

And with a deplorably cheerful wave of the hand he turned and strolled away.

* * *

Simon Verey, crossing London Bridge, saw a slender, fair girl hurrying along in front of him, a covered marketing basket over her arm. He started forward. It had happened so many times in the last two weeks—he would see a fair girl and hurry to accost her, only to find that he was confronting a total stranger. But this time...

'Thérèse!'

She turned and he was looking into the cornflower blue eyes that he remembered. His heart started to race.

'Thérèse,' he said again. He put out a hand but she flinched back. Her eyes were bright and angry.

'Leave me alone! Why must you be forever pestering me? Coming to the house...upsetting *Maman*...fine gentlemen asking for her daughter.' Her tone was scornful. 'What do you think I am, *monsieur*? Because I am penniless and you are a rich lord—'

Simon was stung by the injustice of this. 'That's not fair! I only wanted to see you, to talk to you.'

She shrugged carelessly. 'We have nothing to say to each other, *monsieur*! If you are in earnest, the best thing you can do for me is leave me alone!'

She turned to go, but Simon caught her arm, beyond caution. 'It cannot be true that you do not care! I cannot be alone in feeling thus!'

For a frozen minute they stared into each other's eyes and he saw the doubt and the hesitation and, behind it all, a flash of emotion so vivid that he almost pulled her into his arms there and then. He knew that he had not misread her. Thérèse did care, but—

'It is immaterial how I feel,' Thérèse said, so

fiercely that Simon almost stepped back, yet so softly he could barely hear. 'There are reasons why I cannot have anything to do with you, my lord—'

'Is the gennelman bothering you, miss?' asked a burly carter, and Simon dropped Thérèse's arm, suddenly conscious of the attention their raised voices had attracted.

'No, I thank you.' Her composure was flawless. The moment of intimacy, when he had seen into her soul, might never have been. Simon felt triumph and despair in equal measure. 'The gentleman is about to go. Good day, sir,' and she walked away across the bridge, without a backward glance.

Henry Marchnight called late at Haye House that night and was met by Tredpole the butler, wearing his most lugubrious expression.

'I regret that his Grace is unwell, my lord,' Tredpole said, his face completely blank. 'He is not receiving visitors.'

Since Alex had never had a day's illness in all the time Henry had known him, he treated this with polite incredulity.

'Come now, Tredpole, you can tell me the truth. Where is he?'

'His Grace is in the study, my lord, but—' Tredpole shook his head '—I would counsel against disturbing him!'

Light dawned. 'You mean that he is foxed, Tredpole?' Henry hesitated, suddenly aware that he might never have seen Alex ill, but he certainly had never seen him drunk.

The butler cleared his throat delicately. 'A little

cast away, my lord, and I have seldom seen him in a blacker temper—'

The door of the study crashed open making the hall chandelier vibrate. Alex, his hair ruffled, his clothes dishevelled, was leaning against the door jamb.

'Tredpole? Where the devil are you, man? I'll have died of thirst before I get that second bottle! Who the hell are you chattering to?'

Henry thought that he saw the butler wince. It was impossible to imagine the stately Tredpole chattering to anyone.

'Lord Henry Marchnight is here, your Grace,' the butler said austerely. 'I was informing him that your Grace was not receiving.'

'And I was telling him not to be such a damned fool!' Henry said cheerfully. 'How are you, Alex? Think I'll share that second bottle with you!'

Tredpole moved noiselessly away to fetch a second glass. Alex stood aside with exaggerated courtesy to allow Henry to precede him into the room and gestured him to a chair.

'Well, Henry?'

Henry raised his eyebrows. 'My apologies for interrupting you! Seems you wish to go to the devil on your own!'

That won him a brief smile. Alex pushed the brandy bottle towards his friend.

'I hear you were riding in the Park with Miss Verey this morning,' Henry continued.

The smile vanished. Alex frowned. 'You take a keen interest in Miss Verey's concerns, Harry!'

Henry, his unspoken question resolved, relaxed and sat back in his chair. 'Don't be an arrant fool, Alex!

I love Jane like a sister, but that's all!' He paused, then added, 'Unlike you!'

Alex did not deny it. 'How the hell did this happen?' he said morosely.

Henry poured himself a generous measure. 'No one is immune, Alex,' he said. 'Your mistake was probably to think that you were.'

Alex ran a hand through his hair, still frowning darkly. 'I told her that I had decided it was a mistake to force Philip to marry her. Do you think Philip genuinely cares for Miss Marchment, Harry?'

'Yes, I am sure that he does. Everyone has observed it. What did Jane say to that?'

'She was very happy. Not so happy when I put forward my alternative, which was that she should marry me.' Alex drank deeply. 'What should I do, Harry?'

'Don't ask me, old fellow. You know I'm the last person to ask for advice!' Despite the joking tone there was a deeper bitterness in Henry's voice.

'I collect you refer to Lady Polly Seagrave? You could put that to rights if you chose!'

Henry shrugged. 'Maybe so, but we are talking of your romantic difficulties, not mine! I do not immediately perceive the problem, however. You proposed to Miss Verey and—what happened? Did she refuse you?'

'Not outright,' Alex acknowledged, 'but who wants an unwilling bride? Not I! I am to wait until tomorrow to know my fate!'

'Jane is scarcely indifferent to you,' Henry said with a grin, savouring his brandy. 'And she is very young. Give her time!'

'I have—until tomorrow. This is damnably hard on my pride!'

Henry laughed. 'Come on, Alex, your pride can take it! I see that you intend to spend the entire time three sheets to the wind!'

Alex grinned reluctantly. 'It seems a sound enough plan, Harry! But perhaps a game of faro would be an alternative.'

Henry inclined his head. 'Why not? I may stand a chance of winning for once!'

And they settled down to make a night of it.

Chapter Twelve

The following day saw huge excitement in Portman Square. Lord Philip had arrived at an improbably early hour and had asked, with barely restrained impatience, to speak with Sophia alone. He had followed this with a brief meeting with Lady Verey, after which both she and Sophia erupted into the drawing-room, where Jane had been pretending to read.

'Oh, Jane!' Sophia burst out. 'It is so wonderful! The Duke has given Philip permission to pay his addresses to me and he has come at once to ask me to marry him! He is posting to Wiltshire in a couple of days to see my parents! Oh, Jane!'

'Jane, my dearest, dearest child!' Lady Verey cried simultaneously. 'I am so very happy for you! A Duke! Who would have thought it!'

Jane, who was hugging Sophia, eyed her mother with misgiving. 'Whatever can you mean, Mama?'

'Why, Lord Philip tells me that his brother wishes to marry you, you little goose! Surely that was the purpose of his meeting with you yesterday? Why did you say nothing to me? I knew he was developing a *tendre* for you! You are the most fortunate girl in all of London!'

Jane winced.

'Philip says that we are to be married in four weeks and that he cannot believe his good fortune!' Sophia burbled, her blue eyes huge. 'I have written at once to my mama, begging her to return to Town with him and help me to choose my bride clothes! You will help me too, won't you, Jane? Oh, Jane, we shall be sisters! I am so happy!'

'I told the Duke that I would not marry him,' Jane said.

There was a silence. Sophia's smile faded and she stepped back, staring at her friend in disbelief. Lady Verey turned pale. A pained spasm crossed her face.

'Jane? What are you saying?'

'I told the Duke that I would not marry him,' Jane repeated, wishing that the ground would open up and swallow her whole. It was not precisely true, but she did not want her mother becoming carried away and announcing the two engagements at the same time. Besides, her heart was sore that Alex had apparently disregarded their conversation and decided that the marriage would go ahead. Why had he told her that he would wait for her decision when he evidently intended to ride roughshod over her feelings?

Lady Verey eased her way backwards into the elegant Louis Quinze *fauteuil* and sat down rather hurriedly. Sophia went swiftly to the sideboard to fetch her a drink.

'Time…' Lady Verey said faintly. 'You need time… overpowered by excitement…accustomed to the idea… Thank you, child,' she added, as Sophia pressed the glass into her hand.

'I am sorry, Mama,' Jane said, taken aback that her mother had not pressed for the marriage more stridently. She seemed more saddened than angry. And Sophia—

'Oh, Sophy, I am so sorry!' Jane was overcome by remorse. 'I am so selfish! This is your special day and I would not spoil it for all the world!'

'Never mind that,' Miss Marchment said severely, showing her practical streak. 'I am so very happy that nothing could spoil my mood! But I wish to know what it is with you, Jane—we were all so very sure that you are in love with the Duke, you see!'

'All?' Jane repeated faintly, sitting down rather suddenly in much the same way as her mother had.

'Yes indeed, dear child!' Lady Verey sat forward, fixing her daughter with her wide myopic eyes. 'We have all observed it! Sophia and I were quite certain and even Lady Eleanor was coming round to the same view! And Sophia will tell you that Lord Philip is quite convinced that the Duke is smitten by you! Tell her, Sophia!'

'It's true, Jane!' Sophia said eagerly, coming to kneel by her friend's chair. 'Lord Philip said that Henry Marchnight, who as you know is well acquainted with the Duke, said that—'

'Wait, wait!' Jane besought. 'Has everyone been discussing this?'

'Well, yes, my love!' Lady Verey frowned a little. 'It was quite clear to me at Malladon that Lord Philip and Sophia were set fair to make a match of it and when I mentioned it to Eleanor Fane she told me that I was not to regard it, for she was sure that Alex Delahaye intended you for himself! They say that he has never attached himself to any woman since the death of his first wife,' Lady Verey said triumphantly, inadvertently making the situation worse. 'She was a great beauty, of course, but we all know that her behaviour scarcely graced the Delahaye name!'

'I believe, however, that the Duke was most sincerely fond of her,' Jane said dolefully.

Lady Verey stared. 'But since she is dead, my love, you have no need to think of her at all!'

There was a rustle and Sophia took Jane's hand in hers.

'Dear Jane,' she said gently, 'tell me what is the matter!'

'He does not love me, Sophy!' Jane let out a desolate sigh. 'He is still in love with his dead wife! Oh, I seem to amuse him and he indulges me, but I know he is only wishing to marry me to honour the pledge to his grandfather!' She turned to look at her mother. 'So I will *not* marry him, Mama, for all that I love him so much!'

Sophia's eyes were huge. 'So you do love the Duke! Jane, are you sure? He is so…frightening!'

'Oh, he is not so bad when one gets to know him a little! Yes, of course I love him!' Jane said crossly. 'I love him but he does not love me and I will *not* marry a man who does not love me!'

'Heigh ho!' Lady Verey said philosophically, getting to her feet. 'Fine sentiments, my girl, but you have forgotten a couple of things!'

Both girls looked up at her inquiringly. 'One!' Lady Verey enumerated. 'If Lord Philip has told us you are betrothed to Alex Delahaye he will have told everyone and it will be all over Town! Two! If Alex Delahaye wishes to marry you, I defy even you to withstand him!' And so saying, she swept grandly from the room.

Word of Sophia's engagement spread like wildfire that day, mainly because Lord Philip was proclaiming it from the rooftops. It was something of a sensation. The little country miss, with no money and nothing to recommend her but her pretty face, had caught the younger brother of a Duke who was a hardened rake to boot. Not everyone was kind. Jane knew that Sophia missed none of the nuances, though she smiled bravely throughout until her face ached. Nor was Jane able to do much to help, for many of the malicious remarks made reference to her own short and ill-fated courtship by Lord Philip, so that Jane ended up being the butt of the spite as well.

'Oh, it is not to be borne,' Sophia stormed, her good nature quite banished by a particularly sharp remark from Miss Brantledge. 'I declare I will make Philip live in the country all year round if people cannot curb their tongues! To suggest that I stole Philip from under your nose is the outside of enough!'

Both girls were feeling on edge by the time they reached Lady Marfleet's ball that evening. Jane was very grateful that Lord Philip had decided to postpone his departure to Wiltshire and was there to give her friend some much-needed support. Smoothing down her lilac and silver dress, she wondered whether Alex would also be there. It seemed like days rather than hours since she had parted from him and she knew that he would be awaiting her answer. Her nerves tightened at the thought.

'Miss Marchment!' Lady Jersey, malice incarnate, billowed up to them as soon as they entered the ballroom. 'I must congratulate you, you sly little puss! And Miss Verey! I hear your own triumph is to be announced soon! Such a relief for your dear mama that you will not be eclipsed by your friend!' And with a sharp little smile she glided away to spread the gossip.

It was, in fact, at least three-quarters of the way through the evening when the Duke of Delahaye finally deigned to make an appearance. Jane had not been short of partners and Lord Blakeney was particularly attentive. Nevertheless, she found that she had missed Alex's company more than she had imagined. It did not make her feel any happier, especially when her first view of him was with Lady Dennery hanging on his arm and whispering in his ear. Jane turned a particularly brilliant smile on Lord Blakeney, who blinked with surprise.

'Is this not most enjoyable, my lord?' she gushed, making sure that her smile was even broader as they whirled past the Duke and his fair companion. 'I declare I could dance all night!'

''Pon my word, Miss Verey, I could partner you the whole time too!' Blakeney said, quite carried away by her enthusiasm. 'Splendid idea! Are you free for the next?'

The next dance was a progressive country dance which Jane had intended to keep free for a well-earned rest. Now, seeing Lady Dennery persuading Alex on to the floor, she scorned the idea. So this was what he meant when he said that she should not concern herself with Lady Dennery! He intended to carry on as he had before and she was supposed to close her eyes to it! The hurt and anger rose inside her.

It was some time before the movement of the dance

brought her together with Alex and by then Jane had
had plenty of time to think about how she would deal
with him. Accordingly, she gave him the very
slightest of acknowledgements when he greeted her
and she smiled ravishingly at Lord Blakeney further
down the set.

'How do you do, your Grace? I was—' Again she
broke off as Blakeney passed in front of her and she
paused to exchange a few words.

Alex was speaking. Jane turned a vague, question-
ing face to him. 'I beg your pardon, your Grace, I
was not attending…'

'No.' Alex sounded quite expressionless. 'I was
only observing that Blakeney is a universal favourite!
Only last week it was Miss Dalton who was waxing
poetic about him!'

'Oh, he is most charming!' Jane agreed airily.
'Lord Henshaw has also been most attentive this evening—'

'Spare me a recital of your admirers, Miss Verey,'
Alex said, with the first hint of irritation he had
shown. 'I had thought to claim the right to banish
such suitors!'

Jane raised her brows. 'Had you, your Grace?'

It was the perfect moment for Blakeney to claim
her again, as the figure brought him back to her side
and obliged Alex to move on. For the rest of the
dance she was aware of his inscrutable dark gaze resting on her from time to time and there was something
calculating in it that made her very nervous.

The dance ended and Jane very prettily accepted
Lord Blakeney's escort back to her mother's side.
They did not gct far.

'Sorry to cut you out, old fellow,' the Duke of Delahaye drawled, blocking their way, 'but Miss Verey is promised to me for the next. Miss Verey...' There was a very definite challenge in his eyes.

Jane picked up the gauntlet, taking his arm a little gingerly and allowing him to steer her to an alcove at the side of the dance floor.

'Now, Miss Verey,' Alex said pleasantly, 'you will explain to me why you are playing Blakeney on your line just to thwart me.'

Jane's lips closed tightly. 'I have no notion what you mean, your Grace. I am sure that it would be ungracious in me to deny Lord Blakeney my company when he seeks me out!'

'Indeed! It would do no harm for you to be a little more moderate in your undertakings! Blakeney, Henshaw, Farraday...you will soon have a name as a flirt!'

Jane's eyes narrowed. She had thrown Blakeney and Henshaw in his face and could therefore not complain if he reproached her for it, but poor Mr Farraday, who would not say boo to a goose...

'If we are speaking of flirtations, your Grace, you would do well to look to yourself!'

Alex caught her wrist in a tight grip. They had both forgotten the crowded ballroom and the press of people so close at hand.

'I collect that you mean to censure me for my relationship with Lady Dennery,' he said levelly. 'I should have realised that it was jealousy that prompted your remarks—'

Jane's eyes flashed. This was particularly provoking as it was true.

'I do not care if Lady Dennery wishes to rehearse

her *amours* before the whole Town! I only condemn your hypocrisy in ringing a peal over me!'

'And I do not care to see the likes of Blakeney hanging on your coat-tails! I shall take steps to prevent it in future!'

Their eyes met and held, locked in furious confrontation. Then Alex shook his head slightly.

'I cannot believe… Jane, you try my patience sorely, but I suppose my own behaviour is scarcely exemplary! To tell the truth, I met Lady Dennery in the ante-room, that is all. What I said this morning is true—you need have no concern for her! Now, admit you would not care what company I kept if you did not like me a little!'

The logic of this was hard to refute. His fingers had relaxed their grip and had slid down to take her hand in his. His touch was warm and seductive, reminding Jane of their encounter in the Park. She could feel a smile start to curve her lips.

'Your Grace—'

'Please call me Alex, now that we are betrothed.'

'Yes!' Jane said, suddenly remembering that she had an issue to raise with him. 'I understand that you have already told your brother that we are to wed! That was not well done, sir! I asked for a little time!'

'I know it.' The pressure of Alex's fingers had increased infinitesimally, sending quivers of sensation along Jane's nerves. 'You are mistaken, Jane. I said nothing to Philip, although he may have drawn his own conclusions when I gave my blessing on his match with Miss Marchment! I would not do that when I had given you my word that I would wait for your decision.' He stepped closer. 'Will you give me your answer now, Jane? I do most ardently hope that you will accept me...'

Jane felt as though she was trapped in the tantalising web of her feelings. Alex was smiling with a warmth that did strange things to her equilibrium; she could read in his eyes that he wanted to kiss her and she felt a little dizzy.

'Perhaps I will... But this is Sophia's night, not mine, your Grace. I would not wish to steal her thunder—'

His expression told her that he knew she had capitulated. She saw the blaze of triumph in his eyes, shadowed by a less definable emotion. Jane was swept by excitement followed by near-terror. Alex turned her hand over and kissed the palm, then a dry voice from beside them broke the spell.

'Alex, I am persuaded that you would not wish to draw any further attention to Miss Verey, at least not yet!' Lady Eleanor Fane said.

Alex tore his gaze away from Jane. 'As usual, you are quite correct, Aunt Eleanor,' he said abruptly. 'I will bid you goodnight, Miss Verey.'

'I assume that you have just agreed to make Alex the happiest of men,' Lady Eleanor said comfortably, tucking Jane's arm through hers and steering her towards Lady Verey. 'It is an open secret, particularly the way that the two of you looked this evening! When you were quarrelling I scarce knew whether it would end in tears or kisses! As good as a play, and good to see Alex on his high ropes when usually he is the most moderate of men!'

Jane smiled, accepted the approval and the good-tempered teasing, but a small, cold corner of her heart reminded her that one thing was missing. It seemed that, despite his pleasure at the engagement, the Duke of Delahaye was still not able to tell her that he loved her.

The following day was bright and summery enough to banish even the most melancholy of reflections. They were engaged for a trip to Richmond to watch a balloon launch and Lord Philip and the Duke had offered their escort, before Philip took himself off to Ambergate next morning.

They arrived in the country to discover a crowd already gathered, strolling in the sun and watching the stripy silk balloon rippling gently in the breeze. Four burly men were anchoring it to the ground with thick ropes. Jane jumped down from the phaeton, her troubles forgotten.

'Oh, how wonderful. I would so love to fly!'

'Why don't you stand in the basket and see what its like under the canopy, miss?' one of the aviators suggested. 'Here, let me give you a hand up the steps.'

A few of the crowd clapped as Jane stepped over the side and down into the well of the basket. After a moment, Alex followed her, jumping down inside. It was surprisingly roomy under the huge silk canopy, with strong leather straps that Jane imagined the aviators must hold on to during the flight. There was room for at least three people in the basket and the edge was so high that Jane could barely see over the top. She looked up into the balloon's canopy and wondered what it would be like to feel the ground drop away and watch the countryside receding below you.

A sudden gust of wind caught the canopy and

whipped under the basket. There was a shout and then the crowd was scattering, drawing back. For a moment Jane wondered what was happening and then she felt the edge of the basket tip up, throwing her to the floor. The basket started to drag across the field, lifting from the ground one moment, bumping over the tussocks the next as the wind filled the canopy.

'Oh!' Jane tried to scramble to her feet, but their progress was too rough to allow her to regain her balance. She felt as helpless as a rag doll, tumbled in a heap of petticoats on the floor, tossed from side to side.

'Hold on!' Alex had managed to grasp one of the leather straps in one hand and bent down to pull Jane closer. The basket lifted from the ground and with a whimper Jane clutched at his jacket, turning her face into his chest. Gone were her ambitions of being a fearless aviator. Suddenly solid ground seemed much more appealing.

The basket hit the ground for a final time, shaking Alex's grip from the strap so that he fell with Jane in a heap on the floor. There was silence. Silence and stillness. Jane opened her eyes. Above her the huge canopy was snagged on the branches of a tall oak and as she watched, it gradually crumpled down on top of them, blotting out the blue of the sky.

She felt as though she was covered in bruises, every bone in her body shaken from its socket. Her hat had come off and she had evidently sat on it at some point for it was completely flattened. Her hair was tumbled about her face and she suddenly became aware that her skirts were up about her knees, revealing far too much of her legs to Alex's appreciative gaze. She tried to sit up, only to find that the angle of the basket prevented it.

Jane pushed the hair out of her eyes and tried to straighten her clothing. Her dress had slipped from one shoulder, showing the upper curve of her breasts, and she was sure that she looked like the veriest Cyprian with her hair about her shoulders, her skirts riding up and her dress descending to meet it.

She turned her head to see Alex watching her with a lazy grin that made her heart skip a beat.

He was looking no less dishevelled than she, his black hair hopelessly tousled, his jacket creased and his neckcloth awry.

'You look very nice,' Alex said slowly.

The silk canopy descended with a sudden whoosh, throwing them into a twilight world. In the distance Jane could hear shouts and voices calling, but she paid no attention.

Alex put out one hand and tumbled her back into his arms. Before she could say a word his mouth came down on hers.

It was suddenly like another world, a fantasy world. The shock, the fear and the sudden relief combined in a heady brew. Instead of pushing him away, Jane found herself pulling Alex closer so that their tangled limbs were inextricably entwined. Her lips parted in invitation and she felt the same dizzy, melting sensation invade her limbs as though her whole body was just waiting for his touch.

The kiss deepened with a searing intensity but Jane was no longer afraid. She shivered as the dress slipped further from her shoulders and Alex's fingers skimmed her bare skin. Desire coursed through her. His mouth left hers to trace the line of her neck and the curve of her breast with agonising, irresistible slowness, pausing only as it reached the place where the last wisps of material still covered her. The excitement lit her blood with wildfire. Alex's mouth was rough and urgent as it returned to hers and Jane revelled in its sensuous demand. She had lost all concept of time or reality, only knowing the greatest relief and joy at being safe and in the arms of the man she loved.

Neither of them heard the voices or footsteps approaching and only came to their senses as the silk curtain lifted to reveal the anxious faces of the balloonists and half the crowd. Alex had sufficient time and presence of mind to straighten Jane's dress, but they were still in each other's arms when it seemed that they were surrounded by people exclaiming and crying and reaching in to the basket to help them out.

Alex picked Jane up and handed her out of the basket to the first of the waiting men. Her legs crumpled as she was put gently on the ground and when Alex jumped down and scooped her into his arms again, she made no demur. The fresh breeze cooled her hot cheeks and the bright light made her blink. Suddenly she could feel every ache and bruise, and she did not want to face the barrage of questions and the curious eyes of the crowd. She felt the tears come into her eyes and turned her face against Alex's shoulder. She was not sure whether it was reaction to the accident or the sudden realisation of what she had done that made her want to cry.

Alex strode across the field, making short shrift of the questions of the crowd. It was only when they reached Lady Verey and the others, almost prostrate with anxiety, that Alex allowed his pace to slow.

'Miss Verey is bruised and shocked but otherwise unhurt,' he said, giving a tearful Lady Verey his most reassuring smile. 'We must return home at once, for she needs to rest.'

'What a terrible thing to happen!' Lady Eleanor, normally so resilient, had aged visibly. 'When we saw that the men had had the ropes snatched from their hands, we thought you would take off straight into the sky!'

'Not without the burners going, ma'am,' Lord Philip said practically, 'but it must have been very unpleasant nevertheless. Alex, put her down here.' He gestured towards the seat of his carriage. 'Can you drive, or would you prefer someone to take your phaeton back for you? I notice your shoulder is giving you a little trouble.'

Alex hesitated. 'Thank you, Philip. I must confess that it pains me a little. If you could take my team, perhaps Blakeney would drive your curricle back?'

'I'm flattered you trust me with your cattle,' Philip said a little drily. 'I've been waiting for a chance to try my hand with them, although not, perhaps, under these circumstances! Lady Eleanor, perhaps you and Sophia could travel with me? Lady Verey, I am persuaded that you would wish to remain with your daughter? As would Alex, I make no doubt...'

Lady Verey was already in the carriage, chafing Jane's cold hands and peering into her daughter's face.

'No harm done,' Philip said bracingly, proving himself a staunch support in times of need. 'We'll have you all back in Portman Square in no time!'

Sophia bent to kiss her friend, her blue gaze troubled.

'Oh Jane,' she whispered, 'everyone is talking! They all saw the two of you in the balloon basket and…' she blushed '…they say that he was making love to you! Oh, Jane, you'll have to marry him now!'

Chapter Thirteen

'You'll have to marry him now.'

Jane slept deeply that night; when she awoke, Sophia's words were still ringing in her head. She slipped from her bed and moved across to the window, leaning on the sill. It was still early. The street was deserted and beyond the rooftops the sky was a pale, misty blue and very beautiful.

Jane sighed. She knew that what Sophia had said was true. To be found kissing and hugging in the basket of a hot-air balloon was an extraordinary circumstance that the *ton* would savour to the full. Alex had already made his declaration and now, for the sake of her reputation, the announcement would need to be made as soon as possible...

She opened the window and took a deep breath of the cool air. She ached a little from the balloon accident, but not as much as she had expected. Evidently she had been very lucky.

The house was silent. Jane could imagine what would happen once Lady Verey was awake. Her mother would erupt into her bedroom, insisting on a public announcement of the engagement forthwith, planning the wedding, talking and talking about bride clothes...

Jane dressed quickly and quietly. She had a few difficulties with the buttons of her dress but managed by twisting around as far as she could. It was hopeless to try to arrange her hair on her own, so she tied it back with a ribbon and bundled it under a chip bonnet. Folding her cloak over her arm, she went softly from the room and down the wide stairs.

A housemaid was scrubbing the doorstep and looked up, startled and taken aback, to see the young mistress out and about so early.

'Oh, miss—' she began, but Jane put a finger to her lips.

'Hush, Hetty! I shall not be gone long! Pray do not tell Mama...'

'But, Miss Jane—' the maid protested, only to find she was speaking to thin air. Jane's hurrying figure could just be seen, disappearing down the street and turning the corner. The maid watched dubiously, then, with a sigh, she returned to her scrubbing.

For several days, Jane had had in her mind a half-formed plan to go to Spitalfields and find Thérèse de Beaurain. Simon had maintained that he would not force his attentions on Thérèse since she quite evidently did not welcome them, but Jane loved her brother a great deal, knew that he was unhappy and was determined to try to help him. If Thérèse truly did not care, then Jane was prepared to accept that, but she could see that it would be easy for the French girl to misunderstand Simon's intentions. Jane was sure that she could make Thérèse realise that Simon was entirely honourable, and perhaps persuade her to agree to a meeting.

There was only one fly in the ointment and it was a formidable one. Jane knew that Alex would never agree to her visiting Spitalfields and, now that they were to be officially betrothed, she was sure she would never be able to slip away on her own. This was her only chance.

Jane had thought that it would be only a step to Spitalfields, but that was because she did not really know where it was. She turned down Oxford Street and, by the time she reached St Giles Circus, she felt as though she had been walking for hours. She was obliged to pause for a rest, for her feet had started to ache and, as the morning awoke and the pavements filled, she was starting to attract some curious glances. A young man driving a cart called across to her, but Jane raised her chin and turned haughtily away. She was now far from Portman Square and for the first time, the imprudence of her plan struck her.

'Cab, lady?'

A hansom had drawn up beside Jane. The driver, a fatherly-looking figure, was eyeing her with concern.

'Can I take you home, miss? You should not be wandering about on your own...'

Jane smiled. 'Thank you, sir. You can take me to Spitalfields, if you please.'

The driver looked dubious. 'It's no place for a young lady alone. Be sensible, ma'am, and go home. Where's it to be? Grosvenor Square? Queen's Square?'

For a moment Jane reflected crossly on her lack of foresight in forgetting to borrow some of Cassie's old clothes. It seemed that a young lady was as instantly recognisable on the streets of London as a Cyprian might be. She had not laid her plans particularly well this time, and felt keenly that Alex was to blame for this. She had become so preoccupied by him that it had left little room for other schemes.

'I have business with another lady in Spitalfields,' she repeated. 'Be so good as to take me there, sir.'

The driver scratched his head doubtfully. Then, clearly thinking that Jane was safer with his escort than without, he reluctantly agreed and they set off along High Holborn.

Jane watched in fascination as the streets passed by. Narrow cobbled alleys gave glimpses of cramped squares and tumbling buildings leaning towards each other. Shop signs swung in the breeze and sprawling taverns already seemed packed with humanity. Crowds jostled the coach, good-humoured in the sunshine, peering curiously into the interior. Jane could not have created more of a stir had she been preceded by a butler announcing her progress.

'This is Crispin Street, Miss,' the driver said, in tones of deepest disapproval. 'Whereabouts do you wish to me to set you down?'

Jane's throat was suddenly dry. 'I am not precisely sure—' she began, then broke off as she saw a fair girl emerging from a house a little way down the street.

'Oh, there she is! I am sure of it! I pray you…' she fumbled in her reticule for a coin '…wait for me here! I shall not be long!' She thrust the money into his hand and turned back to the street.

'Thérèse! Wait!'

The fair girl had been about to pass them by with no more than an inquiring look, but at Jane's words she hesitated a moment and her intensely blue eyes rested in puzzlement on Jane's face.

'*Mam'zelle?* I beg your pardon—do I know you?'

'No…yes!' Jane found that she seemed out of breath, her thoughts tumbling. It had all happened too quickly. How was she to find the words to explain? The cab driver was listening with unconcealed interest and a couple of passers-by had stopped to watch. Across the street, a portly man, bulging out of an embroidered waistcoat, lounged in a doorway and watched them out of the corner of his eye.

A frown wrinkled the girl's forehead as she considered Jane's simple white dress and elegant bonnet. 'I think you are a long way from home, *mam'zelle*… Perhaps you would be better to return.'

Jane thought that she was probably right. She suddenly felt very odd, cast adrift in an entirely unfamiliar world. Yet the stubbornness that had brought her this far would not allow her to give up now.

'I am Jane Verey,' she said clearly. 'I believe that you are acquainted with my brother Simon, Miss de Beaurain. I must speak with you.'

The girl's blue eyes had narrowed. 'You are his sister? Can he have sent you here? But no, it is impossible!'

She had started to turn away, but Jane caught her arm in desperation. 'Please! I beg you to listen to me!'

A murmur ran through the growing crowd. Thérèse eyed them with exasperation, her expression becoming even more irritated as it returned to Jane's flushed but determined face. 'Very well, Miss Verey! You had better come with me before they tear the clothes from your back! This way…'

She ushered Jane through a narrow doorway and

up a steep stair. The air was musty and dim out of
the sunshine, and Jane blinked as her eyes accustomed themselves to the comparative darkness.

There was one room only at the top of the stairs,
a long room resembling an attic, with bare boards and
high windows. To the side of the stairs was a table
with materials scattered across it—rich silks and taffetas in red and gold, a contrast to the bare austerity
of the room with its single chair and wooden bed
pushed up against the wall. The bed was occupied,
but Jane did not like to stare with ill-bred curiosity at
the recumbent figure.

'My mother is too ill to be disturbed,' Thérèse said
abruptly. 'I beg you to speak softly, Miss Verey, and
do not wake her! Now, how may I help you?'

Her tone was not encouraging. Jane looked about
her helplessly. She wondered suddenly whether she
was making a dreadful mistake, then she remembered
Alex's words. The proud daughter of the Vicomte de
Beaurain had already rejected one offer of help. She
would need every ounce of persuasion she possessed
to make Thérèse de Beaurain even listen to her.

Jane sat down on the workbench beside the dress
that was clearly Thérèse's latest commission. The
room was spotlessly clean and tidy, the floor swept
and the bedclothes neatly folded around the invalid
on the bed. Jane dragged her gaze away and found
Thérèse watching her with a mixture of pity and exasperation.

'I do not know what can bring you here,
mam'zelle,' the French girl said impatiently. 'I have
already told your brother, the good Lord Verey, that
I do not wish to encourage his interest. He has been
here—sitting in the street, begging entry to the house!

I cannot believe that he has sent you to plead his case!
I repeat, I have no wish be his lordship's mistress!'

The colour flamed in Jane's face. Thérèse's tone
had been heavily ironic, but there was anger in her
eyes—anger and a kind of hopelessness that Jane did
not understand. For two pins she would have rushed
from the house, but the memory of Simon's strained
and despairing face was before her eyes. She spoke
firmly.

'Mademoiselle de Beaurain, I beg you to hear me
out. Firstly, my brother has no notion that I have
sought you out today. I am here because I care about
his happiness and I thought—erroneously, perhaps—
that you might do so too. Secondly, I do not believe
that Simon ever suggested that you should become
his mistress! He is far too honourable a man to do
such a thing!' The sincerity in her voice rang out. 'I
thought that if I could see you…explain to you that
he was desperately unhappy…you might relent and
at least grant him an interview… He loves you!' she
finished desperately.

There was silence. Thérèsc had sat, head bent,
whilst Jane spoke, but now she looked up with a flash
of her blue eyes. 'Do you know who I am, Miss
Verey?'

'Yes! You are the daughter of the Vicomte de
Beaurain, who fled France at the Revolution! You
used to do sewing for Celestine and you were at the
masquerade ball at Lady Aston's, which was where
my brother fell in love with you! You are related to
General Sir John Huntington, who offended you by
trying to offer you charity! I assure you that I am
offering no such thing!'

This time there was reluctant humour in Thérèse's

voice. 'I believe you, Miss Verey! You are remarkably well informed! And is your brother similarly aware of my history?'

'No!' Jane spoke more hotly than she had intended. 'Simon knows nothing and cares even less! He is not concerned over your ancestry or current occupation! He would not care if you were a Duchess or a chambermaid! But I cannot convince you of that.'

A bout of coughing from the bed interrupted them and Thérèse jumped up, hurrying across to hold a beaker of water to her mother's lips. They spoke briefly in French, too softly for Jane to hear, then the Vicomtesse turned on her side, smothering another paroxysm of coughs in her pillow. Thérèse straightened the covers about her mother's form, then came back to Jane, a deep frown on her brow.

'Forgive me, Miss Verey, but I must ask you to leave now. My mother has need of more medicines and I was on my way to fetch them when you arrived.' Her gaze rested on the luxurious silk dress. 'I have my work to do, as you see. You have done your best for your brother, but—'

'Will you not see him at the very least?'

Thérèse was shaking her head. There was a mixture of frustration and anger visible on her face. 'Miss Verey, you do not understand—'

There was a peremptory knocking, then the door burst open to admit a florid man whose yellowing smile Jane immediately distrusted. He was well dressed in a rather gaudy manner, with lace at the throat and wrists, and although he affected the manner and pose of a gentleman, there was something vaguely threatening in his appearance. Jane immediately sensed something defensive in Thérèse's demeanour as the girl stood up, shielding her from his view.

The man executed a bow. 'How d'ye do, my lady? I am come as promised to collect my debt!'

'I told you that the money would not be available before Tuesday,' Thérèse said calmly, but Jane thought she detected a hint of nervousness in her voice. She gestured towards the table. 'I have the work to finish before I am paid and only then can I pay you!'

The gentleman did not seem convinced. He paced the boards, walking over to peer with ill-concealed curiosity at the figure on the bed.

'I see your mother is not in plump currant,' he observed unctuously. 'How would it be if I sent out for the medicine for her—at a price?'

Thérèse cast Jane a swift look. She spoke stiffly. 'I have told you before, sir, that the price is too high for me!'

The gentleman stepped neatly around Thérèse and stopped before Jane. His gooseberry-green eyes, bloodshot and slightly protuberant, appraised her with sharpened interest. With a sudden jump of the heart Jane recognised him. This, she was sure, was the man she had seen at Vauxhall advancing towards Alex with a knife in his hand. He had been with Thérèse when she and Simon had seen them in the gardens, but later he had been alone, creeping down the dark alleys with murder in his mind... She shrank back.

'Barely saw you there, my dear!' the man was saying cheerfully. 'Thérèse, introduce me to you friend!'

'My friend was just leaving, sir,' Thérèse said, and this time there was no mistaking the sharp anxiety in her tone.

'Not so swift, my sweet!' There was an edge to the unctuous voice now. 'So charming a companion! Pray make me known to her!'

Thérèse paused. 'You must excuse us, Mr Samways. Your money will be ready on Tuesday as agreed. Now, by your leave—'

The gentleman stepped forward and grasped Jane's sleeve. She came to her feet with a gasp of shock. There was no mistaking the cupidity and excitement on his face.

'I do believe that you have the real thing here, Thérèse, my dear! Who is she—some society lady come to consult about a new dress? But no...' he peered closely into Jane's face and she could smell his stale breath '...she is too young! A golden child! A pretty pigeon for the plucking!'

'You mistake, Mr Samways,' Thérèse spoke hurriedly. 'My friend is nothing and no one! She cannot interest you—'

'On the contrary!' The gentleman's eyes were avid on Jane's face. 'She interests me extremely! There must be an anxious family somewhere and I am determined to take care of her for them!'

'You will not hurt her!'

There was taut anxiety in Thérèse's voice. Jane, only part-understanding, grabbed her cloak and tried to step past the gentleman. He was too quick for her, grasping her arm.

'A moment, my dear! You are too hasty!' He bent his face close to hers. 'Who are you, eh?'

'I am no one, sir, as Miss de Beaurain has said,' Jane said hurriedly, a catch in her voice. 'I beg you to let me go now! I will be missed!'

'Why, that's just what I'm saying!' Jane could not

mistake the menace underlying his voice now. 'There'll be those who'll pay handsomely to get you back, my dear! Now, be a good girl and tell me who they are! The sooner you do, the sooner you'll be going home!'

Jane's eyes met Thérèse's in a look of horror. It seemed impossible that her errand had brought her into such sudden and unexpected peril. Despite what Alex had said to her about Spitalfields, it had never occurred to her that she might be in any physical danger. It was daylight and there were plenty of people about, and although she had felt uncomfortable in this unfamiliar environment, she had not for a moment thought that there might be those who saw her as a prize, a means of gaining some money... All her thoughts had been concentrated on the interview with Thérèse and the necessity of convincing her to meet Simon again, rather than the hazards that might lie along the way. Now, she realised that she had been naïve and foolish in the extreme.

'I suppose you have brought your jackals with you!' Thérèse was saying furiously. 'How dare you use me to further your dirty little plans! I have told you I shall have no part in your filthy games!'

The gentleman gave her a look of admiration. 'Spoken like a true noblewoman, my dear, a true aristocrat! I ain't offended! Truth to tell, you had your chance to share in my good fortune! I've accepted that you ain't interested, but you'll pay your dues like the rest and keep your mouth shut!'

Thérèse said a rude and idiomatic phrase, the meaning of which Jane could only guess at. Samways was still holding her arm, and now he dragged her over to the wooden chair, thrusting her down on to it.

'I've plenty of time, my dear, but have you? Wouldn't you rather be restored to the bosom of your family?'

Tears stung Jane's eyes. She had only herself to blame for getting into such a ridiculous and dangerous situation.

'I do not understand you, sir!' she said, scrubbing angrily at her eyes. 'This is tantamount to kidnap!'

'No, no, my dear!' Samways swung a chair round and straddled it, resting his arms along the back. 'I have no intention of kidnap or abduction! This is a business transaction—I will keep you here safe until your family can reclaim you!'

'At a price!' Jane said furiously.

Samways shrugged expansively. 'It costs to keep a young lady safe in these parts! You ask the high-and-mighty French missie there!' He nodded at Thérèse, who was standing irresolute, biting her lip. 'She pays me to keep her from the brothels and the whore-houses, which—' He thrust his face close to Jane's '…is where you'll be if your loved ones don't come through with the cash!'

For a moment Jane stared at him, her eyes bright with fury. She was enraged to find herself in such a position of weakness, but there was a strong practical streak in her as well. Common sense suggested that it was in Samways's interests to keep her unhurt whilst he extracted a ransom. She knew her family would pay. Therefore it was sensible to make the process as painless as possible—and face the consequences once she was free. For a moment Alex's face swam before her eyes. She could picture his anger, the black brows drawn with fury, the blistering words that would be heaped on her head.

'I am Miss Jane Verey of Portman Square,' she said haughtily. 'If you approach my brother, Lord Verey, he will see to it that you are…rewarded…for restoring me to him unharmed.'

Samways was out of his chair even before she had finished speaking, rubbing his hands together in anticipation of rich pickings. The sister of a lord! Even better than he had imagined!

'Don't go getting any ideas, now,' he warned, pausing at the door. 'Dolbottle and Henty are watching the house and will persuade you against leaving. If your brother is fond of you, Miss Verey, I reckon you should be home by nightfall!'

'If we are not to go out, you had best fetch the medicine for Madame de Beaurain,' Jane said crossly. 'I do not see why she should suffer unnecessarily!'

Fortunately, Samways seemed much amused by this. 'Medicine for the Frenchies! Yes, milady!'

There was a silence after he had gone out. Madame de Beaurain was asleep and snoring softly. Thérèse moved across to the window and looked out into the street.

'He spoke the truth. His men are everywhere.' Her blue gaze lingered thoughtfully on Jane. 'That was very wise, Miss Verey. You have more sense than most of your contemporaries, who would be having the vapours by now!'

'Thank you,' Jane said coolly. 'Please call me Jane.'

There was a hint of amusement in Thérèse's gaze. 'And you must call me Thérèse. I am sorry that a compassionate errand has put you in such an awkward position, Jane.'

Jane's hazel eyes were bright as they rested on Thérèse's face. 'What did that unpleasant man mean when he said that you paid him to keep you out of the brothels?'

A hint of colour stole into Thérèse's cheeks. 'Just that,' she said shortly. 'Mr Samways is a business man, a man of many and varied interests! One of them is the ownership of a number of whorehouses. I did not care to be amongst his women, Jane, though he offered me the privilege of being his own mistress! So instead I pay him so that I need *not* be a whore! A neat reversal, *n'est ce pas?*'

Jane was momentarily silenced. 'But what…could he..?'

'Oh, yes,' Thérèse said drily, 'he could! He runs this neighbourhood, Jane, and everyone must contribute in some way!'

She sat down and stoically started to stitch the hem of the taffeta dress. Jane stared at her. After a moment Thérèse looked up and gave her a faint smile.

'Does my sang-froid offend you, dear Jane? But you see, it is the way of the world! It is simply that you are usually protected from its harsh realities! Have no fear, Samways will quickly find your family, they will pay handsomely for you and you will be on your way home! A storm in a tea cup!'

'I am not offended,' Jane said, not entirely truthfully. 'If you will pass me the underskirt, Thérèse, I shall occupy myself in helping you. I am not so neat a seamstress as you, but if you give me the bits that do not show…'

There was reluctant admiration in Thérèse's eyes as she pushed the skirt across to Jane.

For a while they sewed in silence, but after a little, Jane said, 'Perhaps you could tell me a little of yourself, Thérèse, to pass the time. I could chatter but I would prefer to hear about you, if you do not mind...'

Thérèse laughed. 'Very well, Jane. Would you like the tale of my life? It starts in gilded luxury in Blois, where I was the pampered only child of the Vicomte and Vicomtesse de Beaurain. I had wardrobes of pretty clothes and servants at my beck and call. I remember nothing of those days for when I was still a baby my father was guillotined and we were forced to flee abroad. We went by night, running away, hiding like thieves... We came to England, where my mother worked for years as a teacher of French and later took in sewing when her health began to fail.' She cast a swift, affectionate look across at the humped figure in the bed. 'I did not go to school— my mother taught me until I was old enough to work, telling me all the time that I should try to better my position and remember whose daughter I was. What I remember is nothing of richness and luxury and everything of poverty and struggle.' Despite the words her face was serene, untroubled.

'Then I became French governess to a family in Kent...' Thérèse shrugged a little. 'It is the old story. I was young and the master of the house was old and importunate and the mistress unable to believe that he was resistible... I was turned off without a reference and for my next governess role I was obliged to take a job further down the social scale with a Cit who wished his daughters to become little ladies...' Another shrug. 'I have no time for rank and fortune—

how could I, given my own circumstances? What value has rank been to me, the penniless daughter of a French nobleman? But these people were not even pleasant—petty, small-minded… In the end they dismissed me because they said they found my manner too high and mighty, but really they were uncomfortable to have a servant higher born than they. So I came back to London and took to sewing, like my mother.' She bit her thread with sudden violence. 'My mother's health was deteriorating. It was that that prompted me to contact the Huntingtons and ask for help. Nothing else would have induced me to beg, for I am too proud.' She met Jane's eyes and smiled a little. 'I know it is my besetting sin! Anyway, we received a grudging invitation to visit. Have you met the family, Jane? They are as proud as we, stiff and unbending, and they were not warm to their French cousins. Well, it would never have worked… I cannot be a poor relation—I would rather earn an honest wage. And so there was talk of ingratitude and pride, and we came back and took a room here. My mother became too ill to work and her medicine costs much, but we manage.'

'And then, a few weeks ago, you went to Lady Aston's masquerade,' Jane said softly. Thérèse put down her sewing slowly. There was suddenly a distant look in her eyes. 'Yes. Oh, Jane, it was a beautiful dress, that one. I have worked for years with silks and velvets, and never felt tempted, but that dress… The old Duchess—' she gave a naughty smile '—I fear she could not do it justice. As soon as I saw it coming together under my hands I had to have it! I tried it on…and then I thought, why not? No one would know…so I ran up a domino as well and went to the masquerade. I had heard the Duchess mention it. And—' she shrugged '—the rest you know.'

'You danced with Simon,' Jane said thoughtfully. 'I saw the two of you. You looked very happy.'

Thérèse evaded her eyes. 'I was enjoying myself. It was like a fairytale and the deception added spice to it all! Just for once…' She shook her head. 'Oh, I cannot say that I was mingling with my equals, in a place I was meant to be, for fate has decreed otherwise! But it was lovely. Then that toad of a man tried to importune me and your brother came to my aid…' Her voice trailed away.

'You like Simon, don't you?' Jane said perceptively. 'Regardless of what you have said, I do believe…'

Thérèse looked away. She was silent for a moment. 'Perhaps if things had been different… Yes—' suddenly she pushed the dress away from her and stood up '—when I met him I thought—there is a man…' there was a smile in her eyes '…and truly, I was tempted for the first time ever, but…'

'But Simon does not want you to be his mistress!' Jane objected. 'He would never insult you so! He wants to marry you!'

'Even worse!' Thérèse said briskly. 'Can you imagine people asking your mother about her daughter-in-law and she being obliged to say that it is the girl who made her dresses?'

'Our family does not care about such things!' Jane said staunchly.

Thérèse suddenly looked very tired. 'Everybody cares about such things, Jane! But there is worse! You have seen Samways—can you imagine him coming to Portman Square and blackmailing me with threats

to tell the *ton* how I paid him to stay out of his whore-
houses… What a delicious scandal that would be!
Now, would you like to share my luncheon? It is only
bread and cheese, but the cheese is French!'

Chapter Fourteen

The afternoon dragged by. Shortly after lunch, a man brought some medicines for the Vicomtesse de Beaurain, and she roused herself sufficiently to take a spoonful at Thérèse's coaxing.

'What is the matter with her?' Jane whispered softly, as Thérèse returned to the sewing-table. She did not wish to pry, but there was something unbearably touching about the patient devotion with which the daughter nursed her sick mother.

'She has a weak chest and is forever suffering inflammation of the lungs,' Thérèse said. 'She needs to go to a hot climate, or to a spa, perhaps, to cure her.' For a moment the tears shone in her eyes, then she blinked them back. 'Now come! I need to finish this dress so that I may pay Samways!'

They talked some more. Thérèse spoke about her experiences as a governess and Jane told Thérèse about her childhood at Ambergate, managing to talk quite a lot about Simon in the process.

'It sounds a delightful place to live,' Thérèse said dreamily, when Jane had finished describing the rolling Wiltshire hills and lush fields. 'But I suppose that all young ladies must come to London to make a suitable match. Are you betrothed yet, Jane? It would seem very likely!'

Jane blushed. She had managed to avoid speaking of Alex and even succeeded in not thinking about him for at least five minutes at a time.

'No! Yes, that is, I suppose I am, in a manner of speaking…'

'Tiens!' Thérèse said, amused. 'Are you or are you not, Jane? You do not seem certain!'

'Well…' suddenly Jane felt like confiding. 'There is a gentleman who made an arrangement with my father that I should become betrothed to his brother.'

Thérèse nodded. 'That I can understand. That also is the way of the world! And then?'

'I did not wish to marry the brother,' Jane said, 'and then he fell in love with my dearest friend.'

'And what happened about the arranged match?'

Jane blushed again. 'Well, the gentleman—he is a Duke—wishes me to marry him now instead of his brother, in order to preserve the family alliance. It was not a good enough reason to persuade me. Unfortunately yesterday we became…in short, I appear to be compromised and will have to agree.'

It sounded quite extraordinary when described in those bald terms and indeed Thérèse was staring at her in the greatest astonishment.

'Mon Dieu, Jane, do not tell me half the story! Who is this Duke, and what is he like, and how on earth did so innocent a girl as you become compromised?'

Jane could feel herself blushing all the more. 'The gentleman is the Duke of Delahaye. He is—oh, how can I describe him? He is accustomed to people falling in with his plans and was not at all pleased when

I opposed them! He is handsome but seems a little grave until one gets to know him, and he has a reputation as a recluse, which some consider to be most odd! But I think—'

Jane broke off, aware that she was smiling and that she had given herself away entirely.

'So you are in love with him,' Thérèse said shrewdly, 'in which case why did you refuse his proposal?'

Jane hesitated. 'Why do you refuse to see Simon?' she countered. 'The reasons are not always simple, are they, Thérèse?'

Their eyes held for a moment, then the older girl smiled and shrugged a little. 'I like you, Jane Verey! I should not, but I do! *Mon Dieu*, why must the Vereys make things so much more difficult for me?'

Jane was glad to turn the subject away from herself. She knew that she had given herself away too easily. It did not matter that Thérèse suspected that she was in love with Alex, but at all costs she had to guard against him finding out the truth. It would be too demeaning, when his affections still lay with his dead wife. With a little pang of apprehension, Jane realised that she would have to face Alex at some point and explain why she had disregarded his warnings to avoid Spitalfields. It was a nerve-racking thought.

'We saw you with Samways at Vauxhall Gardens,' Jane said suddenly, her thoughts of Alex bringing her back to the man who had threatened him there. 'Surely you did not go there with him, Thérèse?'

Thérèse laughed. 'No Jane, you may acquit me of complaisance in Samways's dirty schemes! I had gone to Vauxhall on my own—I was playing truant again, I confess! Samways caught up with me there and tried to persuade me to join him in a spot of enterprise. He was engaged in lifting plump purses from unsuspecting victims and wished to pass them on to me for safe-keeping! I gave him the rightabout and saw no more of him!'

Jane hesitated on the edge of telling Thérèse about Samways's attack on Alex, but held her peace. For all the older girl's worldliness and air of cynicism, Jane suspected that she would be shocked. It was not comforting, however, to think that she was in the power of a man who was so ruthless. Jane hoped profoundly that Simon would pay what was demanded and that she would be home within a few hours.

They chatted a little more, then Thérèse made some broth for their supper and managed to persuade her mother to take a little. A soft conversation in French followed, then Thérèse called Jane over.

'Miss Verey, may I make you known to my mother, the Vicomtesse de Beaurain? Mama, this is Miss Jane Verey.'

The Vicomtesse had the waxy pallor of the very ill. Her slight body made barely a dent under the thin covers. Her eyes, a faded blue that had no doubt once been as vivid as Thérèse's own, were sunk deep and shadowed with pain. Nevertheless, they rested on Jane with interest and warmth. She took Jane's hand in her own.

'Enchantée, mam'zelle…'

'I am sorry that you are so unwell, ma'am,' Jane said sincerely. 'It must be horrid for you. If I can do anything to help—'

The Vicomtesse opened her blue eyes very wide. 'You can help, Miss Verey. You can persuade my foolish daughter to give your brother a hearing. She is pining for him, yet absurd notions of rank and pride keep her silent—'

'*Maman!*' Jane was amused to see that Thérèse had blushed bright red. 'You should not give me away!'

'Pshaw!' The Vicomtesse made a vague gesture, lying back and closing her eyes. 'I want what is best for my daughter, Miss Verey, and I recognise love when I see it. Seven times your brother has come here to speak to Thérèse and each time she has sent him away. Yet afterwards, she cries…'

'*Maman,*' Thérèse said again, beseechingly, 'it is not so simple—'

'Nonsense! It is as simple or as complicated as you wish to make it! That's French practicality!' The Vicomtesse smiled faintly. 'Now let me rest, child, and think on what I have said!'

The candle had burned down. Thérèse started to tidy the room and folded up the sewing with neat, practical movements. 'It is very late,' she said. 'Perhaps Samways will not be back tonight. You should try and rest…'

She dragged out a pallet from under the Viscomtesse's bed and gestured towards it, but Jane was shaking her head.

'I should not sleep,' she said with truth. 'I will doze in the chair—'

The door opened and Jane's heart leaped in her throat. Samways came in, grinning at Thérèse as she looked down her nose at him.

'Good evening, Princess! Well, now, it seems I have a tastier bait than I had thought at first!' He swung round on Jane, who instinctively drew back. 'It seems,' Samways said gloatingly, 'that this little lady is the betrothed of the Duke of Delahaye!'

Jane caught her breath as he came towards her and raised one calloused hand to run it down her cheek. She flinched away. 'I have a grudge against that man,' Samways continued. 'At first I wondered whether it would suffice to send you back to him after an instructive night in one of my clubs... It's a sweet notion!' His shoulders shook at Jane's look of disgusted horror. 'But then I thought not—I'm not a vindictive man—I'll just use you to bait the trap! He will come to save you, will he not?'

'Let us hope he thinks it worth it!' Jane said, with more cold composure than she was feeling. 'I was telling Mademoiselle de Beaurain earlier that it is an arranged match. I pray that his Grace will put himself to the trouble!'

For a moment Samways hesitated, then showed his teeth in a yellow grin. 'You had better pray so, miss! Now, you will stay here whilst I send to his Grace of Delahaye, telling him to meet me here to negotiate the terms of your freedom...'

With a sick flash of memory, Jane saw again that night at Vauxhall, the moonlight glinting on the knife blade. She knew what would await Alex when he came to keep the meeting. Thérèse stepped closer, as though she were afraid that Jane would faint, and put a comforting hand on her shoulder.

'It will be all right, *chérie*...'

Jane swallowed hard. 'What is your quarrel with Alex Delahaye, sir? If you intend to use me in your revenge I believe I have a right to know!'

For a moment she thought that Samways would refuse, but then he smiled again. 'The man robbed me of fortune, that it what I hold against him!'

'Robbed you?' Jane sounded as amazed as she felt. She had not expected this.

'Aye.' Samways passed his handkerchief across his florid face. 'There was a time when I was a gentleman, set fair to marry one of his Grace's relatives! Rich she was—a rich widow ripe for the picking, and sweet enough on me to make the business easy! That was before the Duke saw fit to put an end to it and lose me a fortune into the bargain!'

'A rich widow—' Jane was almost whispering.

'Aye, Lady Eleanor Fane!' The hatred in his voice was almost tangible now. 'That oh-so-respectable society lady was willing to throw her bonnet over the windmill for me—until Delahaye turned me off! All that fortune that would have been mine—none of this scraping and scratching a living…'

Jane sat down rather quickly, her thoughts whirling. It was an extraordinary story. The thought of the severe Lady Eleanor being thwarted from making a runaway match with an unsuitable man at least ten years her junior made the imagination boggle. Yet Samways had said that he had been a gentleman once and his hatred of Alex was all too real…

Dimly she registered that Samways was leaving and instructing one of his men to stay with the girls. Thérèse was objecting at this invasion of her home but was being overruled. The door slammed behind and the man settled himself in the armchair, fingering his knife and grinning wolfishly at Jane. Thérèse, who appeared to have accepted the situation with sudden and suspicious equanimity, was offering him a drink of wine. Jane watched as she moved across to pour it and, behind the man's back, added some of her mother's medicine. Jane stared, then, obedient to a fierce glare from Thérèse, looked away.

They settled down, Jane taking the pallet that Thérèse had indicated and Thérèse herself lighting another candle and sitting at the workbench as though prepared to sit out the night. The presence of Samway's henchman prevented any kind of discussion. On the bed, the Vicomtesse sighed a little in her sleep.

For what seemed like hours, Jane lay rigid on the hard pallet, her thoughts going round and around in her head. It was bad enough to have put herself in a position where Simon could be asked for money for her safe return, but to have brought Alex into danger was an entirely different matter. She wondered whether Samways had contacted him yet, what he would do, whether he could escape the threat and if so, what would happen to her... She knew her thoughts were quite profitless but she could not escape them. A couple of tears squeezed from beneath her eyelids.

'Jane!' Thérèse was shaking her by the shoulder and Jane opened her eyes, dazzled for a moment by the candle flame. 'Come quickly! He is asleep!'

'What—?'

'The poppy juice!' Thérèse said impatiently. 'I thought it would never work!' She stood aside so that Jane could see the slumped figure of the guard, sound asleep and snoring loudly. 'Now, listen. You must get out of that window and climb along the ledge to the end of the building. There is a staircase there that leads down to the street. Samways's men will be about, but in the dark you may be able to slip past. If not, there is a family in the end tenement who will hide you! I would come too, only I cannot leave *Maman* here! I pray you will not be too late!'

'But when he comes back…' Jane was struggling with the stiff catch on the window. 'What will you say, Thérèse?'

'Oh, that I fell asleep and when I awoke you were gone! If it comes to it, Jane, I will do everything I can to help your Duke of Delahaye, but I hope—I imagine—that he is a man who can look after himself! Now, good luck and godspeed!' She gave Jane a brief, hard hug.

Just climbing out of the window was frightful enough for Jane. She had never been afraid of heights, but in the dark she felt frighteningly exposed and alone. The ledge was wide enough to edge along very carefully but when her dress caught on a nail and pulled her back she almost lost her balance, and had to bite her lip hard to prevent herself from crying out. She found that she no longer cared if all of Samways's men were thronging the street below as long as she could get back on to solid ground.

She reached the end of the building at last and stepped carefully down into the dark stairwell, pausing for her frightened breathing to still. There was no sound or movement close by and she began to hope that she had been undetected. The stairs were unlit and she started to creep down, feeling her way down one wall, each step a venture into the unknown.

When she got to the bottom she paused again, before peering gingerly around the corner and out into the street. It appeared to be deserted, which was odd since Samways's men had been swarming everywhere earlier. Jane started to slip along the edge of the building, keeping in the shadows, intent only on reaching the main street and trying to find someone who could help her. She tried to blot out of her mind the dangers of wandering around London at night, the perils that might befall her, the fact that Alex might even now be walking into a trap...

She reached the end of the buildings and there was a pool of darkness before her, blacker than the surrounding night. Jane darted across, almost tripping over a kerb stone and putting out a hand blindly to break her fall. And then she was caught and held in a merciless grip, strong arms sweeping her up and away from the darkness, but she did not cry out or struggle, for as soon as he had touched her she had recognised who he was.

There was light and warmth, and someone was forcing strong spirit down her throat.

'What the hell do we do now, Alex?' Jane heard a voice say.

Jane coughed and opened her eyes. She was still in Alex's arms, sitting on his knee and held close, which struck her as somewhat improper given that the other occupants of the room were Harry Marchnight and her own brother. She struggled to be free, but Alex held her tightly.

'Jane? Has he hurt you? Are you all right?'

'No, I am not hurt,' Jane said crossly, 'but for you squeezing me half to death!'

She saw Simon's tense face ease into a smile as he exchanged a rueful look with Alex. 'She's quite herself,' he observed.

Alex stood up, placing her gently in the chair opposite his.

'We haven't much time,' he said. 'You really are unhurt, Jane? Tell me the truth!'

'Yes, truly!' Jane was shaken and a little awed by what she saw in Alex's face. 'And Thérèse is quite safe, though we must not be gone long! She drugged the man who was sent to guard us, but how long he will remain unconscious is another matter—'

'That was when you escaped?' Henry questioned swiftly. 'And there was only one man left in the room with you?'

Jane nodded. 'Thérèse would not come with me because she would not leave her mother, but she should not be left to face Samways alone! He said his men were everywhere, but—'

'We've taken out all of those who were guarding the street,' Alex said. 'We were intending to ambush the ones in the house with you, though of course we had no way of knowing how many there were. But you say there is only one, and he has been dealt with by Mademoiselle de Beaurain.' He flashed Simon a grin. 'The next time we consider mounting a rescue we will remember that the two of you are well able to take care of yourselves! What did you have in mind for Samways? Hitting him over the head with a sauce-pan, perhaps?'

'Perhaps...' Jane shivered. 'We must go back for Thérèse. Whatever she says, she cannot stay there now!'

'No.' Alex consulted his watch '—and we have little time. I am to meet Samways here within the hour—which I shall do, but with the odds weighted more in my favour than he imagines! Simon, will you escort Jane, Thérèse and her mother back to Portman Square? Harry and I will deal with Samways!'

It was Thérèse who opened the door to Jane's knock. The candlelight was behind her, turning her silver hair to a halo, and her face was in shadow.

'Jane? What has happened? *Tiens*—' she suddenly saw Alex and Henry Marchnight '—*messieurs...*'

Alex tucked the pistol into his belt. 'Your servant, Mam'zelle de Beaurain. I am Alexander Delahaye, Miss Verey's fiancé.'

'Jane is most fortunate,' Thérèse said, with an expressive lift of her brows. 'And this gentleman...?'

Henry Marchnight, languidly elegant as ever, came forward to bow over Thérèse's hand. 'Henry Marchnight, entirely at your service, *mademoiselle*. And here is one who most particularly wishes to see you...' He stepped to one side and Simon came out of the shadows, closing the door softly behind him before turning to Thérèse.

It was an extraordinary moment. Jane, standing within the circle of Alex's arm, saw the arrested expression on Thérèse's face and the still watchfulness of Simon's. She had not had the chance to tell Simon anything of the outcome of her conversations with Thérèse, and now she saw that there had been no need anyway. They had eyes only for each other, utterly absorbed in the reaction of one to the other. Jane, Alex, Henry, the sleeping occupants of the room...all might have been invisible.

'Good evening, milord,' Thérèse said, a little tremulously. Her eyes were suddenly full of tears. Jane realised, with a rush of compassion, that she was very nervous.

'Thérèse.' Simon said.

Very slowly they came together. Simon's arms went around her gently, then he was holding her exultantly to him and there was no need for any further words.

'Time for all that later,' Alex said, with a grin. His arm tightened about Jane for a brief instant, then he became businesslike.

'Mademoiselle de Beaurain, you and your mother must leave here at once. Please could you gather your belongings as swiftly as possible. Simon will escort you back to Portman Square with Jane whilst Henry and I stay to keep our appointment with Samways. Please!' Alex added imperatively, as Thérèse had not moved. 'There is not a moment to lose!'

'You will come with us, won't you, Thérèse?' Jane said, moving forward. Thérèse had not let go of Simon's hand and Jane half-expected him to add his pleas to hers, but he remained silent, his eyes never leaving her face.

There was a moment of stillness, then a voice spoke from the bed.

'My child,' the Vicomtesse said, 'if you refuse now I swear I shall disinherit you!'

She struggled to sit up, coughing a little. 'Pass me my wrap, I pray you, *monsieur*,' she instructed Alex. 'I shall then feel respectable enough to undertake the journey!'

Thérèse nodded, a little smile on her lips. 'There is nothing here that I wish to bring,' she said, and Jane thought that she was speaking of more than just her belongings. 'I have a small bag—so…' she pulled it out from under the bed '…and that is all.' She turned to Simon. 'I fear I come to you in nothing but the clothes I stand up in, my lord!'

Simon's smile was full of tenderness. 'That is enough for me, my love! Now, will you go first and

I shall carry your mother down. The carriage is behind Crispin Buildings. Harry, if you could help us before you come back to stay with Alex…?'

'What will you do with him?' Thérèse asked, eyeing the slumped figure of Samways's henchman. It looked to Jane as though he had not moved since she had gone.

Alex laughed. 'We will leave him there! Samways will return to find an empty room, an unconscious guard—and Harry and myself waiting for him!'

At the last moment, before she started down the dark stair for the last time, Jane turned to look back at Alex. She wanted to run to him and tell him to be careful, that she loved him, that if he was killed she could never feel happy again. But there was something stern in his expression, as though he was already thinking of the encounter to come, that made her bite the words back and she could only hope that she had the chance to tell him when next she saw him.

Their arrival in Portman Square was as dramatic as anyone might have wished. The whole house was in uproar, with all lights blazing and all the servants still awake and milling around whilst they waited for news. Jane, whose preoccupation with Alex's safety had almost led her to forget that she had been held to ransom, hung back, suddenly embarrassed.

Simon helped the Vicomtesse from the carriage and sent a startled footman running to waken the doctor. Thérèse followed him into the hall, while Jane brought up the rear.

Lady Verey and Sophia had been in the drawing-room, but both came hurrying as Simon strode into the hall, their strained faces breaking into smiles.

'Jane!' Sophia hugged her friend with heartfelt relief. 'Oh, Jane, we were so worried! How could you do such a thing?'

'Thank God you are safe, Jane! And—' Lady Verey broke off as she caught sight of Thérèse and her mother. 'Who—?' she began, only to have the question comprehensively answered as Simon, oblivious to all around him, swept Thérèse into a ruthless embrace.

'My apologies, madam, for this unexpected intrusion into your home,' Vicomtesse de Beaurain said calmly. 'It must seem most singular and indeed it is, but—' A spasm of coughing shook her and Jane and Lady Verey both stepped forward to help her.

'Do not try to talk any more, ma'am,' Jane said soothingly. 'Mama, Sophia, this is the Vicomtesse de Beaurain and that—' she nodded towards the slender figure of Thérèse, still locked in Simon's arms '—that is her daughter, whom Simon intends to marry!'

'A fortunate thing too, after such a display!' Lady Verey said, trying not to smile. The two mothers exchanged looks of qualified approval. 'Well, well, no doubt we shall hear all about it in the morning! Please come this way, ma'am, and I will show you to your bedchamber. Is that Dr Tovey arriving? Excellent!' And with the air of one who can take any number of surprises in her stride, Lady Verey led her unexpected guests away.

'Oh, Jane! It is so romantic!' Sophia curled up at the end of her friend's bed, her face lit with happiness. 'Why, it is plain to see that they love each other to distraction! And Simon has only met her three times! Barely spoken to her! And yet he knew at once that she was meant for him...' Sophia gave a pleasurable little shiver.

Jane felt tired and wan that afternoon. She had hardly slept for fear that Alex's plans had gone awry and even now he and Harry Marchnight were lying dead in a pool of blood somewhere. She knew that sooner or later she would have to face the repercussions of her actions in going to Spitalfields and bringing all this trouble on them. And the final straw was the air of extravagant romance that seemed to be invading the house, with both Sophia and Simon floating happily on their respective clouds of rapture. Examining her feelings, Jane felt left out and a little envious.

'I came to tell you that your mama utterly forbids you to get out of bed until Dr Tovey has confirmed that you are quite well,' Sophia continued blithely, unaware of her friend's ill humour, 'and that the Duke of Delahaye has sent a message that both he and Lord Henry are quite safe, the man is taken and he will call to see you this evening! I will leave you to rest now!'

Jane lay back against her pillows with a heavy sigh. She had no need of a doctor to tell her that she was tired but otherwise unharmed. It was her heart that was sore. Sophia and Philip had triumphed over adversity to become betrothed and now Simon had found his Thérèse. In comparison her own engagement, based on Alex's desire to make the alliance his grandfather wanted, was distinctly unromantic.

Jane got up and dressed slowly, choosing a dress of pale mauve then discarding it because it made her look sallow. After she had tried a second one of jonquil muslin and a third of pink, she resigned herself to the fact that she was too pale for anything to look flattering and settled for her oldest dress. Cassie arranged her hair in a simple knot and then she was as ready as she would ever be to face the world.

The rest of the family were taking supper when Jane went downstairs, but she did not feel like eating and slipped out into the courtyard garden. It was cool and the sky was just starting to turn the pale blue of evening. She sat by the fountain and listened to the water splashing into the pool below. She could hear Sophia and Thérèse laughing together in the dining-room. They were already fast friends and with the common ground of weddings and trousseaux, they had plenty to talk about. Jane smiled. Sophia had no malice in her and had already accepted Thérèse without reservation. I am lucky in my friends, Jane thought, and for some reason the thought made her sad and a tear trickled from the corner of her eye and ran down her cheek.

'Jane?'

She had neither sensed nor heard Alex's approach and now she jumped, rubbing her cheeks dry with a hasty hand. In the gathering dusk he looked tall and a little unapproachable and as always, Jane's heart gave a little skip upon seeing him. He looked tired, she thought, which was no great surprise. He took a seat beside her on the stone bench, half-turned towards her with his arm along the back of the seat. For some reason his presence suddenly made feel Jane shy.

'I am glad that you are well,' she said softly. 'I have been worrying…'

'Have you, Jane?' Alex gave her a searching look from those very dark eyes. 'I confess I am a little fatigued, but nothing that will not mend. And Samways is taken. You need have no more concern over him.'

'I was more concerned over the danger to yourself than any threat to me,' Jane said, honesty overcoming her reticence. 'You are the one he sought to kill, after all! I confess it reassures me to think him locked away and unable to do you any more harm!'

'You should not seek to minimise the danger to yourself,' Alex said heavily. 'Did he speak to you of his clubs, Jane? Did he tell you about the brothels he owns and the girls he ruins for his own profit? Did he say that if Simon had refused his ransom you would find yourself at the bottom of the Thames? And did you think of any of those things when you went rushing off to Spitalfields on your mission to unite Thérèse with Simon?' There was a note of warm anger in his voice now. 'I can scarce believe, after all I told you of the dangers of that particular neighbourhood, that you chose to go there alone!'

No one had yet reproached Jane on her conduct, for they had all been too relieved that she was safe to blame her for her foolishness. Alex, however, did not seem inclined to let the matter go easily and Jane felt the tears prickling her eyes again.

'I was only thinking of how I might help Simon—' she began defensively, only to be interrupted.

'I can well believe that you thought of nothing else! Nothing of the danger and the difficulties you caused everyone else and the fear of your mother—'

'Oh, do not!' Jane's composure was fading fast. 'I know I have been foolish! Pray do not remind me! And I am sorry for all the trouble I have caused, but I do believe that Samways would have found another way to reach you if it had not been through me! He had his own quarrel with you and I was only the means he tried to use to gain revenge!'

There was a little silence. The water splashed softly. 'Did he tell you the nature of his grudge against me?' Alex asked, at length.

'A little.' Jane looked away, to where a thin sickle moon was rising above the rooftops. 'That is, he told me some tale of Lady Eleanor Fane, which I took to be all a hum! It did not seen in character at all for Lady Eleanor to be taken in by such a man!'

Alex shifted on the seat. 'Part of what he told you is true enough,' he said soberly. 'I would like to tell you the tale if I may, Jane. Peter Samways was the son of a clergyman who held a living from my father. My father even paid for his education on the understanding that Samways would also go into holy orders. When he declared himself temperamentally unsuited to the priesthood my father found him a position in the household of a friend and later, when Lady Eleanor was widowed, he became her secretary. I do believe that there developed between them an affection that flourished despite the disparities of age and position.'

Alex sighed, trailing his fingers in the shallow pool. 'Who can say what might have happened? Certainly Samways believed that the match was his for the making! And Lady Eleanor's wealth with it! I had no doubts that he was a fortune-hunter,' Alex said ruefully, 'but I would never have intervened had I thought she was happy. You must believe that, Jane!'

'I do believe it!' Jane was taken aback by his vehemence. 'Besides, it would have been no wonder had you objected to so unequal a match—'

Alex made a slight gesture. 'Oh, there are many who would not have thought twice about putting an end to his pretensions! And I confess I was uneasy. Yet I would not have interfered. But then Lady Eleanor came to me in some distress, reporting that some small items had gone missing from her household—small sums of money, items of jewellery, including a locket with a picture of her late husband. We suspected one of the servants and we set a trap.' He sighed. 'Samways was caught red-handed. I had to turn him off.'

'He bears a heavy grudge against you for it,' Jane said thoughtfully. 'What happened to him after he left Lady Eleanor's service?'

'I believe that he made a bid to fix her interest despite what had happened,' Alex said. 'No doubt he thought to gamble on Lady Eleanor's affection for him. His failure to win her no doubt added to his bitterness. He took a post as clerk in chambers in Holborn and I heard that he had been dismissed for fraud. I imagine his downward spiral continued from then onwards. Samways dropped out of my sight for many years and I thought of him no more. Then one day a little above a year ago, he sought me out to ask a favour. On the strength of the fondness my father had had for him, he asked for my help in finding gainful employment. Against my better judgement I agreed to help—only to find that he had never intended to pursue an honest career. His intention was to defraud his employer in short order and I was left with the embarrassment of explaining away my lack of discretion to those I had counted my friends. It was profoundly difficult.'

A bird sang close at hand, its golden liquid notes

falling on the still air. The lights of the house were growing brighter now. Alex shifted a little, his face in shadow.

'I had thought that I had seen the back of him, but it seemed that was not so. A few months later he contacted me again with an unsavoury proposition. He implied that there had been some improper relationship between himself and Lady Eleanor all those years ago but promised to hold his peace on receipt of ten thousand pounds. I told him to spread his gossip and be damned. I did not believe it could hurt her—she is too respected and it was a long time ago. Anyway, Samways took his dismissal badly. I do believe that he holds me to blame in some manner for all his bad luck and that was when his resentment was fuelled into a rage strong enough to seek my life.'

Jane shivered. 'When I saw him at Vauxhall—'

'Yes, I think that he would have tried to kill me that night had you not intervened. It was a perfect opportunity—he would never have been caught. And I had already had one ''accident'' whilst out shooting, when a stray bullet had grazed my arm and the man who had fired it was never found. I began to ask some questions about Samways—with my connections it was not difficult—and I found out about the brothels and the blackmail and all the other unpleasant activities that he has dabbled in.'

Jane shivered again. 'And Lady Eleanor? Does she know anything of this?'

'I am glad to say that she does not. Nor does anyone else except Simon and Harry Marchnight. To them and to yourself I have told the whole truth, but everyone else believes that your kidnap was just the work of an opportunistic criminal.'

'Then I will never tell,' Jane said stoutly. 'As you said before, the escapade reflects no credit on me. The least said, the better!'

'You have kept many secrets for me,' Alex said and there was a smile in his voice now. 'I must thank you for that, Jane! You have been the soul of discretion and I am sorry that I was so angry before. It is simply that when I heard that Samways had you in his power I was so very afraid for you.' He took her hand and the warmth sent little shock waves through her. Absorbed in the tale he had to tell, she had almost forgotten the physical impact he had on her.

'I wanted to speak to you of our marriage,' Alex said, a little huskily. 'I had thought that it might be a little difficult with three weddings in the family, but your mama has hit on a scheme! She thinks that a triple wedding at Ambergate in a month or so would be just the thing!'

'A month!' Jane, suddenly confronted by the imminence of the marriage, felt as though her breath had been taken away. She had imagined that first Sophia and Philip would wed, then Simon and Thérèse and finally, perhaps, she might have to start thinking of her own wedding. Something close to panic rose in her. She would have to explain her doubts to Alex, tell him that she did not feel comfortable marrying him when his affections were still engaged elsewhere. No doubt hundreds of other girls would not care a jot and would be carried away with excitement to be in her position, Jane thought miserably. It was only she, loving Alex as she did, who could not accept second best. She remembered that she had told Alex that night at Almack's that she would be happy to marry where there was respect and liking; no blame could attach to him for thinking that he was offering her precisely that and she should therefore be happy.

'Jane?' Alex was watching her face and there was an expression on his own that she did not understand. His voice was very quiet. 'Is something the matter?'

His very gentleness made Jane wish to cry.

'I am just tired,' she said hastily. 'The shock of the last few days...'

'Of course.' For some reason she thought that he sounded as though he did not believe her. 'Jane, if there is anything wrong you must tell me—'

There was a step on the path and then Sophia's voice said gaily, 'I beg your pardon, but Lady Verey fears Jane will take a chill sitting out here in the dusk! She asks that you both come in and join us in the drawing-room.'

'Of course,' Alex said again. He stood back to allow Jane to precede him and she was very conscious of his regard as she stepped past him. She did not know whether to be glad or sorry for Sophia's intervention, but she did know that, sooner or later, she would have to tell Alex the truth.

Chapter Fifteen

Ambergate, drowsing in the June heat in the middle of its water meadows, seemed just as it had always been. After a whirlwind four weeks that had seemed to comprise of nothing but social engagements interspersed with dress fittings, Jane felt like collapsing into its peacefulness and never waking again.

Life had changed so much as a result of her engagement. She was the recipient of more invitations than there were hours in the day, fêted and courted, her company and opinion sought on everything. It would have been enough to turn her head were she not isolated in a growing misery that seemed to blot out all else. It seemed that the more sought after she became, the more she felt distanced from Alex. It had begun with their conversation on the day after her rescue from Samways and each new day seemed to push them a little further apart.

In public, Alex was an attentive suitor, forever seeing to Jane's comfort, introducing her to new people, guiding her through the minefield of social contact that inevitably awaited the lady he had chosen as his wife. In private—but there was no 'in private'.

Now, when their betrothal might have allowed them a little latitude, they never met alone. Alex never took her driving and did not even call in Portman Square to see her. Jane felt as though they were drifting further apart at the very time they should have been seeking to be closer. Alex had become once more the enigmatic stranger of their first acquaintance, and Jane felt that she had barely managed to glimpse beneath the surface before he had withdrawn from her.

She could not understand it. He was so kind to her when they were in company, so concerned that she should not feel overwhelmed or out of her depth. It seemed that he did care for her, or at least cared that she should be happy. Yet there was no sign of any deeper emotion, nor even a sign of any of the passion that had flared between them in the past. Jane contemplated the idea of an empty, indifferent relationship with Alex and found the thought intolerable.

Her feeling of isolation seemed magnified by the cruel contrast provided by Simon and Thérèse, and Sophia and Philip. Both couples were so blissfully happy and in love that Jane could hardly bear to be near them. Philip was a changed man, relaxed and laughing, watching Sophia with adoring eyes. Simon and Thérèse were still in the first flush of love, their affection tinged by a sense of wonderment. The delight experienced by all her friends, plus their conviction that she should be feeling the same as they, left Jane more lonely than ever and very afraid that her marriage to Alex would be a hollow sham.

On the night before they left London for Ambergate, Alex had hosted a dinner for the family at Haye House. Sophia, her face flushed with excitement, had regaled everyone with the tale of the Eve of St Agnes.

'So Jane and I agreed that we would put the legend to the test and I went to bed without any supper and did not look behind me, just as the tale demanded, and I dreamed of such a very handsome man!' She turned glowing eyes on Philip. 'So tall and fair, and so very much like Philip!'

There was general laughter.

'And what did you dream of, Jane?' Alex asked silkily, an intent look in his dark eyes. Jane looked away.

'I did not dream that night, sir.'

The smiles of the others faded as they sensed the constraint between the two of them, but Sophia was still so buoyed up with the astonishing felicity of the story coming true that she had not seemed to notice.

'Oh, Jane! How can you say that? When you dreamed of Alex—' she blushed a little to use the name of her future brother-in-law '—and now you are betrothed to him! You see! It must be true!'

Jane smiled a little at her friend's vehemence. For a moment she forgot the ring of faces around her, Alex looking at her with the same watchful intent as before. 'The truth of it is, Sophy, that it was the real Alexander Delahaye I saw and no dream! He was visiting Ambergate that night. I peeked around my bedroom door and saw a man in the corridor—a man I thought seemed all darkness and shadows, as though he had stepped straight out of the legend...' She paused. 'I was very young and he looked quite stern and frightening, yet curiously compelling to me. Oh, I thought him handsome! And I went back to bed and he stalked my dreams that night...' Her voice trailed away as she suddenly became aware of the silence around her and how far she might have given herself away. Then Lady Eleanor Fane stirred and said approvingly, 'A charming story, child!' And she realised that everyone had taken this as the proof that she was head over ears in love with Alex.

Henry Marchnight clapped him on the back, grinning.

'You're a lucky man, Alex!'

'Why, so I think,' Alex said expressionlessly, his eyes never leaving Jane's face.

The party had broken up early, for they were all to make the journey to Ambergate the following day—all but Alex, who declared that he had business that would keep him in London for a little longer. Jane's spirits had sunk to such a low ebb that she wondered whether the business could involve Lady Dennery. She had no reason to suspect so, but doubt and jealousy gnawed away at her.

Returning to Ambergate had brought with it some kind of solace. Whilst Lady Verey and Lady Eleanor plotted and planned to make it the biggest and most impressive wedding that the county had ever seen, Jane wandered across the fields or sat in the gardens, looking at the mellow old house where she had lived all her life. Even this, Jane knew, would change on her marriage. She would become the mistress of half a dozen fine houses and Simon and Thérèse would take possession of Ambergate. Lady Verey was already cheerfully contemplating a move to Amber House, the Dower house at the end of the drive.

Jane traipsed back to the house just as dusk was falling. It was two days before the wedding and she could hear the voices of Lady Eleanor and Lady

Verey endlessly extolling the virtues of orange blossom and white lace:

'We will ask dear Jane when she returns. Where has the child got to? I declare, she hasn't eaten all day! It isn't natural, this indifference to her own wedding! Why, both Thérèse and Sophia are *aux anges*, but Jane mopes about as though we were planning her funeral!'

Jane paused in the hallway. She felt too miserable to want any supper and the temptation to seek refuge in her room was overwhelming.

The grandfather clock struck ten. Lighting a candle, Jane trod softly up the stair. She reached the corner at the top and turned down the shadowy passageway. She heard a door open below in the hall, but did not look behind, and once in her bedroom she undressed quickly, blew out the candle and jumped into bed.

Sleep eluded her. For a while she tossed and turned, dozing, her mind full of images of Alex. She heard the rest of the house preparing for bed and then silence. Jane's stomach suddenly gave a loud rumble.

With a sigh she slipped out of bed, reached for her wrap and stole downstairs to the larder. There was half a chicken, some fresh bread and a new pat of delicious butter out on the slab and suddenly she felt ravenous. When she had eaten as much as she could, and washed the whole of it down with a beaker of milk, she felt much better. Picking up her candle again, she retraced her steps into the hall and back up the stairs.

The moonlight was very bright. Somewhere deep in the woods, Jane heard an owl call once, then again. The treads of the stair gave softly under her feet. Suddenly, although the night was warm, Jane gave a shiver. There was the creak of a floorboard behind her and she hesitated. She had a strange conviction that there was someone following her, but it seemed nonsense. She had heard no steps and there were always strange noises at Ambergate, which was a very old house indeed.

There was an unexpected breath of wind and the candle flame guttered, then went out. Jane spun around. This time, she was sure that there was someone behind her, but the whole of the stairs were in shadow. With a little muted squeak, Jane shot down the passage and reached the shelter of her bedroom doorway. Her curtains were not quite closed, allowing a pool of silver to dapple the floor. She turned to shut the door against whatever restless spirits seemed to be abroad that night, but as she did so, a figure slid through the doorway and a hand touched her arm, warm and very much alive.

'Jane?'

'Alex!'

Jane was so relieved that her ghost was, in fact, real that she was almost annoyed with him.

'What ever are you doing here?'

'I could not sleep.' Alex leaned against the door jamb, surveying her from head to foot. 'Nor, it seems, could you?'

'I was hungry,' Jane whispered, putting the candle down on the chest and wondering whether he intended to stay there for long. 'Lady Eleanor is only two rooms away. We must take care not wake her up.'

'Then I had better close the door,' Alex agreed, suiting actions to words.

This had not been precisely what Jane intended. She wondered what on earth Lady Eleanor would think if she knew that her godson was in Jane's bedroom, for all that they were supposed to be marrying in a few days' time.

'I did not even know that you had arrived from Town,' Jane said, still whispering. Alex lit the candle and turned to face her. He was still fully clothed, in casual but elegant garb, and his gaze, as it travelled over Jane, only served to emphasise her own state of undress. She jumped quickly into bed, burrowing her cold toes under the covers, watching with deep misgiving as Alex sat down on the side of the bed facing her.

'I arrived whilst you were out this evening,' he said, still looking at her. 'I was hoping to see you, but when we realised that you had come straight up to your room, I thought that I would wait until the morning. But then I could not sleep and decided to take a walk, as it was such a clear night. It was as I was letting myself back in that I heard a noise and realised that I was not the only one abroad.'

He took Jane's cold hands in his.

'Jane, I know that there is something wrong. You must tell me what it is. Your mother was saying only this evening that you are pining for something, and I knew even before we left London that there were difficulties. Is it that you are sad to be leaving Ambergate? It will be a wrench for you, I know, but I am sure that you will always be welcome here. And you will have a new home of your own.'

A huge lump seemed to be blocking Jane's throat.

She thought of the familiar warmth of Ambergate and the imagined cold vastness of the Delahaye estates, and shivered.

'I do not want a dozen houses of my own!' The words burst from her. 'I do not want to be a Duchess and have people bowing and scraping, people I know would not care a rush for me if I were plain Miss Verey! I want none of it!'

Alex had gone very still. His face was in shadow. He still held her hands and his grip had tightened, though Jane made no attempt to pull away. Her eyes, bright with tears, held his defiantly.

'What do you want then, Jane?'

'I want you to love me!' Jane wailed, bursting into tears as she finally admitted to the root cause of her misery. 'I want you to love me as much as I love you! That's all I have ever wanted and without that the rest is not worth a penny!'

Alex let go of her hands abruptly and pulled her into his arms. Jane was too unhappy to resist and for several seconds she just cried against his chest whilst he murmured endearments into her hair. Then, recalling what she had just said, she pulled back and glared at him.

'Oh! You are forever making me say things that would be better unsaid! How dare you?'

Alex did not reply. He turned her face up to his and kissed her. His lips were very gentle, teasing the corners of Jane's mouth with a featherlight touch before raining a path of tiny kisses along the sensitive line of her jaw and the soft skin of her neck. Jane shivered again, but not from cold. It was fortunate that she was already sitting down, she thought hazily, for the burning sweetness that was coursing through her blood made her tremble.

'Alex—'

'Shh! If you make a noise, Lady Eleanor will hear you and doubtless be scandalised!'

'Oh!' In her strangely weakened state, Jane felt herself fall back against her pillows. Alex leant over her.

'And I do love you,' Alex continued, his words muffled against her throat. 'My darling Jane, I love you so much I would have thought it was utterly obvious to everybody!'

'Oh!'

'Is that all you can say?' Alex smiled wickedly down into her dazed eyes. 'I am used to far more accomplished repartee from you, my love!'

His mouth captured hers again and Jane lay back against the yielding pillows with a little sigh. She reached out to him, sliding her hands over the firm muscles of his back beneath his jacket, feeling the heat of his skin through the linen shirt. It was delicious and intoxicating and entirely improper.

Jane was aware that her nightdress, high-necked and virginal as it was, constituted scant barrier against a determined approach, and already Alex's deft fingers were unfastening the laces, brushing the flimsy cotton aside and drifting gently over her exposed skin. As he traced the curve of her breast, Jane arched in pure pleasure, digging her fingers into his back. Improper or not, she certainly did not want him to stop now.

'Jane, we must stop this now if I am not to break all the rules of hospitality and seduce you in your brother's house!' Alex's voice was hoarse, his eyes glittering with a desire that could not be hidden. 'God forgive me, I never intended it so, but I can scarce help myself!'

He removed himself to the end of the bed, very forcibly. 'I need to talk to you, Jane, but this is evidently not the time and the place since talking is not uppermost in my mind! Now, do you still doubt that I love you?'

Jane could feel herself smiling in the darkness. 'No…'

'And I shall not show so much restraint on our wedding night, I promise you!'

Jane drew the covers up to her chin. She felt warm and happy and very much loved. 'I should think not, your Grace!' she said primly.

They met at breakfast, when both behaved as though the previous night's encounter had never occurred. Thérèse noticed that Jane could not meet her fiancé's eyes, but her rosy colour and slight smile suggested that she was in no way displeased to see him. After the meal they escaped from company with indecent haste and strolled towards the walled garden.

'Why did you ever imagine that I did not love you, Jane?' Alex asked. There was a certain expression in his eyes that made Jane feel suddenly breathless and, as she remembered the events of the previous evening, the colour came into her face again. Her doubts seemed so foolish now, in the bright light of day and secure in the knowledge that Alex loved her. Yet at the time they had seemed horribly real…

'Well, first there was your pledge to your grandfather—'

'What of it? I am sure that I am pleased to fulfil his wishes, but I would not let that dictate my marriage!'

'Oh! But that cannot be so! You said that our marriage would be a neat solution!'

Alex looked rueful. 'I did say that, I know! It is partly correct, of course, but it hid the most important truth, which was that I had wanted to marry you myself almost from the first moment. It took me a little while to realise, for I was not accustomed to seeking the company of women—' He broke off. 'Why the reproachful look, Jane?'

'I did not wish to bring Lady Denncry's name into this,' Jane said, mock-sorrowfully, 'but it seems I have no choice! If you did not seek her company, then how would you describe your conduct?'

Alex laughed. 'Very well, I concede I made a bad mistake there! She threw herself at my head and I— well, I was trying to distract myself from the curious hold you appeared to have over me! Needless to say, it did not work! But,' he added hastily, 'she was never my mistress!'

'Hmm!' Jane looked severe. 'I believe she had her eye on your strawberry leaves!'

'They will look nicer on your head, I think!'

Jane tried not to smile. She had not yet finished her inquisition. 'There is a more serious charge against you, however. What of your love for your wife?'

'For whom? I collect you mean for Madeline? Yes, I suppose I should tell you about her.' Alex stopped smiling and Jane felt her heart start to race. Now, she was sure, he would be honest with her and tell her that no matter how much he loved her, he had never ceased to care for his beautiful Duchess. He gestured to her to sit down in the rose arbour.

'It's true that I loved Madeline very much when I first married her,' Alex said. 'She was beautiful and I was young and not very wise. Even when matters started to go awry between us I kept hoping that I might yet make all well, that I might make Madeline love me again. It was a long time before I realised.'

'Realised what?'

Alex shrugged. 'Why, that Madeline was incapable of loving anyone except herself. She had nothing to give; she wanted more and more, until she was insane with greed. Greed for riches and power and love, but without paying any price in return.' He shook his head. 'It was then that my love, which had been twisted out of all recognition, finally died.' He looked up suddenly to meet Jane's sympathetic gaze and took her hands in his. 'I told you once not to pity me, did I not? That was not because I had any feelings left for Madeline, but because I had already started to care for you! It was not pity I wanted from you, Jane, but something far stronger!' His voice dropped. 'And more passionate!'

'I thought—' Jane stopped and started again. 'At Malladon, when you showed me her picture, I thought you were going to tell me that you still loved her. I thought that you kept the portrait in so prominent a place to remind you...'

'I never go to Malladon,' Alex said simply. 'The house was let until a few months ago and it was never a favourite home of mine. I had forgotten that Madeline's picture hung there! That evening, I was going to tell you what had happened between Madeline and myself, and to tell you that I loved you.

Then you ran away and I thought that it was too soon to make my feelings known!'

'If only I had known! My own reluctance sprang only from the belief that you wanted to marry me for all the convenient and none of the romantic reasons!'

Alex's lips twitched. 'We have made a fine mull of things between us, but I hope that in future we shall achieve a better understanding! I certainly intend to devote a great deal of time to doing so!'

They sat for a while in the sunshine. 'I am so glad that everything is all right,' Jane said contentedly. 'I kept looking at Sophia and Thérèse and feeling so envious of their happiness, when all I wanted was mine for the asking!'

The old church at Ambergate was bright with orange blossom and lilies on the day of the wedding. The three radiant brides emerged on to the village green on the arms of their proud husbands and were showered with rose petals and good wishes. As they paused beneath the lych gate, Lady Sophia Delahaye turned a glowing face to her sister-in-law the Duchess and gave her an impulsive hug. Her eyes were as bright as stars.

'Oh, Jane! I can scarce believe it! Is this not fine?'

* * * * *

NICOLA CORNICK

is passionate about many things: her country cottage and its garden, her two small cats, her husband and her writing, though not necessarily in that order! She has always been fascinated by history, both as her chosen subject at university and subsequently as an engrossing hobby. She works as a university administrator and finds her writing the perfect antidote to the demands of life in a busy office.

FROM REGENCY ROMPS TO MESMERIZING MEDIEVALS, FALL IN LOVE WITH THESE STIRRING TALES FROM HARLEQUIN HISTORICALS

Pick up these Harlequin Historicals and partake in a thrilling and emotional love story set in the Wild, Wild West!

On sale May 2002

NAVAJO SUNRISE
by Elizabeth Lane
(New Mexico, 1868)
Will forbidden love bloom between an officer's daughter and a proud warrior?

CHASE WHEELER'S WOMAN
by Charlene Sands
(Texas, 1881)
An independent young lady becomes smitten with her handsome Native American chaperone!

On sale June 2002

THE COURTSHIP
by Lynna Banning
(Oregon, post–Civil War)
Can a lonely spinster pave a new life with the dashing town banker?

THE PERFECT WIFE
by Mary Burton
(Montana, 1876)
A rugged rancher gets more than he bargained for when he weds an innocent Southern belle!

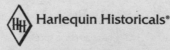

HHH Harlequin Historicals®